SUPER FAKE LOVE SONG

Also by David Yoon

Frankly in Love

DELUSION
STUDIO CITY
RUINS OF GRAY
TOPANGA
MISS MAYHEM
ANGEL CITY
HOLLYWOOD
VENICE
CULVER CITY
THE DROPPED-D SEA
INGLEWOOD
SMOG THE DRAGON
GARDENA
DELGADO BEACH
SWAMP OF DEFEAT
PLAYA MESA
GLASS ISLAND
CARSON IKEA
POINT WHITTIER
TORRANCE
THE SIREN SHREDDER
MYSTICAL REALMS OF
SOUTHERN CALIFORNIA

DAVID YOON

putnam

G. P. PUTNAM'S SONS

G. P. Putnam's Sons
An imprint of Penguin Random House LLC, New York

Visit us online at penguinrandomhouse.com

Library of Congress Cataloging-in-Publication Data is available.

Printed in the United States of America
ISBN 9781984812230

1 3 5 7 9 10 8 6 4 2

Design by Eileen Savage. Text set in GT Sectra.

To nerds
and anyone else just trying to be themselves,
but first, nerds

Contents

III

IV

V

Showing off is the fool's idea of glory.

—Bruce Lee

If you find the false, you find the true.

—Gary Gygax

SUPER FAKE LOVE SONG

What is the most embarrassing thing you have ever done for love?

Once upon a time, a girl sent flowers to herself from a fake secret admirer to draw attention from a boy, only to be found out by the boy's friend's mother, who owned the flower shop.

Once upon a time, a boy crashed his car with that of a boy's just for a chance to talk to him, only to send them both to the hospital and get charged with gross negligence.

Once upon a time, a girl faked a French accent at her new school to pique the interest of a Francophile girl, only to be busted by the arrival of an actual French student.

Once upon a time, a boy faked being the front man of a rock band in order to impress a girl, only to—

Origin

Every superhero has an origin story. Every villain has an origin story.

Every loser has an origin story, too.

Did you know that?

I do.

My time of judgment officially fell one moment in middle school. This one moment clearly defined me as a loser. This one moment cast my loserdom into cold carbonite.

I was thirteen. My family had only recently moved from the tiny humble hamlet of Arroyo Plato to the sprawling opulence of Rancho Ruby.

I had returned from Math to find my locker hanging ajar, its padlock somehow picked. We had lockers in middle school—I missed the backpack hooks of my old school of yesteryear and their implicit belief in the goodness of society—and I liked to keep my paladin figurine on the topmost shelf to visit between classes.

A paladin was a warrior blessed with the power of divine magic.

I had scraped the figurine into form by my own hand from a small block of plaster, then painted it, then sprayed it with a clear coat to protect against scratches.

The sword. The shield. The sigil. The spurs.

It was my one and only copy; I hadn't learned how to cast molds yet, or electroplate, or airbrush, or any of the other things I would later master.

On this day, I opened my locker to discover the figurine had gone missing. In its place was a line, drawn in white chalk, leading down and away. Scrawled instructions read:

THIS WAY SUNNY DAE

I knew this clumsy handwriting; I suspected it was that of Gunner Schwinghammer, who had been born as a fully grown man-child and wowed the adult administration with his preternatural ability to catch and run a football with high school–level acumen. While my friend count never grew beyond two—Milo and Jamal—Gunner's friend count was always increasing.

And indeed, as I followed the line past the water fountains and down the breezeway, I glanced up to see Gunner following me with glittering eyes.

I shook him off. Gunner weighed fifty-two thousand pounds; I weighed six. Gunner was royalty incumbent; I was a serf with stinking mud caked on my boots.

For now, I could only hope that the figurine hadn't gotten dinged beyond the point of reasonable repair.

I continued to follow the line of chalk as it skipped over

cracks and jumped down a curb and into the fresh stinking black of the parking lot.

ALMOST THERE PUBIC HAIR

How far did this stupid line go?

As far as the last car, and into the eraser-red concrete of the baseball area. Down three quick steps, careening right into the shade of an empty dugout.

Around me, the indifferent sun was busy sparkling the dew of another beautiful morning laden with the scent of fresh-cut grass, which was actually a distress chemical released by the mutilated blades in an anguished effort to repair themselves.

The line finally came to rest in the perpetual darkness beneath the fiberglass benches.

PRIZE-A-PALOOZA

YOU TOTAL NERD LOOZA

What I saw was worse than all the looks and all the whispers. What I saw would always be worse than all that Gunner would come to offer: the outright name-calling, the cafeteria-tray flipping, the body checks in the hallway. All the stuff that would follow me past middle school and across the quad into the domain of senior high.

What I saw was my first warning ever.

Paladin Gray had been worn down to a nub, because the figurine itself had been used to draw the line that led me here.

This, the line warned, *marks the end of your childhood.*

From that day on, I understood.

I understood that here, in Rancho Ruby, no part of my thirteen-year-old self was up to standard. I understood that from now on, every day was a new day in the worst possible way: each day I would be challenged, and each day I would likely fail.

I could not afford to cry—everywhere was now a dangerous place—so I kicked a hole in the orange earth with my heel and dropped the chunk in. I covered it over. I stomped thrice to mask the seam.

And I stepped back into the sun to survey the new realm before me.

I

Mimic octopuses change shape and hue.
When they are scared, they become something new.

Spark

I was now seventeen.

I now lived on the other side of the quad, at Rancho Ruby Senior High.

It was Monday. It was school.

What was there to say about school?

Lockers. Class bells. The pantheon of student archetypes: the introspective art girl, the loud jock, the rebel in black. Put your phones away. Will you help me cheat on the quiz. Who will sit next to me at lunch. The kind teacher. The mean teacher. The tough-as-nails vice principal with the secret soft spot.

There was the hot girl, Artemis, whose locker was next to mine, who answered every one of my *Good morning*s with a broadcast-quality eyeroll.

There were the nerds, who were me, Milo, and Jamal.

There could of course be no nerds without a bully—for the bully makes the nerd—and mine was and would ever be Gunner.

Gunner, the human Aryan Tales™ action figure. Gunner (orig. *Gunnar*, Nordic for "warrior"), now the superstar feature back of the Ruby High Ravagers, celebrated for his high-RPM piston quads and record number of berserkergang end-zone dances.

Gunner would invade my table at lunch to steal chips to feed his illiterate golem of a sidekick and tip our drink bottles and so on, like he had routinely done since the middle school era. He called it the *nerd tax*. By now I was able to instinctively avoid him and his sidekick, with an outward annoyance that was actually barely disguised fear.

What a cliché.

I regarded Ruby High through skeptical eyes, as if it did not really exist. It was a school like many other schools in the country, all repeating similar patterns in similar fashion, again and again throughout all ages, world without end.

Track and field—*track* for short—was where I could lounge with my two best-slash-only friends in the Californian golden hour, picking clovers for fifty minutes straight before performing a few minutes of burst activity: long jump (me), shot put (Milo), and high jump (Jamal).

Ruby High was a football school. Track was what donkey-brained football superstars and their sycophantic coaches did to obsessively fill every minute of every hour with training. No one gave two dungballs about track. No one came to track meets.

I loved track.

Track fulfilled the Physical Education requirement with almost no effort.

"Here comes Coach Oldtimer," said Jamal. Coach Oldtimer's real name was We Did Not Care What His Real Name Was.

"Pretend you're stretching." He opened his arms and mimed shooting invisible arrows, *pew, pew.* Jamal (third-generation Jamaican-American) was stretched so tall and thin, he was nearly featureless.

"Oh, stretching," I cried.

Milo (third-generation Guatemalan-American) lay flat and gently rolled side to side, flattening the grass with his muscular superhero body, which he had done nothing to achieve and did nothing to maintain. He even wore thick black prescription glasses as if he harbored a secret identity.

I, Sunny (third-generation Korean-American), bent my unremarkable physique to vigorously rub calf muscles as tender and delicate as veal, rub rub rub.

Together, we three represented 42.85714286 percent of the entire nonwhite population of Ruby High. The other four were Indian, Indian, East Asian, and nonwhite Hispanic, all girls and therefore off-limits, for Milo and Jamal and I did not possess the ability to talk to girls. At Ruby High, we were the lonely-onlies in a sea of everybodies.

"Stretching stretching," I said.

"Go away Coach go away Coach," said Milo under his breath.

But Coach Oldtimer did not go away. Coach, an older white man with the face of an enchanted tree scarred by the emerald fires of war, drew near. He'd been with the school since its founding six thousand years ago.

"I like this little dance you guys got going on right here," said Coach. "Miles, you sure you don't want to run tight end for the football team? Quick, strong guy like you?"

"It's Milo," said Milo.

"I'll join football," said Jamal.

Coach gave skinny Jamal an eyeful of pity. "It gets pretty rough," he said.

"Toxic masculinity," coughed Jamal into his fist.

"What?" said Coach, pouting.

"How can we help you, Coach Oldtimer?" I said.

Coach shook off his bewilderment and maintained his smile. "It's huddle-up time to give all you boys the dope on next week's track meet with Montsange High."

A football jock in the distance cupped his hands to his face and juked an imaginary blitz. Gunner.

"Give us the dope, Coach!" said Gunner. Then he gave a crouched Neanderthal glance over to the girls' track-and-field team to see if they noticed. They did, spasmodically flipping their long flawless locks of hair in autonomic limbic response.

Track was what mouth-breathing football cheerleaders did to ensure they remained visible to donkey-brained football players for every possible minute of every day.

I sat up. "I'm not sure our performance will be significantly enhanced by your dope."

Finally Coach's smile fell. "Your friggin' loss." He stalked away.

"Final grades are decided by attendance, not performance," I called.

"Friggin' nerds," muttered Coach Oldtimer.

"We're not nerds," I whined.

"Okay, nerds," said Gunner.

"Nerds," said some of the girls in the distance.

"Nerds," whispered the wind.

"Why does everyone keep calling us nerds?" said Milo, and

made a worried face that asked, *Did someone find out about DIY Fantasy FX?*

He was referring to our ScreenJunkie channel, where for three years we had been posting homemade videos showing how even the most craft-impaired butterfingers could fashion impressive practical effects from simple household materials for their next LARP event.

LARP, or live action role playing, was when people dressed and acted like their Dungeons & Dragons game characters out in real life.

We did not LARP. We could never. In this temporal plane, we would only get discovered and buried alive under a nonstop torrent of ridicule. As it was, we made sure to never show our faces in our videos—my idea.

Jamal leaned in. "So there's some pretty exciting audience activity on our channel."

"Give us the dope, Jamal!" yodeled Milo, and gave an ironic glance over at the girls' team, who glared back at him like tigers in the sun.

"We finally broke a hundred," cried Jamal.

Me and Milo exchanged a look. One hundred ScreenJunkie followers. One step closer to advertisers and sponsorships.

"And," said Jamal, with a wild smile, "we sold three tee shirts! Three!"

Me and Milo exchanged another look, this time with our mouths in twin Os.

"And finally," said Jamal, hiding his glee behind his very long fingers, "Lady Lashblade *liked* our 'Pod of Mending' episode."

"She liked my glitterbomb," I said.

"She liked your glitterbomb," said Jamal.

I gripped the turf like it had just quaked.

Everyone knew how influential Lady Lashblade (best friends with Lady Steelsash (producer of *What Kingdoms May Rise* (starring actor Stephan Deming (husband of Elise Patel (head organizer for Fantastic Faire (the largest medieval and Renaissance-themed outdoor festival in the country)))))) was.

"That is huge," said Milo.

I hugged Jamal, who recoiled because physical contact was not his absolute favorite, before hugging Milo, who was big on hugging as well as simply big.

"We gotta keep going with new episodes, you guys," I said.

"Heck yeah we do," said Jamal, with a grin as wide as his neck.

"We gotta brainstorm our next custom prop," I said.

Milo pushed up his glasses. "Right now?"

"Right now," said Jamal.

"So, I was thinking, what if we made a—" I was saying when a football glanced off my temple.

"Catch," said Gunner.

"Asswipe," I muttered.

"What?" said Gunner. "What did you call me?"

Coach Oldtimer reappeared upon a fetid cloud of menthol rub. "Ladies, take a powder."

"He started it," I said, instantly wishing I hadn't sounded so whinging. I pointed at my temple and the football on the grass.

"I don't care who started it," said Coach Oldtimer. "Warm-ups, let's go."

"Coach said warm-ups, nerds," sang Gunner, who caught up with Coach Oldtimer to share a side-hug and a laugh.

I heaved myself up. "Right as I was pitching my idea."

"Asswipe," said Milo, loud enough to make Gunner glance

back and make Milo cower. This made as much sense as a pit bull backing down to a Chihuahua—Milo was big and strong enough to easily kick Gunner back into first grade if he wanted.

"To be continued, you guys," I said. I broke into the world's slowest jog, still rubbing my temple. "To be continued!"

I ran my long jumps and averaged three meters, a new personal low.

Milo threw the shot put *n* meters, *n* being a number Milo neither remembered nor cared about, because shot put meant about as much as playing Frisbee in the dark with a corpse.

Jamal got the high bar stuck between his legs while midair and abraded the groin muscle next to his right testicle.

But who cared? Who cared about track, or Gunner, or his football? What was important was that DIY Fantasy FX had reached some kind of tipping point. Its next phase was about to begin.

The week accelerated until it became a multicolored blur smearing across time and space. This happened whenever I focused hard on a new prop project. You could say this was what I loved most about DIY Fantasy FX: the effect it had on time.

I spent my school day sketching prop ideas on the sly, then holding my phone under my desk to text photos of those sketches to Milo and Jamal. In this way we held our design meetings.

Materials too expensive and not common enough, Milo would say.

Totally fun FX but maybe not quite feasible for a real-world use case? Jamal would say.

No but how about this one, I would counter, moving my previous concept into a cloud folder named Idea Archive. The folder contained more than a hundred note clippings spanning my entire friendship with Milo and Jamal.

Milo was the Production Adviser. Jamal was the Promoter.

I was the Idea Guy.

Our group chat was named the SuJaMi Guild, for Sunny, Jamal, and Milo.

In Chemistry, we three huddled in the back of the classroom and drew on notepads while the rest of the students boiled strips of balsa wood or whatever those bucktoothed lemmings had been told to do.

Me and Milo and Jamal were strictly B students.

"Excuse me," said Ms. Uptight Teacher. "What do you three think you're doing back here?"

I thought fast. "It's STEAM."

STEAM referred to any activity that involved Science, Technology, Engineering, Arts, and Math. Falling off a skateboard could be STEAM. Eating tacos could be STEAM.

Ms. Uptight Teacher peered at my scribbles. "Huh?"

"STEAM," I insisted.

"STEAM," said Jamal.

"Okay, but—" said Ms. Uptight Teacher.

"STEAMSTEAMSTEAM," said me and Milo and Jamal.

She left us alone to brainstorm in peace.

While picking clover in the golden Friday afternoon light of another track practice, me and/or Milo and/or Jamal—it was hard to remember who said what first—came up with Raiden's Spark: electroluminescent wires spring-launched from a wrist-mounted device.

"It fulfills our CREAPS requirement," said Milo.

"Cheap parts," I said, counting on my fingers.

"Readily available," said Jamal, counting on his, too.

"Easy to assemble," said Milo, nodding.

"Awesome effect," said Jamal, nodding, too.

"Portable," I said.

"Safe!" cried Milo.

"We got ourselves a plan, Karaan," I said, referring of course to the god of all lycanthropes.

I reached out both arms to exchange high fives with Jamal and Milo at the same time. Jamal's was gentle as a baby's kick. Milo's could break a cinder block.

"Hey," yelled Coach Oldtimer. "Let's get lined up for sprints, pronto."

"In a minute, beef strokinoff," I snapped, irritated.

"Jeez, you guys, come on," said Coach, waving his clipboard in vain.

I turned back to Milo and Jamal. "I'll get building over the weekend."

"Early start," said Milo. "Bravo."

"The early bird rips the worm from the safety of her underground home and bites her in half while her children watch in horror," I said.

I spent all Saturday shuttling back and forth between home, Hardware Gloryhole, and Lonely Hobby in Dad's sapphire-blue-for-boys Inspire NV, an electric car that cost triple the average annual American salary and was crucial to *looking the part*. Mom had one, too, in burgundy-red-for-girls. She was forever taking it in for service because *The more expensive the car, the more attention it needs—but the more attention you get.*

Armed with supplies, I holed up in my room.

Here in my room, I felt safe. I felt free. Free to be 100 percent me. I had all the things I loved surrounding me, all hidden away in Arctic White airtight storage containers.

In my room were maces and shields and swords. There were dragons and dice and maps and pewter figurines, all painted in micro-brush detail. There were elven dictionaries and fae songbooks. There were model pliers and glue and solder guns and electronics and wood.

I banged containers open and closed, and gathered the tools I'd need. I had a whole system. I preferred opaque containers because I did not want anyone to see, and therefore judge, the things I cared deeply about. The things that made me me.

I flipped my face shield down and got to work. I soldered. Glued. Test-fired. Live-fired. I took notes in my lab book. I crashed asleep, sprang awake the next morning, and kept right on going. I fell into a fugue state deep enough to alarm even Mom, who took a full ten-minute break from her twenty-four-hour workday to cautiously offer a plate of simple dry foods to keep her younger son alive.

Mom tapped her ear to mute her call—a gesture gone automatic over the years. "Even nerds gotta eat," she said. She was working, even though it was a Sunday. She wore a cream-colored work blouse incongruously paired with yoga pants and horrible orange foam clogs, because *Video meetings are from the waist up.*

"I'm not a nerd," I said from behind my face shield. "I'm an innovator *for* nerds."

"Right, Jesus, okay," said Mom, hands raised.

By the time Monday evening came around, I was up to version twelve of the Raiden's Spark. I turned off the lights. I aimed my hand at the door, thumbed a button, and let fly a ragged cone of neon-bright wires.

The wires streaked across the stone chamber in a brilliant flash and wrapped Gunner's steel helm before he could even begin a backswing of his bastard sword. The rest of my party cowered in awe as a nest of lightning enveloped Gunner's armored torso, turning him into a marionette gone mad with jittering death spasms, with absolutely no hope for a saving throw against this: a +9 magic bonus attack.

The wires of Raiden's Spark retracted smoothly into the spring mechanism via a small hand reel. Gunner lay steaming on the flagstone.

I turned the lights back on. I flipped my face shield up. I blinked back into my room.

I opened my lab book, which I had meticulously decorated into the hammered-iron style of medieval blacksmithery.

DIY FANTASY FX—SUNNY DAE

From the tiny arms of a tiny standing knight I took a tiny sword that was not a sword but a pen, and muttered words as I wrote them.

"Raiden's Spark, success."

Fakery

"You're not wearing that," said Mom.

"I always wear this," I said.

"Not to dinner at the club, you're not," said Mom. She had traded her usual WFH yoga pants for a long gray wool skirt.

I looked down at my clothes. Glowstick-green vintage Kazaa tee shirt. Cargo shorts the color, and shape, of potatoes.

Dad appeared in a suit and tie, which is what he always wore. He put down his phone, sighed at my room and its many white plastic storage containers, at the newly completed Raiden's Spark, and at me. He shook his head.

"Still with the toys," he murmured to Mom. "Shouldn't Sunny be into girls by now?"

"The book said kids mature at their own pace," murmured Mom back.

"I hear everything you're saying," I said. "And the Raiden's Spark is hardly a toy."

Dad went back to his phone. Dad also worked twenty-four-hour days. Dad and Mom worked at the same company, which they also owned and operated.

"We're at the club tonight," said Mom. "Please wear slacks and a button-up and a blazer and argyle socks and driving loafers."

"And underwear and skin and hair and teeth," I said.

"And a tie," said Dad, eyes locked to his screen.

"Get your outfit in alignment—now, please," said Mom, and turned her attention back to her buzzing phone.

I changed my clothes, hissing. Then I prepared to descend the stairs. I hated stairs. People slipped and fell down stairs. Our old place back in Arroyo Plato had not been cursed with stairs.

Gray, my older brother, once called me fifteen going on fifty.

He didn't call me anything now.

Dad's blue-for-boys Inspire NV wound silently through the spaghetti streets of our neighborhood: Rancho Ruby.

Rancho Ruby was developed all at once in the late nineties as a seaside mega-enclave for the newly wealthy. It was the setting for *Indecent Housewives of Rancho Ruby*. It had its own private airstrip for C-level executive douchebags of all denominations.

If you thought Playa Mesa was fancy, that meant you'd never seen Rancho Ruby.

Rancho Ruby was 99.6 percent white. We, the Daes, were one of the few minority families, and one of two Asian families, possessing the wealth required to live in such a community.

Being a minority in a crowd of majority meant having to prove yourself worthy, over and over, for you were only as credible as your latest divine miracle. For Mom, this meant seizing the lead volunteer position at my school despite her unrelenting work schedule. For Dad, this meant pretending to care deeply about maintaining an impeccable address setup and swing amid the endless poking and ribbing at the Rancho Ruby Country Club.

Mom and Dad's company, Manny Dae Business Management Services, was started by Dad's late father, Emmanuel Dae, a first-generation Korean immigrant who gave his only son his name, his charisma, and his client list. Once upon a time, the company was run out of his old house in Arroyo Plato, which after his death became our house.

This was the time when big brother Gray and I would rattle the floors of the old craftsman with our stomps and jumps and sprints. When clients—all immigrant mom-n-pops from the neighborhood, understandably intimidated by American tax law—would happily toss back any toy balls or vehicles that happened to stray into the living room, where Mom and Dad held meetings in English, simple Korean, and even simpler Spanish.

It was also the time when Gray helped me make my first costume—a tinfoil helmet—so that I could play squire to his knight. Together we conquered the backyard lands and stacked the corpses of pillow goblins ten high, often joined by customers' children enchanted by Gray's charms. Even back then, Gray had charisma like no other.

Magic missile! Gray would scream. And I could practically see it!

Magic missile!

But.

Mom and Dad—hustling like hell all over every county in Southern Californialand—landed their first C-level client with C-level cash. After that, they could not imagine going back to the mom-n-pops with their handwritten checks and collateral jerk drumsticks.

Landing a few more C-level clients—all in Rancho Ruby, all acquired through word of mouth—enabled them to move us into the seven-bedroom monstrosity we lived in today.

"We're here," said Dad.

I jerked awake. The Inspire NV had taken us to the cartoonishly oversize carriage house of the Rancho Ruby Country Club. Three young valets—one for each of us—helped us out of the car. They wore hunter green. They were all Hispanic.

"Sup," I said to my valet.

"Have a wonderful evening, Mr. Dae," said the valet. He looked about twenty-one. Gray was twenty-one.

Dad handed him the key fob. "I appreciate everything you and your team do," he said.

The valet, unaccustomed to such sincerity, brandished the fob with a smile.

"Of course, Mr. Dae," said the valet.

Lion's-head doors opened to reveal a heavily coffered oak corridor leading us toward the restrained din of a dark velvet cocktail lounge and beyond, deep into the cavern of the dining room proper to sit in deep leather booths as rusty crimson as a kidney.

A waiter—dressed in real steakhouse whites with a real towel draped over his forearm—led us to our booth.

"Thank you, Tony," said Mom.

"My pleasure, Mrs. Dae," said Tony. "Medium rares all around, extra au jus?"

"You know us so well," said Mom.

The dining room murmured away, for this was where the serious networking happened; I watched Mom and Dad as they alternated between scanning the room and checking their phones, scanning and checking.

"Now, will we be needing this fourth place setting?" said Tony the waiter.

"Not tonight," said Mom. She'd been saying this for three years now.

Tony began stacking the place setting.

In order to distract Tony, I pointed and said, "Is that stag head new?"

Tony glanced back at the wall, giving me time to palm a miniature teaspoon.

"That thing's been creeping me out for years," said Tony.

I glanced at Mom and Dad, but they of course did not notice my pilferage.

Tony whisked the plates and utensils away. That fourth place setting had been meant for Gray. It was sweet that the staff still put it out, just in case.

Gray had forgone college against Mom and Dad's wishes. He was living forty minutes away in Hollywood, the glowing nexus of every dazzling arc light crisscrossing Los Angeles, and well on his way to becoming a rock star.

I imagined Gray, lit from all sides by flashbulb lightning.

"Honey, did you get my Hastings Company email?" said

Mom, tapping at her phone. "They're asking about reseller permits."

"What the hell do we know about reseller permits?" said Dad.

"Just make something up, Mr. CEO," said Mom.

"Fake it till you make it," said Dad, and he high-fived Mom.

Then they returned to their phones.

"Sunny," said Mom. "Did you get my email about later tonight?"

"Uh," I said.

"I sent it this morning?" said Mom, growing disappointed in her son. Tony swept a drink in front of her, and she swept it to her mouth for a sip in a fluid motion without breaking eye contact with me.

I was terrible at email. I would leave it unchecked for days at a time. Email was the awkward transitional technology between snail mail and texting. Pick one or the other. Even the word *email—electronic mail—*sounded vintage, like *horseless carriage.*

Mom frowned. "Your morning email is what sets the tone for the rest of your day."

"Email is fundamentally incompatible with my workflow," I said.

Dad raised his eyebrows as he worked his phone. "I got your email, dude. The Sohs, right?"

"Yap," said Mom. Something appeared on her extremely large smartwatch, and she flicked it away. "So, to reiterate what was in the email: Our old friends from college, commercial development consultants, you've never met them, are here from London for the next three to six quarters, working on this ginormous mixed-use project in downtown LA, but, and, so, we got Trey, who should be here tonight, to score them a condo just down the street, anyway, their daughter, Cirrus, you've never met her, same age as you, she'll be at Ruby High starting tomorrow, so we figured you could show her the ropes, because we and the Sohs have always done favors for each other."

"Sohs?" I said.

"Jane and Brandon Soh, S-O-H," said Dad.

"Cirrus isn't gonna know anyone," said Mom. "So I figured you could be her orientation buddy."

"I'm the world's worst orientation buddy," I said, because it was true. My main interest was in cataloging the imbecilic spectacle of human folly, not justifying their inane rules and customs with explanation. I bit a nervous fingernail.

"Friends in need, Sunny," said Dad, eyes on screen.

I hated meeting new people. New people terrified me.

"Tha-anks," chanted Mom.

Dad looked up from his phone and narrowed a hunter's gaze. "I see Trey Fortune," he said. "Right there."

"Take the conch," hissed Mom. She swatted his shoulder. "Go, go, go."

Dad holstered his phone, took a breath, and whispered a little prayer: "Keep a super-duper positive attitude."

"There's my CEO," said Mom. She patted his back.

Then Dad slunk off into the dark. Within moments, he reappeared with Trey Fortune.

Mom shot to her feet. "It's so good to see you, Trey," she chirped.

I groaned silently and rose, as etiquette demanded. "Hi," I said.

"Love the tie, Gray," said Trey Fortune.

I could only blink at the man.

"I mean Sunny—my goof," said Trey Fortune. "You and your brother are practically twins."

I wanted to point out that Gray was five inches taller than me and eight points handsomer, but I could not. I said nothing. For a good couple of seconds, too.

"All Asians are technically identical twins, at the genetic level," I said.

Trey made a horse face: *Did not know that!*

Dad, who often confused my jocularity for unhinged derangement, erupted into the fakest laughter in the annals of laughing, dating all the way back to the prehistoric walrus. Mom picked up on Dad's cue and laughed as well. Together they laughed loud enough to cover up their mortification at their son.

The laughs did the trick, and soon Trey Fortune was laughing right along.

All of us laughed, except for me.

Later.

Back in my room.

As I changed back into my cargo shorts and placed my dress slacks into a white plastic storage container, a miniature teaspoon fell out.

I smiled.

I took the little spoon across the hallway to Gray's room.

I walked in. I sat on the bed, which was perfectly neat from years of disuse. When Gray moved into his own apartment in Hollywood, he took only what he needed from this room and left the rest sitting wherever it sat, giving the place the feel of a ship abandoned mid-dinner:

Posters, old vinyl, three guitars, a bass, amps, club flyers. Graffitied Docs in the closet; a frayed wardrobe of black pants and tee shirts, all still hanging; a leather jacket.

Gray had left it all without a second thought, creating a ruin frozen in time. A Tomb of Cool.

I opened Gray's old desk drawer. It was full of tarnished teaspoons, all stolen from the country club by either me or him over the years. It had been our little gag ever since we moved to Rancho Ruby. We had performed this small act of disobedience without fully realizing why. Without fully understanding that it was our small way of claiming this new, unfamiliar neighborhood as our own.

I dropped the spoon in and slid the drawer shut.

Who knew what Gray was up to these days? I imagined him on a stage bathed in light. I imagined him in a slick studio booth, transfixing a team of producers with his rock star magnetism.

Gray had been in a few bands in high school—pop, rap, folk, whatever was trending at the time—but the Mortals were my favorite. They were dark. They were metal. Gray played a growling dropped D, as metal demanded. They had played the legendary Miss Mayhem on Sunset; Gray was only eighteen at the time.

We are mere Mortals, Gray would boom into the mic. *And so are you.*

Behind an amp head I spied a royal-yellow club flyer taped to the wall.

THE MORTALS—OCTOBER 15—FINAL NIGHT OF
THE 2ND ANNUAL ASIAN AMERICAN AND PACIFIC
ISLANDER ROCK AND ROLL FESTIVAL SPONSORED
BY KOREATOWN AUTO MALL—AT THE WORLD-
FAMOUS MISS MAYHEM ON SUNSET STRIP
IN HOLLYWOOD, CA

It had been torn; a corner dangled.

I looked in Gray's closet. I pushed aside a bulging cardboard box full of unsold Mortals merch: tee shirts, lighters, stickers. I found a thermal long-sleeve shirt adorned with skulls. I slam-danced out of my loathsome blazer and tie and put it on. Was it still cool?

Felt cool to me.

I turned, brushing against a guitar that chimed with dissonance. One of these days I should teach myself how to play beyond the six chords I already sort of knew.

Atop an amp sat a darkly glittering thing.

Gray's Goat of Satan ring.

Metal cool and fantasy nerd, forged as one into a chrome-plated steel homage to Baphomet himself.

When the Mortals were active, Gray's two bandmates would bring their matching rings together in a sacred fist bump and growl the prayer:

To metal.

I put the ring on, relished the weight of the thing.

Elf shot the food! said my phone. It was a ringtone from an early primitive arcade role-playing game. I peered at it, wondering if Gray had felt his ears burning miles from here.

It wasn't Gray. It was Dad, texting me from downstairs.

Cirrus Soh is here!

Immortals

I made my way downstairs, where the front door was already open. Beyond where Dad stood, I could see a ghostly girl straight out of a Japanese horror movie lurking in the dark beyond. Instinctively I clutched at the banister with both hands.

"Hello?" I said.

Dad gestured, and the girl-ghost slowly stepped in. She turned out to be a real girl: heavy charcoal eyeliner, blue lips, in white jeans and a white tee shirt with the words I NO KUNG FU and an illustration of a hand with two fingers—middle and index—held straight up.

Her gaze traveled around the house slowly, as if she had just emerged into a crypt, and came to rest. On me.

"Hey," she said, as if perplexed by my existence.

I relaxed my grip. I approached. I kept a good eight feet away from the girl. "You're not a ghost."

She cocked her head. "Are you?"

"And we're off and running!" cried Dad with a hand clap. He glanced at ~~my shirt~~ Gray's shirt, blinked, then moved on, oblivious. "Cirrus, this is Sunny, Sunny, this is Cirrus."

My palms immediately grew hot and moist, like they did whenever I was confronted by a pretty girl.

You just said she was pretty.

Well, she is.

I never said I thought she wasn't.

We're actually all in violent agreement.

Cirrus let out a huge moan of a yawn.

"I'm just in from London," she said, "so I'm good and knackered."

"Great," I said. What was *naccud*?

"So it's *Sunny*," said Cirrus, nodding seriously at Dad. "I thought you were calling him *sonny*."

"Yeppers, Sunny Dae," said Dad with a sideways laugh. He turned to me. "Sunny, Cirrus is—"

"Daughter of Jane and Brandon Soh," I said, like an automated information kiosk. "They are our new neighbors. You are old friends."

"Your name is Sunny Dae," said Cirrus, thinking. "And your brother's name is Gray Dae. Sunny day. Gray day."

"You were named after a variety of cloud," I said. I added a smile to make that statement seem less whiny, but it did not help.

Dad stared at his son and this girl, waiting to see what happened next.

Cirrus seemed to relax a millimeter. "It's nice to meet you." She stuck out a hand.

I lunged to receive it. "Nice to meet you, too." Then I lunged right back.

"Intros made!" shouted Dad to himself. He turned to Cirrus. "Anything you need, any school intel, fun hot spots around town, you just ask Sunny."

"Everything here is so foreign and exotic," said Cirrus, peering around with mock theater. She smiled. "But really. Thank you, Mr. Dae. Thank you, Sunny."

The way she said my name was as shocking and brilliant as a thousand diamond beams of white starlight all converging at once on my dumbstruck face.

"Yeah of course you got it hurr," I said in a single breath.

"Sunny'll take good care of you," said Dad, who gave my back an irritating forehand and then vanished.

We stood in our socks in the foyer.

"Great," I said to Cirrus.

"Yow," Cirrus said, jumping at a buzzing phone in her pocket. She smiled at it, and began typing. "Sorry, it's AlloAllo. Are you on AlloAllo?"

"No, yes, I used to be, not that much," I said, fairly certain she was talking about an app. I suddenly felt intensely stupid for not knowing what AlloAllo was, and fervently promised myself I would sign up as soon as possible even if it meant relinquishing all my privacy and basic human rights in the process.

I knit my fingers at my quaking belly. Just above Cirrus's collarbone I noticed a tiny triangle of skin, pulsating at a rate definitely slower than my own heartbeat.

"Looks like my friends in Zurich are up," said Cirrus. She

finished up, put the phone away. "They're such morning people over there."

"I know," I said.

I know?

"You've been?" said Cirrus.

"Not for a while," I said.

What was I saying? I had never left Southern California in my entire life.

Moths were batting away at the porch lanterns, so I shut the front door. "How long you in the States for?" I said, marking the first time I'd ever referred to America as *the States*.

"Right up until I leave," said Cirrus with finger pistols and a shake of her long black hair. "Seriously, though. Probably until I graduate. I mean *we*. One sec."

She pulled out her phone again, smiled, typed. "School just let out in Sydney. Oi, Audrey, oi, Simon."

"Sydney is in Australia," I said resolutely.

Cirrus tucked her chin at her shirt. "I'm actually wearing Simon, speak of the devil."

Her shirt once belonged to Simon? Simon was the name of her shirt?

"Great," I said, making this the third time I used the word *great*. I was struggling very hard now. Cirrus was cool. Cirrus was so, so cool. She had just arrived from London. She had friends all over the world. Friends who did cool things and were therefore also so, so cool. She came from an entirely cool world. She did not belong in such an uncool house in an uncool neighborhood with an uncool loser like—

"My friend Simon made this tee shirt," said Cirrus. "Amazing artist. Youngest ever to show at White Rabbit Gallery. He made it for my other friend. Audrey. She's got this brilliant metal band protesting Asian stereotypes, called I No Kung Fu. Get it?"

"I like art," I said, wiping my forehead. *Say something interesting.* "I hate Asian stereotypes."

I said interesting! Interesting!

I knew no artists. I knew no musicians, other than long-gone Gray. I knew no one cool.

I wanted to blurt out, *My brother is a musician!* but managed to restrain myself. Instead, I found myself asking the most non-interesting question possible.

"Where, uh, what are your parents working on, doing?" I said.

"A big mixed-use thing downtown," said Cirrus, "because apparently Los Angeles doesn't have enough luxury malls and luxury condos."

"It doesn't?" I said.

"That was a joke," said Cirrus.

Now my ears ignited, because normally I had at least intermediate to advanced skill at identifying jokes.

"Hahahahahaha," I said, busted as hell. "Anyway, malls are cool."

Cirrus gave me a perplexed smirk: *You know better than to call that sort of thing cool.*

I scrambled to refurbish my last statement. "I meant *cool* in the sense that this new mall will help humanity finally get their carbon footprint big enough to make the Amazon rain forest the planet's hot new desert," I said.

"Jesus, you're cynical," whispered Cirrus, impressed.

By this point, my feet were as hot as my hands and my ears. My body was all-hot.

"How is the UK?" I said. *UK* stood for United Kingdom. Then I remembered Brexit, and the possibility that the UK would no longer exist, and wished I could do it over again to prove I wasn't an ignorant American.

Cirrus thought. "Lots of history. Bit crowded. Bit rainy. Not like here, which is lovely."

"Sure, cool cool cool cool," I said. I made a mental sticky note to add London to my weather app to compare.

"I like your shirt," said Cirrus.

Instantly my chin shot down to my shirt and shot right back up. I'd forgotten that this shirt was not my shirt. This was Gray's shirt. It was quite tight.

And she *liked* it.

"Oh, this stupid old rag?" I said, far too loudly. The *old* part was true. I didn't mention the part about it being Gray's and not mine. Maybe that was the *stupid* part. I picked at Gray's shirt's sleeves.

"The skulls give it a throwback vibe," said Cirrus.

I had no idea what the hell that meant, so I focused on her shirt instead.

"What does that hand gesture mean?" I said. I held two fingers straight up, middle and index, like it showed on her shirt.

Cirrus demonstrated by holding up two fingers herself, then curling her index finger down so that only the middle one remained standing.

"It means *this*, but in Australia," said Cirrus.

I lowered and raised my index finger: middle finger, two fingers, middle finger, two fingers. "So, eff you, eff you, eff you, eff you."

Cirrus did this thing where she covered her mouth with the back of her hand to laugh—she had the velvet laugh of a villainess—and for a moment I stood spellbound. Finally I put my hand away like an amateur magician stashing his last, best trick.

Cirrus slowly flexed one leg after another, as if tired from standing for a long period of—

You let her stand in the foyer this whole time?

"How about we go sit in my room!" I cried, and headed up the stairs.

"Sounds great?" said Cirrus, and followed.

I reached the landing and hesitated. An image flashed in my mind: Cirrus, sitting in my room, amid my stacks of white plastic storage containers. Cirrus, opening the containers one by one. Loudly saying,

Got lots of swords and shields and nerdy stuff. Are you one of those big mega-nerds?

I halted abruptly enough to have Cirrus literally bump into my back.

"Oop," said Cirrus, sidestepping me to slide into my room.

Except it was *Gray's* room.

"Ohhhhahhh," I began, without finishing.

Gray's door was always open, because that's how Gray liked things. The door to *my* room was always shut, because that's how I liked things.

My door was blank and unadorned. My door could have led to anything—a linen closet, a brick wall, an alternate universe.

You only get one chance to make a first impression, Mom liked to say. It was characteristically shallow advice, but there was a truth to it that I only now realized.

I followed Cirrus, heading left into Gray's room instead of right into mine.

Cirrus had already made herself at home in Gray's salvaged steel swivel chair. She drummed her fingers on her thighs, as if eager to be introduced to the room's history.

I started to say something, then stopped.

I started to say something else, then stopped.

I started to—

Cirrus eyed me with growing concern.

"So are you—" she said.

"These are guitars," I said suddenly. I craned my neck back to look at them. I stretched, sniffed, did all the things amateurs do when gearing up for a big lie. "They're my guitars."

Cirrus brightened. "Wait. Are you in a band?"

"Phtphpthpt," I said with a full-body spasm. "It's just a little band, but yes: I am."

Cirrus looked at the guitars again, as if they had changed. "Very cool."

I heard none of this, because my lie was still busy pinging around the inside of my big empty head like a stray shot. Shocking, how easily the lie had slipped out.

"You're more than cool," continued Cirrus. "You're brave. Most people barely have hobbies, if they bother to try anything at all. Most people let the dream starve and die in the kill-basement of their soul and only visit the rotting corpse when they themselves are finally on death's door wondering, *What was I so afraid of this whole time?*"

"Jesus, you're cynical," I whispered.

Cirrus spotted something behind ~~my guitars~~ Gray's guitars: the torn Mortals flyer. "Is that you?"

I cleared my throat, which was already clear. "That's, uh, my old band," I said. "We split up. I'm working on a new thing."

"Cool-cool," said Cirrus, nodding blankly.

Then she flashed me a look.

Not just any look.

The Look.

I recognized the Look from when Gray was still at school. The Look was a particular type of glance Gray got often—a combination of burning curiosity barely masked by bogus nonchalance. Everyone badly wanted to know Gray; everyone pretended they didn't.

The Look was the expression people gave to someone doing something well, and with passion. It was an instinctive attraction to creativity—the highest form of human endeavor—expressed by emitting little hearts out of our eyes. It was falling a little bit in love with people who were fashioning something new with their hands and their imaginations.

I had always wondered what it would feel like to get the Look, and now I realized I had just found out.

The Look was pure deadly sweet terror, and it felt *incredible*.

I instantly wanted another.

Cirrus moved on, her face neutral again. She nodded at something on Gray's old guitar amp. "What's that?"

"My ring?" I said.

It was slightly easier this time, calling it *my* ring, as if lying were a thing that became easier with practice.

I let her hold the Goat of Satan ring. She leaned forward, accepted it, put it on.

"It's heavy," she said, amazed.

"It's the Goat of Satan," I said. The goat's name was Barthomat, Birtalmont, Baccarat—

"And then you make a fist and say 'To metal,'" I growled.

"To metal," she growled back. Then she studied the ring with a pensive eye, as if it reminded her of something sad. She took it off, handed it back. I put the ring on with a deftness that implied I'd been wearing the thing for years. My finger absorbed her lingering warmth. For an idiotic moment I felt like we had just somehow kissed.

"So what's your new band called?" said Cirrus.

She threw me the Look again before turning to gaze at nothing in particular. I realized what she was doing. She was *wanting* for something from me, while *pretending* her question was no big deal.

My mind seized up. I fiddled with my fingers at my belly, which had gone a little sour. I shoved my hands into my pockets, only to find it was too hot for pockets. So I took them out again and just kind of rested my fingertips on my ribs. Many people sat like this all the time, except those who didn't, which was everybody.

"Our working band name," I said, "is the Immortals."

Immediately I wished I could take it back.

Cirrus smiled. "So you *were* the Mortals. And now you are the *Im*mortals."

"Okay, shut up."

"And I thought I was lazy," she said with a chuckle.

"I know, I know," I said, with a wild marionette's shrug. "We wanted to maintain brand recognition?"

"No, I like it," said Cirrus. "Also it's got this dorky Dungeons & Dragons vibe, like *Fools, you cannot defeat the immortals!*"

"You're just being nice," I said, openly knitting my fingers now. *Dorky,* she said. *Dungeons & Dragons,* she said.

"I am," said Cirrus, then laughed until she had to place a hand on my shoulder for support, at which moment I decided she could laugh however long she wanted. All night would be fine by me.

"Seriously, though," she said. "I could never put myself out there like that. I'd love to see you guys at your next gig."

All I could do was shrug and turn the ring around and around. *Baphomet.* The goat was called Baphomet.

"Ffshhhffshssh," I said, nodding and nodding.

Cirrus grew quiet. She seemed to be considering something, and gave a wan little chuckle to whatever thought was in her head. She opened her mouth to speak.

My gut quivered. I felt I was about to learn something deep and interesting and extraordinarily personal from this new girl. And only fifteen minutes into our very first conversation! The first conversation of many!

But her lips drew a thin tight line, and nothing came out.

Cirrus's eyes had reset. It was as if a Topic of Conversation dial selector had just been switched to OFF by an unseen hand. Her phone blooped again—more AlloAllos—but she didn't seem to hear it at all.

I blanched. Had I just inadvertently disappointed her in some opaque way? It was entirely possible—ask my parents—but at the moment I could not fathom what that way could be.

"I should head back," she said, and stood.

"Cool," I said, blinking. But this was not cool. She was here, she was about to speak, and now she was suddenly leaving.

"See you tomorrow at school?" she said.

"Uh, sure," I said. I wanted to kick myself, but I did not know why, or if I even needed to.

So I just watched as Cirrus Soh floated away down the stairs to let herself out without a sound.

Research

Name: Cirrus Soh
Ethnic background: Korean-American
Language skills: unknown (traces of British accent)
Social media footprint: apparently immense, must delve into AlloAllo
Other details: unknown, so many questions

Mamba

I woke up with a yell:

"Uhh!"

I had had a dream. I sat in a beautiful green field full of five-leafed clovers. Cirrus sat by my side. A curtain of hair blew into her amber eyes, and she drew it back, and a flying football glanced off her temple.

Nurrrrrrrrrddddddz, said a demonic Gunner.

The bedroom door opened, and Dad poked his head in with his eyes closed.

"I'm respecting your privacy and asking if everything's okay," said Dad.

I reached over to silence my analog bedside clock (sleeping beside your phone has been proven to give you cancer), which had been buzzing. I removed my sleep cap and clutched it to my chest.

"Just a bad dream," I said through my night guard. "You can open your eyes."

Dad opened his eyes but kept them discreetly downcast. "I know how mornings can be for young men, and also how certain dreams can produce certain reactions, which is totally cool and understandable, especially with a new girl in the picture."

"I need you to not be here," I said.

"Yap," said Dad, and vanished with a look of relief.

I peeled my night guard out of my mouth and dropped it into its dedicated bowl of distilled water. I slid my bare feet into my high-density memory foam slippers, wrapped myself in a heavy robe to protect my body from the irksome chill of the morning, and began rummaging among my white plastic containers for something clean to wear.

I hesitated at my ManSkirt® utility kilt—an ideal choice for a hot day like today, but blood-soaked bait for the Gunners of the world—and reached for my usual potato cargos instead. But they would not do. Not for my first day as Cirrus's orientation buddy.

Cirrus had left so abruptly last night. I reviewed our conversation as best as I could in my mind. But I could not tell if I had said or done anything off-putting. Had I driven her away somehow right as we were getting to know each other? I hoped I hadn't been inadvertently insensitive. I harbored the secret fear that I could sometimes be inadvertently insensitive.

I put on my vintage Kozmo.com tee shirt—an original from the dot-com era—which normally I liked because of its edgy orange and green color scheme, but it now felt stupid and incorrect. All my clothes felt stupid and incorrect.

I opened the door, checked to make sure the hallway was clear, and went into Gray's room. There I unearthed a black

Linkin Park vee neck with moth holes artfully perforating the shoulder and lat areas.

I put it on. Its long-long sleeves were perfectly too long and perfectly frayed. I ran a hand through my matted hair, raising it into spikes. My cargo shorts of course looked completely incongruous, so I replaced them with a pair of black skinny jeans as snug as the Ring of Baphomet now on my middle finger. I wrangled a guitar over my shoulder. It hung low on my hip like a minigun.

I looked in the mirror. Everything was too tight—I could even see my *package*—and air passed through the moth holes to touch my skin in dozens of unfamiliar places, but I could not help but feel a little wilder, a little more lithe, like a mamba just wriggling free from the flaky gray tube of its old self.

"To metal," said I to my reflection.

"Breakfast," screamed a voice from below.

I scrambled. I did not want my parents to see me playing dress-up in Gray's clothes.

I hefted the guitar back onto its stand. I peeled off the shirt, and now the jeans, hopping, hopping, and shoved them under the bed. I changed back into my shorts and my Kozmo.com shirt. My old familiar clothes now felt baggy and tired and just kind of *indifferent*. I prepared to descend the staircase into the day that lay beyond.

But I stared at the black clothes lurking under the bed. They were far from indifferent—they were *different*. They beckoned. They impelled me to stuff them deep into my backpack to take to school.

I traveled carefully downstairs, ate a bowl of oatmeal—

steel-cut for a lower glycemic index—and bid my parents *à plus tard*.

My parents said nothing. They did not notice my unusually stuffed backpack. They were scrolling that long, daily scroll of the American information worker that stopped only when it was time to sleep.

In the garage I strapped on a helmet and donned my skid pads, which, after years of practice, now only took less than a minute—a tiny investment of time for a huge return on physical safety and, yes, style (ask any X Games athlete). I adjusted my backpack straps for even weight distribution. I stood on the platform pedals of my Velociraptor® Elite elliptical bicycle.

But I paused.

There was that Japanese proverb: *The nail that sticks out gets hammered down.*

(At least the Japanese were open about their conformist groupthink. The American version would be more of a hypocritical camp cheer:

In-di-vi-du-al-i-ty! Be ev-ry-thing you can be!

Long as you are just like me!)

I hated my old ten-speed. I hated how inefficient it was, how it squashed the perineum and abraded the groin.

But I stripped off my helmet and skid pads and took it anyway.

Ten minutes later, I slammed the horrid bike into the school bike rack. Then I eyed the old storage shed at the far end of the lot. I hopped a low hedge, casual as a bank robber, and slipped into the dusted-out, rusted-out vacuum of the shed.

Two minutes later, I emerged like a mamba into the light of

a tall grass field. The black vee hugged my chest and shoulders. The pants hugged everything else. My black shoes, being the wide-toe-box variety, actually matched in a teen-Frankenstein's-monster kind of way.

"To metal," I whispered, and entered the school.

As I walked, I felt like an astronaut approaching a steaming gantry. Eyes flicked toward me, followed, and flicked at each other in astonishment.

To metal.

I kept my eyes up, chin high, and walked. I felt a confidence buoy my limbs. Could the clothes be unlocking that feeling? Had they for Gray? They were just clothes. But still.

All around, people were giving me the Look.

I giggled to myself. Was it that easy?

"There's the—" I said.

"—cafeteria," said Cirrus.

We left the concrete outdoor amphitheater, keeping to the right to avoid swimming upstream in the fast-moving current of students: introspective art girl, loud jock, et cetera.

"Over there is where they—" I said.

"—admin and nurse's office," said Cirrus.

"I'll just watch you guide yourself around campus," I said. I shifted my books and stuff to my other arm. I had left my Pets.com backpack in my locker. I made a mental sticky to check if there were any of Gray's old backpacks in his closet.

Cirrus, in contrast, carried nothing. No bag, no lunch, not even a class schedule. Just her in a neat black dress and sunglasses, looking like she'd ditched a wake.

It occurred to me that between her black dress and my black outfit, we matched nicely.

She eyed me with her big lenses. "I like your shirt."

"Thanks," I said. "I like your shirt, too. Your dress. Dresses are basically long shirts."

"No," said Cirrus.

"Why did you leave so quickly last night?" I asked, but not really. Instead, I said nothing as we walked, keeping an eye out for Gunner or his goons until we reached my locker.

"This is me if you ever need to find me," I said, pointing. Hot Girl Artemis appeared and snapped her head at the sight of Cirrus.

"Who are *you*?" said Artemis, quickly shifting to Evaluate & Compare mode. She then performed a secondary scan of me, in an effort to map the exact nature of our relationship.

I froze. I held my poise as best I could. For a nauseating moment I wondered if she would betray my charade—her smooth gynoid countenance breaking into a fit of monotonic laughter: *The mega-nerd is trying to be cool for the weird new girl!*

"You first," said Cirrus coolly.

"Ecgh," said Artemis with revulsion. "What?"

"That's how it works," said Cirrus. "You introduce yourself first. Then you let the other person reciprocate."

Maybe it was because Artemis could not match any criteria in her meager database to link me and Cirrus together in any meaningful way; maybe, in the wretched control bridge of her heart, she calculated that Cirrus represented no threat to her preprogrammed objectives.

Whatever the case, Hot Girl Artemis's haphazardly coded

algorithm must have deemed this encounter not worth a nanosecond more of her runtime, for she spat out a final *Ecgh*, disengaged her E&C scan, and executed a walkaway: a huff, a locker door slam, a flawless strut.

"Nice to meet you, too," said Cirrus.

"Sorry about her," I said.

"Every school has one," said Cirrus.

Her phone buzzed, and she answered. "You might like this," she said. "My friend in Japan is in a feminist grunge band called Hervana."

She showed me a video of four impossibly cool girls playing to a crowd waving their arms in unison.

"My god, they're incredible," I said.

Cirrus backhanded my shoulder. "From one rock star to another."

"Ha," I said.

In Cirrus's mind, I fit in with her international network of creative hipsters constantly pinging her from all around the globe. In her mind, I was just as cool as them. Maybe, I suspected, even more so.

Cirrus did not know that, in reality, I was but quarry for meat-eaters such as Gunner. She did not know that I used to be a reputational liability for my own brother, who avoided me in school. She did not know that I single-handedly made up 33.33 percent of the nerd caste at Ruby High.

I knew this whole thing was wrong.

But I *loved* it.

"Ugh, more AlloAllos," said Cirrus. She typed for a bit before putting her phone on mute and stuffing it away. "Enough."

"You have lots of friends," I said.

"I've been to lots of schools," said Cirrus with a shrug.

We kept walking until we reached the center courtyard of the school. Cirrus stood atop a bench to survey things with arms folded.

"If that's the one hundred block there," she said, squinting, "then that must be two hundred. Then three. And so on."

I raised my eyebrows: *You are correct.*

"Gym there," she continued. "Locker room. Weight room. Industrial classes there. They usually like to keep pipes and vents and stuff all in one part of the school."

"It's like you can see the matrix," I said.

"All schools are the same," muttered Cirrus. "Sometimes I feel like I'm just appearing in the same place. Again and again. Just alternate realities in an infinite multiverse."

Up until this point in my young life I had never heard anything more romantic.

I sat on the bench, only to realize I looked like an upskirt creeper. So I stood and leaned as rakishly as I could on a nearby trash can, only to realize it stank of barf gone leathery solid in the heat. I returned to my original place and held one hand over the other like some kind of drunk valet.

I cleared my throat. She shot me a look, as if I had just materialized.

"So do you miss your mother country?" I said, cool as can be.

"Huh?" said Cirrus.

"Jolly old England?" I said, faltering now.

"I'm not from-from there, actually," said Cirrus.

"So, uh," I said. "What's your background?"

Cirrus looked at me. "Background."

"Where were you born, blablabla, ha ha," I said, laughing for absolutely no reason.

"Right, this question," said Cirrus, drawing forth a ready answer. "Born in Sweden mostly by accident. Technically, I'm a citizen there. But also my dad was adopted by a family in Germany. So I have a second passport. Mom's American. So."

"Nice," I said, as if I understood what any of that meant. Inside, I was spellbound.

"Most everywhere is basically the same," she said.

"Totally," I said, with a bogus Jedi-wave of the hand.

"Kids want friends, grown-ups want a house and a job," said Cirrus.

"We're all just people," I said.

"If it's different you're looking for," said Cirrus, "then hike Masoala, or try those live butod grubs in Sabah." She widened her face with amazement. "I like bugs, but those are like *No, thank you*, you know?"

"I know," I said, absurdly.

"Then again, I also couldn't do live baby octopus in Korea, so maybe I just have a thing about food that's still moving, you know?" said Cirrus.

"I know," I said again, as if I did.

"I'm talking a lot, aren't I," said Cirrus.

"I'm easy to talk to," I said, and was immediately delighted at this sudden display of genuine wit against all odds.

"I have to admit I still get a little nervous when I just get to someplace new," said Cirrus. "So thanks."

"Day nodda," I said.

My smile held steady, but my mind was spinning faster and faster, having been dazzled by her kaleidoscopic cosmopolitan cool.

How many kinds of people had Cirrus met, I wondered, and in how many places? How many archetypes in the student pantheon?

Had she met other Sunnys before Rancho Ruby? Nerd Sunny, Super Macho Sunny, Cool Sunny, Fake Cool Sunny? One Sunny being just okay, but at least better than the other, and so on?

And how was this Sunny?

I began to feel increasingly unspecial.

The bell clanged. Just like it clanged at schools everywhere.

"So your next class is—" I said, but Cirrus wasn't listening.

"Those two guys are staring at us," said Cirrus.

I spotted Milo and Jamal, and made tight fists behind my back. "Let me introduce you to my friends," I said.

"Hiiiiiii," moaned Jamal, jamazed.

"Wowwww," said Milo, milozmerized.

My two best friends wore what they normally wore, which was to say a combination of low-performance joggers and blank polos that were so normcore, they went through dadcore and into weekend dadcore beyond.

I should fix their wardrobe, I found myself thinking, then shook off the thought.

Their abject incoherence must have charmed Cirrus, because she covered her mouth with the back of her hand—such a refined gesture—and laughed.

"Hallooooooh to yooooou tooooo," she said, her eyes as big as eggs. "You must be the Immortals."

Jamal and Milo looked puzzled, as expected. I nodded with great earnestness from behind Cirrus. *Just say yes.*

Milo clued in first. "Yes," he said.

"That's us," said Jamal, dutifully mimicking my bobbing head.

"Very cool," said Cirrus.

Milo and Jamal exploded with gasps of nerd pleasure bordering on the profane. They were unaccustomed to this word *cool*, and now laved at it like dogs discovering fallen chocolate.

I pantomimed a dual-blade decapitation with my hands. *Knock it off.*

They stopped. They awaited further instruction.

I lowered downward-facing palms slowly, as if calming a cross-eyed horse. *Be cool.*

"Cirrus," I said, "is a Soh, the daughter of old friends of my parents. They just moved to Los Angeles to mastermind the next great architectural icon."

"It's a mall," said Cirrus.

Milo gestured with his hands. "When did you get in, your plane? Airport?"

Cirrus stifled another giggle. "Sorry. I'm still jet-lagged, so I might find everything amusing right now. I've been in beautiful Rancho Ruby less than a week."

"Jet lag's like Whatever The Flip," said Jamal with a shrug so unorthodox he had to take a sidestep to maintain balance. "W-T-F dubs tha eff."

"Sorry to cut in, but I only have a few minutes to show her the rest of the school," I said quickly. "Shall we?"

"Nice to meet you," said Cirrus to Jamal and Milo.

"Nice to meet you," they howled back.

As I led Cirrus away, Jamal glared at me: *What the hell?*

I bobbled my head back: *I'll explain later!*

But I had no idea how I would do that without sounding like I'd lost my mind.

Solution

That evening, I changed out of Gray's clothes, put on my regular civvies, and strapped on my helmet and skid pads. I launched out onto the serene night streets of Rancho Ruby on my Velociraptor® Elite elliptical bicycle, which was propelled using a fluid striding motion on large foot platforms. The comfort level was vastly superior to the track-style fixies ridden by fools—you never saw mature men riding those, that's for sure, and for darn good health reasons.

Velociraptor® Elite. Stand Up for Fitness.

I wore my wired headphones (Bluetooth headphones caused brain cancer, source) and listened to someone named David Bowie, whom I had just discovered. He sang "Let's Dance." I agreed, and danced while cycling. My helmet-mounted lamp danced back and forth in time.

"Under the moonlight," I sang. "The Cirrus moonlight." I was a pretty proficient singer, brag if I must. I was in choir in junior high; I could precisely hit notes with the divine purity of a prepubescent altar boy.

When I reached Jamal's, I cruised up the herringbone driveway, through the carriage house, across a moonlit atrium, and into the guest villa garage, which was already open and waiting for me.

"There you are, fast and furious," said Jamal, adjusting a hanging bedsheet.

"We've been waiting for this all day," said Milo, setting down his video camera.

The two stopped what they were doing and faced me.

"For what?" I said, although I knew what.

"For you to explain yourself," said Jamal.

I smiled a brittle smile that almost betrayed my mounting nerves. I of course needed to tell them about my lie. But I also needed to tell them about my solution.

"I will," I said. "I promise. But first, let's do our important work."

"You're killing us," said Jamal.

I held my hands in prayer. "Important work with my two best friends whom I love and can trust with even the most embarrassing admissions, no matter how desperate and pathetic."

"Impressive," said Milo, and locked his camera into a tripod.

We three fell into a familiar rhythm: Milo, the visionary director, adjusted settings and framed the shot to show only my arm and the rest of the minimal set designed by Jamal. We recorded a wide shot, a slo-mo shot, and a close-up of the Raiden's Spark device and its parts.

I recorded the narration, because I had the best voice for that sort of thing. Jamal edited everything together at his giant workstation: the title cards, the footage, the narration, and a sweeping fantasy music track, performed by Jamal himself on the keyboard in the corner.

We played it back.

"Perfect," said Milo, who had the best eye for reviewing video. "Upload it."

Jamal uploaded it, and tagged it, and did all the irritating computer crap needed to make sure it was easily findable, because Jamal had the best brain for that sort of thing.

Finally we sat back, slammed open imported Japanese Ramune sodas, and basked in the satisfaction of another episode completed while a carcinogenic wireless speaker played what Milo called *real music*, not the *ear toxins* trending online. We sat with our feet up on the same big orange pouf, the three of us in radial formation like the arms of a scientifically ludicrous but nonetheless sweet 1.21 gigawatt flux capacitor.

"Lady Lashblade's gonna give us a share," said Jamal. "I can feel it."

We toasted: "To Lady Lashblade."

But I was remembering another toast in my mind: *To metal.*

Jamal, having just read my mind effortlessly, said, "So."

"Earlier today," said Milo, "a beautiful new student named Cirrus asked us if we were immortals."

"She asked us if we were *the* Immortals," said Jamal.

"Correct, *the* Immortals," said Milo.

My stomach performed a brand-new break-dance move called the Idiot.

I just smiled fiercely like I was fighting massive gas.

"Ha ha, ugh," I said. I wished I could fabricate something on the fly, something less cringey than the truth.

Jamal eyed me. "You don't look okay."

"I don't feel okay, so that makes sense," I said with a laugh.

"What's wrong?" said Milo.

This was bad. When Milo asked *what's wrong*, he did not let go until the question was fully answered. He was like a bulldog. A big, gentle bulldog that clamped down on unexpressed emotions and shook with rabid fury until they'd been ripped free and were dripping wet in his powerful jaws of compassion.

"It's nothing," I said, and winced at my error. *It's nothing* was bloodscent for Milo.

Milo's emotional jaws squeezed harder. "Tell us what it is, Sunny Dae."

I wrapped my arms around my ears. "Sorry, you guys are breaking up on me."

"Not if we're *texting*," said Milo.

Checkmate. I felt Milo's teeth pierce my psychic skin.

I sagged limp like fresh kill. I gave in. I explained the whole situation. Friends of my parents, my role as orientation buddy. Cirrus's overwhelming coolness. Her confounding beauty. Her trenchant wit.

"She's very comely," said Milo.

"Comely?" said Jamal.

I turned to Jamal. "I seem to have misplaced my quizzing glass, Mr. Jamal."

"I believe you misplaced it in the drawer housing your spats and garters, Mr. Sunny," said Jamal.

"Something wrong with the word *comely*?" said Milo.

Jamal triumphantly jabbed at the air. "I knew something big was behind your wardrobe change," he said.

"I wish I had someone to orient," said Milo.

"I love her," said Jamal.

"Shut up," said Milo. "Sunny has dibs."

"There's no dibbing. Cirrus doesn't belong to me or anyone."

"Then let me love her," said Jamal.

"She's just so ding-dang *cool*," I said. "That's all. We barely even know each other."

I twisted my mouth into a grimace as I recalled the other night, Gray's room, the lie. "And anyway, I'm not exactly the guy she thinks she knows."

Milo looked at me quizzically.

"Oh, I lied to her," I sighed in mournful song.

Jamal raised his eyebrows. "Already?"

"Shut up, butt face," I said.

"*You* shut up, tiny weird-ass face on your mama's face's butt," said Jamal, parrying with confident ease.

"That's enough," said Milo, and eyed me to continue.

"I told her I was in a band," I said. "Because I wanted to seem cool."

Milo and Jamal looked at each other for a moment to take in this information.

"Hence, the Immortals," said Jamal to Milo.

"Sunny's brother's old band was known as the Mortals," said Milo, stroking his chin.

"That is remarkably flagrant," said Jamal.

"And derivative," said Milo to Jamal.

"Shut up," I said.

"Why do you think you want to emulate your brother, specifically?" said Milo.

"I'm not trying to *be* my brother," I said. "It's just I thought I could I don't know rahh."

Jamal and Milo just looked at me and waited.

I dug my hands into my eyes. "I was there, she was there, she thought my room was Gray's room, and I just kinda let her! All those guitars! I was nervous, okay?"

"It is perfectly okay to be terrible with girls," said Milo. "We are all terrible with girls. We know this about ourselves. You were just grasping for the only successful model of male sexuality you have ever known, and that was Gray. You are okay."

"I'm so stupid," I said. "I'm so stupid I think *umami* is something babies say when they're surprised."

Jamal loved playing I'm So Stupid, and joined in. "I'm so stupid I thought *butt floss* meant there's actual teeth in our butt holes doing the cutting work."

"Incredible," I said, and granted Jamal victory.

"It is perfectly okay to feel stupid," Milo said very, very gently. "Because the fact of the situation is, admitting your lie to her would be almost as creepy as having lied in the first place."

I nodded: *Exactly.*

"I really admire watching you work," said Jamal to Milo.

"Revealing your spur-of-the-moment deception would only serve to masturbate the situation," said Milo.

"Exacerbate," said Jamal.

"I'm here to tell you that all you did was make a mistake any one of us could've made," Milo continued. "You're not stupid. Just desperate. And incoherent."

"We're incoherent around girls, too," said Jamal. "Just like o hai baby ng fnzzt shhphtphbpht."

"Dur hurr hurr pleez choose mee I'm a virgin hauhauhau-hau," said Milo.

"Are we doing anything to sausage your anxiety?" said Jamal.

"Assuage," I said, gazing at my two best friends.

I took a long sip, which was impossible given the design of the Japanese Ramune soda bottle, so I just kind of held the bottle to my upturned head and geared up for my pitch.

"So, I thought I would just tell Cirrus the truth," I said.

Milo took a swig. "That is the hard road, old friend. A difficult trial that only the holiest of paladins such as yourself—"

"But then I thought of a solution," I said.

Jamal stared at me sideways. "No," he said slowly.

"Just listen," I said. I crouched low and held my hands out. Milo and Jamal recognized this as my Idea Guy hear-me-out pose.

"I thought it was a question of maintaining a lie, which is unsustainable, or confessing to the lie, which is sociopathic," I said. "But I have found a third path."

Jamal took a step back. "I know what you're going to say."

"Hear me out," I said. "Bands break up all the time."

"No," said Jamal firmly.

I gripped the air tighter.

"I should be getting home," said Jamal.

"This is your home," said Milo.

"Hear me out," I said. "It's so simple. We learn a song or two. We hang out in the music room at school. Cirrus just happens to find us there. And we can be like *Oh hey, Cirrus, what's up, we were just practicing.*"

"And how long do we do this for?" said Jamal.

"That's the thing!" I cried. "The three of us pretend to have a fight. Creative differences, money, doesn't matter. The band breaks up. Problem solved."

Milo opened his palms like a book. "As the Immortals die, so does your lie," he said.

Jamal aimed a long flat palm at my head. "You want us to help you so you don't lose the girl."

"Not that she's even mine to begin with," I said. "But something like that."

"Listen," said Jamal. "You know neither of us wants to see you get hurt by the situation you so inelegantly created in the first place."

"Tough truths," I said. "I appreciate that."

Milo placed one hand atop the other. "You are talking about layering on a new lie to fix the old lie."

"Only temporarily," I said. I swiveled to aim my hands at Jamal like a turret cannon. "You could play bass."

"Never before in my life have I played bass," said Jamal.

"But you play piano!" I said. "How different can it be? Piano is essentially a percussive instrument, and many consider bass guitar to be one as well! Six of one!"

Jamal tilted his head this way and that, struggling with my reasoning.

I rotated to Milo. "And you're athletic! I bet you could totally keep a beat on drums!"

"Never before in my life have I played drums," said Milo.

"You could totally learn," I said. "For just long enough."

I glanced wildly between the two. Milo tapped a foot, then the other, then slapped perfect sixteenth notes on his thighs with his hands, as if testing his body's capabilities. He shrugged his big muscly shoulders. He smiled.

"Could be fun," said Milo.

"Stop," said Jamal.

I clasped my hands. "I love you guys. So much."

"You make it impossible when you say that," said Jamal, squeezing his narrow head.

"We love you too," said Milo. He brought me in for a crushing hug.

I stretched an arm toward Jamal. "Come on. Please."

Jamal underwent a seizure for three seconds, then joined the hug. "You owe us."

"No you don't," said Milo. "Don't listen to Jamal."

I pushed them back to regard their faces. "Thank you."

"So we do this for a little while," said Jamal. "Just long enough to make her believe it. And then it's back to our regular DIY Fantasy FX programming."

"I promise," I said.

Jamal and Milo accepted, and I taught them how to share a fist bump and make the pledge *To metal*, just like Gray and his Mortals used to do.

I bid them farewell. I rode off into the night.

"Under the moonlight," I sang, pumping my legs. The air felt *great*. Everything was a slight downhill from Jamal's house, and the breeze was at my back, and I was flying free.

I would go home, hole myself up in Gray's room, and fiddle with all his equipment. I would orient myself. I would prepare.

I would practice guitar. Maybe even try singing at the same time. I would plan my big plan.

I reached home, activated the WhisperTrak belt-drive garage door, and dismounted. I entered the house silently so as not to wake anyone.

But everyone was still awake. I could hear them. When I walked into the great room, I could see them, too.

"Hey," said Gray.

II

A snake sheds its skin as it stretches in size.
What's left behind is a ghost with no eyes.

Regroup

"Uh," I said.

Mom and Dad sat on the couch with Gray, looking sleepy and pained.

Having Gray as a big brother was like being related to a teen pop star in hiding. Gray, with his sharp feminine jawline; his messy ponytail of blue carbon hair; his fine musculature, as precise as anime line art. He wore a short-fringe suede jacket and necklace of opal and turquoise and silver. Evidence of some sort of neo-country rock outfit, perhaps.

Seeing Gray suddenly before me after months of absence made me probe my own jawline (which was round) and my own musculature (which was largely missing) with dissatisfaction.

Gray sighed through gritted teeth. "Whatever you're thinking, Sun, do me a favor and save it."

Gray could have no idea what I was thinking, which was *Did I leave any of my stuff in his room? Did I leave any of his stuff lying out suspiciously?* I stifled the urge to glance up the staircase.

Instead I looked down and noticed two big duffel bags and a guitar bag.

"Are you . . . back?" I ventured.

Gray thumped a fist on the soft couch arm. "I'm here with all my worldly possessions late on a friggin' Tuesday night. Think, Sun."

"Gray," said Mom. "Be gentle with your brother."

Mom had been telling me and Gray to *be gentle* ever since we were little.

I rubbed my arm as if he'd just punched it. "Nice to see you, too, jeez."

Gray sneered—*Fsss*—and rose. He hoisted a duffel on each shoulder, then took his guitar.

"Going to bed," he said.

But he didn't head upstairs. He went *downstairs* instead, to some other room in the vast finished basement no one ever used. His footsteps faded into the big silence of the rest of the house.

I felt a cool wave of relief that quickly turned into puzzlement. Why didn't he go upstairs to his room?

"What is going on?" I said after he was gone.

"His band broke up," said Dad. Amazingly, he was still wearing his headset.

"Which one?" I said.

"There were multiple?" said Dad.

Mom took Dad's tiny headset out of his ear, turned it off with a careful squeeze, and tossed it into a crystal candy dish. "His roommate hooked up with his other roommate," she said. "Then they up and moved to Seattle. We told him he could stay here and regroup as he gets set up with his next band."

For how long? I wanted to say.

"Gosh," I said instead. Gray had just been through some disappointing nonsense, after all. (Still: Didn't mean Gray had to snap at me like he did.)

"Had to happen sometime," said Dad.

"Don't ever say that to Gray," said Mom.

"Roger that one hundred percent, dude," said Dad. "All I'm saying is music is not exactly a super-duper stable source of income."

"Music is a brutal business model," said Mom.

"Absolutely," said Dad.

"I *am* glad he's back," said Mom.

"Yap," said Dad. "Me too."

"Me too," I did not say. I was already dreading future interactions with him.

Despite this, I found myself creeping alone downstairs after Mom and Dad went up to bed. I entered the basement, so pristine it still exuded new-carpet smell. I'm not sure why I did this. I think I wanted to spy on him. Catch clues about his new life. I felt like I knew so little about him now, and here he was.

I reached the bottom of the stairs. I peeked in. He sat in the billiard room on an ancient poo-colored lazy chair. He was playing some old video game with the volume up loud.

Reload!

Ten seconds!

You lose!

"Goddamn it," said Gray. His eyes looked like someone else's. They looked rabid.

He caught sight of me. His eyes did not soften or change. These were his eyes now.

"Hey," I said, more out of surprise than greeting. I knit my fingers at my belly.

Gray glanced down. "You going through my old crap?" he chuffed.

His Goat of Satan ring. It was still on my finger.

"No," I whined, suddenly thirteen years old again, the age when we grew irreversibly apart. I waited for Gray to start pummeling me with questions. *What the hell were you doing in my room? What else have you gotten yourself into? Did you start dressing up as me to get some girl?*

But Gray asked no such questions; Gray simply returned to his game. "Whatever. It's all junk up there."

I fumed. It wasn't junk. It was *important*.

But if Gray didn't think so, was it?

Gray played. He acted like I wasn't there. For an absurd moment, I wished Gray *would* start interrogating me. I wished he *would* find out about my stupid mistake with Cirrus, and maybe even make fun of me, even if it made me feel awful.

Because all Gray did was ignore me, and that felt awful, too.

Gray glanced back with annoyance. At his little brother still fidgeting in the doorway.

"Leave me alone," he said, and flung the door shut.

When I peeked into Gray's old room the next morning, it was still exactly as I had left it. Untouched. A lost temple. Gray must have stayed in the basement billiard room all night.

Just to make sure, I made the long journey downstairs, where Mom and Dad were already babbling away on a call, then farther downstairs to the level below. I went to the billiard room door and listened.

Snoring.

I opened the door silently. Gray was still on the recliner, controller in hand. The game console was still on. At least the television had had enough sense to put itself to sleep. The room smelled stuffy and hot. Still, even in his sleep-dead state, Gray looked cool. He had changed into an impossibly on-trend tracksuit covered in grenades and Snoopys; he wore a velvet designer bucket hat (available for $200) slumped over his eyes.

I closed the door. I had wanted to make sure it was safe to search Gray's wardrobe without interruption, but I hadn't expected to feel depressed as a result. Gray was still not really here, even though he was physically here now.

At breakfast, Dad looked up from his phonetablaptop shuffle and wondered:

"Should I go check on Gray?"

"Let him come up on his own," said Mom.

I said bye to a monotone chorus of *Nn*s from my parents and rode the ten-speed to school. Once at the bike racks I dismounted and changed outfits: a digital black camo shirt with slashed jeans.

Part of me wished Gray could see how cool I felt, without seeing the part where I was borrowing his clothes.

Back in high school, Gray had already been a rock star. Less than a year after we moved to Rancho Ruby, he managed—despite being the single solitary lonely-only in his *entire class*—to charm his way into becoming universally popular across all the subgroups in the pantheon: jocks and preppies and thespians and student body politicians and so on.

It was around that time that Gray stopped talking to me in public. It goes without saying that Gray and I no longer went on dungeon adventures together, either. In private, we gradually stopped stealing spoons.

It took months for me to understand Gray's increasing distance: As a high schooler, he could not afford to be seen talking to a middle schooler, much less a nerd like me. His surplus of cool would only be depleted by my uncool, and he needed every bit he could get.

I guessed I could understand that. What else could I do?

I would watch my big brother's performances from the back of the auditorium, as mesmerized as the rest of the crowd. Gray: leaning his blackly ripped and distressed and studded self against the mic stand as if it were a staff, chopping away at his guitar to engulf the audience with its sparks.

I had seen with my very eyes twelve white girls on the front line fall instantly in love with Gray. This was well before K-pop burrowed its way into the heart of American mainstream media and laid eggs there; the world had never seen a star who looked like Gray. Gray never paid the girls much attention. He would stare above the crowd with Gatsbian intensity, perhaps at the bright green EXIT sign way in the back. His obliviousness only made the girls want him more.

Now, wearing the very same clothes that Gray had worn back in his high school rocker days, I felt regal. I felt sparky.

Jamal and Milo goggled at me.

"I think this rock persona actually suits you," said Milo.

Jamal looked down at his sweatshirt and sweatpants and walking sneakers.

"Have I been Florida Man this whole time?" he said.

"Gray's closet has lots of clothes you could try," I said. "He's back, by the way."

Milo and Jamal froze.

"Is everything okay?" said Milo.

"He's in between bands," I said. "Other than that, it's hard to tell anything when the guy won't talk to you."

"So, still kind of a dick," said Jamal.

I shrugged: *Yep.*

"Does Gray's return present problems for our plan?" said Milo.

"You mean Sunny's plan," said Jamal.

"Hey," said Milo. "Friends in need."

"I know, I know," said Jamal.

I thought of Gray ignoring me. "It shouldn't present any problems," I said. "On that note, how about we give the whole music thing a try ourselves in the practice room after school?"

Jamal and Milo looked at each other: *O-kay.*

Elf shot the food! cried my phone. I made a mental sticky to temporarily switch to a more conventionally acceptable and therefore more boring ringtone.

Will you be my lunchmate? wrote Cirrus. I ate with the guidance counselor in her office yesterday and it was 1930s Berlin in there.

I smiled the most ridiculous smile ever. I showed it to Jamal and Milo.

Jamal looked at me, awestruck. "That means you're married."

As you wish, I wrote back.

Foot-ball

Are you ready for a real American lunch at a real American school?" I said.

I found Cirrus standing on a concrete berm by the outdoor amphitheater, which was already imprinting in my mind as a sacred site of great significance and origin. She observed the rivers of braying teenfolk with arms folded and the hard eyes of a desert shepherd.

"Show me all of your country's secrets," she said with a smile.

I was feeling bold, so I held out a hand to help her down. She just slapped me five and jumped.

"I get to sit with the cool kids," she said.

I faked a rakish snarl. "Come on."

I felt a swagger rising within me. I was walking with the mysterious and beautiful new girl, who happened to live just down the street, no big deal.

My swagger froze and shattered as soon as I glimpsed the

lunch area. At the far end were Milo and Jamal glaring up at Gunner, who, right on cue, snatched away Milo's basket of fries and tipped his sports drink into his tray for good measure. His hairless, gray-skinned sidekick cackled through rotting teeth:

"Nerd tax."

The sight gutted me of all confidence, leaving it to splatter and curdle all over the floor.

I began to hyperventilate. Cirrus thought I was cool. She thought I was brave. Because she thought I was something I was not. Because I'd told her I was someone I was not.

If you became friends with someone who turned out to be someone else, did that mean you'd have to start all over again with the real them? Would you even want to?

"Over here," I said, veering us off-course toward a blank wall concealed by planters.

I sat down on the ground. Cirrus cheerfully followed, not knowing any better. She did not know this area had no coolness to it whatsoever. How could she?

I wished I could rewind time and simply say,

This is actually Gray's room. Not mine.

But time travel had not yet been invented and never would be, no matter how many lazy-brained sci-fi movies fantasized about it without proper peer-reviewed study.

This was a stupid, stupid problem, and I kicked myself for having created it.

I peered and watched Gunner saunter away in the distance. Milo poured out his flooded tray into a drain in the floor with practiced care. I felt bad that I hadn't been there to help absorb and defuse the abuse. Instead, I was safe here with Cirrus. It felt selfish of me.

Cirrus and I opened our bags and investigated our lunches. Cirrus unwrapped what looked like an al pastor cemita sandwich, but on pretzel bread—quite the twist. I groaned with an almost sexual desire at the sight of it.

"What is that?" I said.

"An experiment," said Cirrus. "My parents let me pick whatever I want for grocery delivery, since it's mostly just me in the house anyway. I wind up messing around with food just for kicks."

I revealed my lunch: pita sandwiches filled not with gyros but leftover bulgogi and dabs of sambal oelek. Lunches were always random, slapdash affairs haphazardly assembled with whatever I could find in the refrigerator. But they were always good, too.

"Trade, trade, trade," said Cirrus with big eyes.

We traded. We ate.

"This is amazing," I said.

"*This* is amazing," said Cirrus. "And not too wet."

I looked at her.

"I'm not a huge fan of wet foods," said Cirrus. "Cereal, most soups, tuna salad sandwiches."

"I'm glad," I said.

"We definitely have the best lunches out of any of these genetically engineered philistines," said Cirrus.

One person's usual is another person's brand new.

A sudden wave of nausea swelled. Because right now I was very much liking being with Cirrus. And I could tell she was liking being with me. Or what she thought was me.

"So is it considered cool to sit here because Americans

aspire to set themselves apart from the rest of the herd?" said Cirrus. "I saw an ad that said something like that."

"Americans are brainwashed from an early age to believe that they are blessèd children of God with total sovereign autonomy and unlimited individual control over their destinies no matter what systemic prejudices or disadvantages they might have been born into, which in turn allows their government to forsake all social responsibility and focus on groveling facedown in the gutter to let the great amoral capitalistic parasites slither through the diseased streets of the nation's corpus unimpeded and unquestioned," I said.

"Cool," said Cirrus. Then she broke into cackles. "You're weird."

Had I gone on and on? I sometimes had a tendency to go on and on.

I remembered my outfit. I remembered I was *cool*.

"Honestly, I eat here because it's quiet," I said. "I don't need to hear a bunch of screaming about which filter looks better."

"Or whose hair makes a candidate more electable," said Cirrus.

"Or how our team needs to score more points than the other guys to win at football," I said. "The answer is more. The answer is always more."

We cackled together, two crazies holding up a wall. We ate.

"That's something I've been curious about in your exotic land," said Cirrus. "American foot-ball. It seems very important here."

I pulled out my phone, scrolled around the horribly designed school website, and showed slick professional photos of our team to her.

"It is," I said. "The whole school revolves around the sport."

"The one where boys in super-tight, super-sexy pants hold endless outdoor meetings about the fate of an inflated pig bladder while pretending to not have hidden desires for one another," said Cirrus.

I stopped mid-chew and gazed at her, amazed. Because she was amazing. "That's the one," I said.

"Not that other football, where openly racist hooligans jeer each other over which player pulled off a foul with the most convincing theatrics," she said with a sly smile.

Gazelles wished they could leap high enough to match the grace of her wit.

"Six of one," I said, and smiled back.

"I also saw something about a Hawking dance?" said Cirrus.

I groaned. "Sadie Hawkins. The revolutionary concept behind that event is that the girl asks the boy to attend, not the other way around."

"Reminds me of White Day in Asia," said Cirrus. "The revolutionary concept behind that is that the girl gives chocolates to the boy."

"That's it?" I said.

"Doesn't take much," said Cirrus.

"Mind blown," I said, and we cackled some more.

"So I guess we have some to-do items in our cultural orientation queue," said Cirrus.

I found myself smiling so much that my head exploded with light that consumed our planet to transform it into a new rival star.

Cirrus ate her last bite, wadded up the eco-friendly, compostable wrapper, and swished a trash can ten feet away with ease. She lobbed mine, too: swish.

She glanced again at my phone.

"It looks like the next American foot-ball match is tomorrow night," said Cirrus.

"It is," I said warily.

"What's a foot-ball match like?" she said.

"They're a spectacular example of what happens when an entire culture represses their sexuality under the banner of sport," I said.

In truth, however, I didn't know—I had never attended a football game. Why would I waste time on that kind of bull-sparkle?

"Foot-ball sounds like it would be hilarious to watch," said Cirrus.

And with that, I decided O hell yes, I must now go to a *foot-ball match.*

"I'll swing by your house tomorrow and we can witness it together," I said.

It was one of the bravest things I'd ever said in my whole life. Not just because I had never gone to a high school football game before, but also because I had never asked a girl out to anything ever. Now I just had. And the girl was named Cirrus.

She leaned back. She *considered* me.

"I meant to say earlier that I like your outfit," she said now with a smile that could revive crops withered by atomic fallout. "Do you have a gig tonight or something?"

"Nah," I said. "It's just Wednesday."

Bam!

It's! Just! Wednesday!

"Well," said Cirrus with a tilt of her head. "I think you look really cool."

Everything went silent but for the lingering *ell* of Cirrus's *cool.*

you look really coooolllllllllll

". . ." said Cirrus. ". . . . ."

I marveled as a nearby skateboard slid to a halt without a sound. A study group broke into mute laughter. Classroom doors silently flapped open and shut.

"?" said Cirrus. "? ?, ?!, ?!?!"

The world returned with a whoosh and a pop, and I realized Cirrus had placed a hand on my shoulder.

"Hello?" said Cirrus.

"Heyyyyyyy—" I said. "—yyyyyyyyyyy—"

"—yyyyyyy," said two voices, joining in.

Milo and Jamal, looking down at me like *There you are.* We rose from our hidden lunch spot.

"Where's your outfits?" said Cirrus, indicating their rudimentary choices in clothing.

They glanced at me with their brows lowered just a millimeter, just enough to let me know they were fully committed to my charade. Thank god for Milo and Jamal.

"We keep things basic when we're off-duty," said Milo, "because we're not the front man."

Cirrus looked at me with fresh eyes. She mimed screaming into a mic. Then she punched my shoulder.

The bell rang.

"Front man," she said, and left.

"Bye," I said slowly, as if I had just learned basic greetings.

I smiled as Cirrus vanished into the commotion surrounding us.

"Higher cognitive process express, now boarding," called a woman. The vice principal. "Let's motivate."

"Motivating," I called back. We launched into a walking speed of 0.25 meters per second.

"You look like the real thing," said Milo.

"I do?" I said, picking at my shirt.

"She punched you," said Milo.

"I wish someone would punch me," said Jamal.

"I'm never washing this . . . what's this arm muscle called?" I said.

"You might not have that muscle yet," said Milo.

"Listen," said Jamal, suddenly serious. "Have your fun and whatever, but I'm warning you right now: Don't go crazy."

"It's just a black shirt and black pants," I said.

"What I'm saying," said Jamal, "is that if she gets too used to this version of you, she'll run away when our plan completes and you go back to being the real you."

"Thanks?" I said.

"We play, we pretend to argue, we break up," said Milo.

"And then everything goes back to normal," said Jamal.

"Okay," I said.

But it wasn't okay. I liked how the clothes made me feel. I even liked the attention, which was a surprise.

"First Immortals practice after school," I said, in my best front-man pose. "Let's rock the thing out with extreme urgency."

Gee

"So this is the music room," said Jamal.

"We never come here," said Milo.

It was true. We never hung out in the music room at school. The only people who came here were students focused on marching band, orchestra, or jazz. The music room was a state-of-the-art chamber, with cable lassos and a mixer board and speakers and doors that latched close like airlocks. It was serious. It had an aroma of seriousness.

No one was here now, because classes had ended for the day.

Aside from the hum of the lights above in the music room, the whole school was tranquil but for the distant bark and whinny of the color guard practicing their knock-off martial routines somewhere. It felt cool being here late, having the place to ourselves.

You think it's cool to be at school after hours. You are a super mega-nerd.

Part of the music room had timpani, upright basses, a piano: everything you'd need for a classical performance.

The other part had a drum kit, an amp, guitars, a mic: everything you'd need for rock and roll.

Mr. Tweed, the music teacher, said we could stay as long as we needed to, because Mr. Tweed knew that music had the power to remind humankind to be human and kind.

There was a large poster with cartoon instruments of every kind looking at us with googly eyes. In unison, they all declared MUSIC IS MAGICAL!

I rapped the brass crash cymbals with my knuckles. They were part of something that looked like drums but was stacked vertically, like a sparkly garbage can with a fancy lid.

"Cocktail drums," I said, like a reverent tour guide. "Prince played these."

"No," said Jamal. "He would never."

My reluctant co-conspirators stared at me, waiting for guidance.

"How about we just familiarize ourselves with the tools of the trade?" I said.

"Did you really just say *tools of the trade*, Dad?" said Milo.

Jamal hoisted a bass guitar and inspected it as if it were a musket. "Tell me how this thing works."

I found an electric guitar and slung it over my shoulder. "Wear it like this."

Jamal threw it over his torso and stumbled for balance under its weight. He plucked a few strings. "There's no sound."

I plugged him into an amp, turned it on, and provided fresh earplugs to protect the delicate hair cells deep within the cochlea, which, once damaged, would never grow back. I did the same for my amp and ears.

Milo was crouched at the drums, muttering to himself. "This foot pedal must activate the bass drum. This must activate the dual cymbal assembly. Okay."

Milo settled onto the drum throne like a rookie pilot. He brandished two sticks. "Okay."

Jamal and I looked at each other. "Okay."

"What now?" said Jamal.

"Wanna play a G?" I said.

"Show me."

I pointed at my guitar. "These bottom four strings go in ascending order from E, to A, then D, then G. Your strings do, too."

"This is way different from *Guitar Poser VR*," said Jamal.

"Hold your hand like this," I said. "Grip it like this."

Jamal quickly processed these instructions. With his index finger he held down the third fret of the lowest string, which was fat as a metal cable. "Three half steps up from E means G would be here," he said. He plucked.

Geeeeeeeee, hummed the amp.

Jamal palmed the string silent. "I guess it is kind of percussive."

"Count us in," I said to Milo.

Milo beamed, as if he had always harbored a secret dream of counting a band in with his sticks. He bashed them together. "One, two, three, four!"

GEEEEEEEEE

Milo crashed everything he could before him: snare, toms, cymbals.

Me and Jamal strummed away at our one mighty chord. We even vamped a little. Like rock stars.

GEE GEE GEE GEEEEEEEEEEE

I leaned into a mic and sang rock-and-roll nonsense: "Baby baby baby baby!"

My pulse was going. I could feel Jamal and Milo's energy too. From just one G chord. Imagine adding another!

"How about E?" I shouted.

We paused to gingerly walk our fingers down, squeaking and squonking along the way as we counted one fret, then two, only to discover that E was an open note that required no digital pressure whatsoever. The amps patiently waited with an electric hum. Milo counted us in again, which was not strictly necessary.

EEE EEE EEE EEEEEEEEEEEE

The three of us continued to do this with other simple chords. Together, we made an imprecise, ultra-dorky form of music, but music nonetheless. We did not shred. Far from it.

Still. I could see us getting better. I could see our timing improving.

BOOM! BA-BOOM! TSHH!

Milo stood at the odd drum kit and shouted, "We! Are! The—"

He twirled his sticks a half revolution before dropping them because his drumstick-twirling skills were extremely poor.

"—Immortals," muttered Milo, bending down to retrieve the sticks.

When Milo got back into position, I could see a happy flush in his cheeks. In Jamal's, too. They had played but the simplest, dumbest music—but I could tell they already thought it was fun.

"And I thought rock and roll was dead," said Mr. Tweed. He

had entered the room with an armload of spiral-bound music books, and we hadn't even noticed. He threw a devil horn salute, cool as can be. "Since when did you three get into music?"

"It was sudden," I said.

"I assume this is for the talent show?" said Mr. Tweed.

"Huh?" I could feel the eyes of Jamal and Milo on me like red sniper sights. I glanced at them, shook my head. "There's a talent show?" I said, with genuine ignorance. I had no idea there was a talent show.

"You're gonna have to bring it. The school rented out Miss Mayhem on Sunset, gonna be big."

Miss Mayhem. In my mind I saw the royal-yellow flyer on Gray's wall:

THE MORTALS

AT THE WORLD-FAMOUS MISS MAYHEM

ON SUNSET STRIP IN HOLLYWOOD, CA

The same place Gray and the Mortals played years ago.

"Do you, uh," I said, "do you actually think we'd be good enough to play Miss Mayhem?"

"With your classic rock falsetto?" said Mr. Tweed. "Sure."

Falsetto, from the Italian *falso* meaning "false," is when a singer fakes a higher voice above their natural range. There was nothing *falso* about my voice—it was just naturally high. I'd never felt proud of it until just now.

"Ahem," said Jamal.

He was glaring at me: *Absolutely not.*

I glanced over at Milo, whose face said: *What Jamal said.*

"We're actually metal, not classic rock," I said.

"Buncha hellspawns, very nice," said Mr. Tweed. "So, Jamal and Milo: As bass and drums, you are the backbone. Keep your eyes locked. Communicate. Your job is to give your front man Sunny here a rock-solid stage to headbang on. That alone will elevate you above the dance gangs, Ariana-bes, and honey-baked Hamiltons."

"That's really great advice, thank you," I said.

Jamal looked pained. "Wait a sec—"

"I've seen a lot of talent shows, you know what I'm saying?" said Mr. Tweed with a side-pshaw. "I would love it if you guys rocked it *the-hell-out* for the sake of my weary soul."

And he held out a paradise-pink flyer.

RUBY HIGH TALENT SHOW—AT THE
LEGENDARY MISS MAYHEM ON SUNSET STRIP
IN HOLLYWOOD, CALIFORNIA—
NO PRESSURE LOL

"We will rock you," I said, secretly addressing Cirrus.

"We will not even think about it," corrected Jamal.

Mr. Tweed clocked the whole situation before him with his brown eyes and chuckled to himself. "Did you know that all serious rock stars started out as total self-taught nerds?"

I looked down at myself and at my friends and wondered: *Are we that obvious?*

"The cool comes later," said Mr. Tweed. He polished his tortoiseshell rims. "Trust me."

"Huh," I said, gospel-nodding.

"What is happening—" whispered Jamal.

Mr. Tweed slapped a hand on the large poster on the wall. "Say it with me."

"Music is magical," we chanted.

"This room's yours, day or night," said Mr. Tweed. "Door code is six, six, six."

"Number of the beast," I said.

"Stay metal, Sunny boy," said Mr. Tweed.

Salsa

I changed back into my civvies, rode home, and stared at my fingertips—fingertips that had gone red and sore from the pressure of the fine wires of the guitar. I smelled them.

They smelled *metal.*

"Hello?" I said.

No response. I remembered Mom and Dad were at the country club for yet another vapid convocation of douche-nozzles crucial to unlocking millions in potential new business.

Gray appeared, holding two plates and a pizza box.

"Mom said we have to eat dinner together," said Gray, and vanished outside.

It was dusk on the back patio, and the landscaped terraces of our yard looked out onto a rolling valley so full of villas and marching cypress you could almost believe you were in freaking Tuscany if not for the blue rectangles of outrageous home theaters flickering here and there.

I stared at a lovely fountain of two marble dolphins

regurgitating upon six marble turtles, who didn't mind. The mood lights awoke, realized what time it was, and immediately set themselves to Romance Mode. I wished it were Cirrus sitting across from me. Eating with Cirrus would be very Romance Mode.

Eating with Gray was very not Romance Mode.

We ate and filled the air with the wet despondent music of our chewing.

"This pizza sucks," said Gray suddenly.

"You're sitting in perfect weather in September in the sprawling backyard of a brazillion-dollar home eating celebrity-chef pizza summoned by an app," I said. "But your pizza sucks."

"Brazillion is the low end for Rancho Ruby," said Gray.

"Housing crisis?" I yodeled. "What housing crisis?"

I had been hoping to get a laugh out of Gray—I used to love making him laugh—but he only hung his head. "Whatever, you don't understand," he said.

"Try me," I said.

Gray just chewed. He thought of something and laughed a dark and disgusted laugh. Something else struck him, and his expression quickly became one of sorrow. He was having a whole inner dialogue right in front of me. Now he froze up. He looked like he wanted to cry.

"Hey," I said. "What's going on?"

"It's nothing," said Gray. "There's nothing to talk about, so why would I, just think for one single second, Sunny, use your stupid brain."

Unlike with Milo, for me *It's nothing* was ice-cold water splashed upon the fire of my compassion.

"God, fine," I said, and tore at my pizza.

Gray inhaled and exhaled loudly as he masticated, producing a super-gross sound of a man buried in food trying to eat his way out, and flung a pizza rind onto the lawn. A squirrel appeared immediately and dragged it into the bushes.

"Whoa," said Gray.

"It's like the little guy was waiting for it," I said.

We both chuffed to ourselves. Then I remembered I was supposed to be annoyed with Gray. But when I looked over, he wasn't annoyed with me. He looked heavy with sorrow all over again.

"I need salsa," said Gray, and left.

I did not follow. I decided I would finish my pizza, put my plate away, and *give him space.*

But I barely got in three more bites before Gray came jogging back, his eyes thrilling at something in his hand.

"Dad went back to this crap?" said Gray, and brandished a jar.

"Yep," I said. "La Victoria salsa. I guess he gave up on the fancy stuff."

Gray had a strange habit of pouring salsa on pizza, and he now did so with an almost tearful glee.

Maybe a little salsa was all Gray needed?

"God," he said. "I haven't had La Victoria in forever."

He took a bite, sending his eyes rolling into the back of his head. "It's so good. Try some."

After a moment of hesitation—when was the last time I had shared food with Gray?—I took a bite.

"That tastes like regurgitated minestrone on top of grilled cheese passed through a hot hair straightener," I said. "It's great."

"La Victoria, dude," said Gray, chewing and nodding excitedly. "*Keep it on the top shelf so it doesn't freeze, boys,* remember?

Next to the Vlasic spears and Grey Poupon in our crappy fridge? Back in Arroyo Plato?"

"The Frost Giant!" I cried, reeling from the memory of the refrigerator door that sometimes couldn't shut against all the billowing overgrown ice. I could see little bits of our old kitchen in Arroyo Plato plopping into view like drips of watercolor. "Remember how Mom and Dad used to hoard Diet Pepsi when it was on sale? Remember Coors Light?"

"I Can't Believe It's Not Butter!" said Gray. "Tapatío."

"Hot Pockets," I said, shooting out my fingers with each word. "Shrimp Cup Noodles—Lunchables—Easy Cheese—Pepperidge Farm pot pies—"

"Hormel corned beef in those weird trapezoid tins," said Gray. He narrowed his eyes, hit by a dark vision: "*Vienna sausages.*"

"Nasty!" I said.

"You cried when we left our old house," said Gray.

"You cried too," I said. "So shut up."

We both sat there with eyes dancing. I saw myself in my enchanted tinfoil helm again, following Gray the Gallant down the hall with a yardstick for a sword and a torn sam taeguk fan as my shield.

I wondered if Gray remembered our adventures, too, but did not ask, because I was terrified he would say *Not really* or, worse, *We were such nerds*. I had the feeling he and I remembered our childhoods very differently.

But I knew we both remembered every inch of our old Arroyo Plato house, and all the cheap junky food in it.

Our laughter sighed away—as all laughter eventually does—and Gray poured more salsa on another slice. He took a bite. He chewed.

"Ten bands in three years," declared Gray.

I stopped. I listened.

"You know some places only pay you in booze?" said Gray. "Hollywood is a trip."

I continued to say nothing. Gray was in a delicate state, and I wanted him to keep talking. I wanted to know about his music. I wanted to know about his life.

"Fakes, flakes, and straight-up snakes, man," said Gray, shaking his head. His face sharpened. "LA's not as big as people think. There's only so many clubs and so many hours in the night. It's such a scene. That was the name of my last band. *Endscene.*"

It made me uneasy seeing Gray like this. Gray was once the unofficial king of Ruby High.

"This next band's gonna kill it," I said, speaking from the experience of constantly improving DIY Fantasy FX videos, one by one. Creative work was not the triumphant sartorial yawp people imagined; it was a steady, relentless drip that led to things like Lady Lashblade, and ideally beyond.

"My next band," chuffed Gray.

"It will," I said. "If not this band, then the one after that."

Gray winced at this. "Sun—"

"You got this." I discovered I had leaned way forward. I was eager for anything from Gray. A smile, a nod, even an irritating ruffle of my hair.

But Gray just flung his pizza rind away, this time deep into the sagebrush.

"Dad said he's gonna put in a good word for me at the club," said Gray to the horizon.

My eyes quizzed. *Good word?*

Gray looked down and away, his mouth snarled with loathing.

"I'm done eating," said Gray, and flung his chair down. He left and vanished back downstairs.

I looked at the stricken chair.

I folded the pizza box closed. I reset the chair. The sun melted away. I wished I hadn't said anything. I wished I had talked about anything else: squirrels, or old video games. I was blaming myself for upsetting Gray. Why was I blaming myself?

Because I just couldn't understand why Gray wasn't like he used to be.

Midnight. I crept into Gray's old room. I sat in the blueness of the darkness there and breathed. From the basement I could hear Gray playing his video game at full, hearing-impairing volume.

On one of Gray's guitars were tiny words in Gray's precise handwriting, arranged as an infinitely repeating wheel.

Beauty Is Truth Is Beauty Is Truth Is

I took the guitar off its stand, plugged it in to the amp, and put on headphones. I tuned down to a dropped D. I played a simple metal riff I remembered from the Mortals.

The guitar body shone in the dark. Its strings flashed in parallels sixfold.

I played okay.

I played and played, struggling to remember how to climb

up and down the pentatonic scale, the foundation for rock guitar solos everywhere for all time. I came up with a few riffs of my own—some dumb, some clearly derivative, and some actually sorta cool.

I noticed a milk crate full of cables and effects pedals and whatnot, and set the guitar down to dig around.

I found a framed picture that had lost its glass: a photo of me and Gray marred by orange streaks of dried battery acid.

I found an ancient piece of technology: a cracked iPod bound by its own charging cable gone sticky with grime. On the back, a strip of gaffer tape with *The Mortals scratch tracks Property of Gray Dae* written in white.

I unwound the filthy cable, plugged it in. From its paltry number of basic apps, I tapped one I'd never heard of: SongEdit Free. A barebones multitrack editor. I imagined Gray—the Gray I once knew—recording impromptu sessions in his bandmate's van, or maybe backstage, or maybe right here in his bedroom late at night on a night like this.

I unplugged my headphones from the amp and plugged into the iPod, which looked comically thin and small and obsolete. But at this moment, it felt like an alien relic containing all the secrets of a lost society.

For now here were all the tracks the Mortals had ever performed, in various states of development. I already knew almost all of them. The ones I didn't know were named Vocals Rough or Random Beats 08 or Untitled Project 32—scratch ideas full of stops and starts that could not even be called songs.

And there, at the very top of the list—meaning the most recent—was a file called Beauty Is Truth Final.

I hit Play.

To understand my reaction to this track, it would help to understand the typical Mortals song, which like all power pop punk hewed to a precise click track and traditional song structure to produce something like:

VERSE 1 → CHORUS
VERSE 2 → CHORUS
BRIDGE → CHORUS

"Beauty Is Truth" did not hew to traditional structure. It did not hew to anything. It was seven minutes long—twice the length of a typical song. Its tempo fluctuated anywhere between anthem slow and mosh-pit fast. It jumped around all over the place, ignoring genre boundaries. Mapped out, it looked like this:

FREEFORM INTRO → VERSE 1 (ROCK) →
CHORUS A
EDM BREAKDOWN → CHORUS B →
VERSE 2 (ROCK)
BRIDGE 1 (TRAP) → VERSE 3 (ACOUSTIC) →
BRIDGE 2 (A CAPELLA)
FINAL CHORUS → OUTRO (TECHNO)

I finished the track. I examined the iPod with amazement. I tightened the headphone band on my head.

And I listened again.

The song got better. I could not understand how it did that.

By the fourth listen, I knew enough of the lyrics to mouth along. As I did, I held the framed photo of me and Gray, and I discovered I wanted to cry a little.

As far as I knew, Gray worked on this song in secret during his senior year of high school. The song had never been performed onstage. It lived only on this forgotten device. Gray hadn't told anyone about it. Why not? Did he think people wouldn't like it?

Why hadn't Gray ever told me about it?

The song ended—again—and I found myself shaking my head with wonder.

The song was the most Gray thing I had ever experienced. It was pure Gray.

Like characters in a game, all people are born endowed with specific magicks. Unlike games, however, that magic depletes over time without careful cultivation and care. Very few people possess the strength to hold on to the magic for very long. It gets even harder as the vine of magic grows thinner and thinner, eventually becoming as thin as a desiccated branch that breaks off with a snap.

Gray's song—"Beauty Is Truth"—was magic.

I wished I could tell Gray that, but Gray didn't seem to be listening to anyone right now.

Sleepy. I doffed the headphones, stood the guitar upright. Clicked off the amp.

Beauty Is Truth Is Beauty Is Truth Is

Did the wheel start with *Beauty*? Or *Truth*?

I went to my room and lay on my bed. I hadn't put on my sleep cap or night guard or anything yet, but found I didn't care right now about halitosis or proper cephalic thermoregulation or the perils of unchecked bruxism.

I just lay there missing Gray, even as he slept just two floors away. I looked at the orange-stained photo of us.

I took a tissue and carefully wiped as much of the orange off as I could, set the photo aside, and clap-clap, turned out the light.

Shame

Thursday. After school.

With fingers still sore from music practice, I adjusted my desk lamp and opened my notebook.

DIY FANTASY FX—SUNNY DAE

I took the tiny pen from the tiny knight and wrote *Prop ideas.*

I had ten minutes before it was time to head to Cirrus's house before the football game, so I figured I would get some brainstorming done.

I spent the next four minutes doing nothing but tapping the pen.

Tap-tap-tap. Tap-tap-tap.

Cir-rus-Soh. Cir-rus-Soh.

I looked at the page. It was freckled with ink.

Knock-knock, went the door, and Dad poked his head in. He wore a suit. He was staring at his phone.

"Dinner's downstairs if you're hungry," said Dad.

"I'll just get something at the football game," I said.

Dad looked up with alarm. "Since when do you go to football games?"

"Cirrus has never seen one," I said.

"Cirrus?" said Dad.

Dad lowered his phone and gazed at me with crystal eyes.

"Dad," I said.

Dad gazed at me with crystal—

"Dad!" I said.

"Right," said Dad, "anyway, so, cool, hey, I wanted to ask your help."

"Press volume up, volume down, then hold the side button," I said.

"Not my phone," said Dad.

"Up up down down left right left right B A Start," I said.

"The Inspire NV has forty-eight cameras both inside and outside the vehicle, all constantly recording, with audio," said Dad.

"How is that okay?" I said.

Dad shook a finger. "And! Did! You! Know! All the videos are on the Inspire customer portal."

I squinted. "Did you want to show me thrilling footage from your commute?"

Dad gripped his phone. "Someone keyed my car. What kind of GD MF-ing A-hole SOB would pull this kind of BS on me?"

"On the car, not you," I said.

"God, the optics!" said Dad.

"Optics?" I said.

Dad pinched his nose. "Now everyone's gonna think, *What did that guy do to deserve getting keyed like that? That guy must be some kind of douchebag!*"

"It depresses me how people blindly believe their car is an expression of their value as a human being," I said.

"You're not helping," said Dad. "Anyway: I can't seem to log in to the Inspire portal."

"Did you use your finger?" I said. "Did you use your face?"

"I don't do that stuff," said Dad.

Jhk jhk, went my phone. I had changed the ringtone from *Elf shot the food!* to a snarling snippet of Dave Grohl's electric guitar from a Foo Fighters intro.

Ready when you are, wrote Cirrus. Ride your bike.

You got a bike?!? I wrote back.

Jhk jhk. Cirrus sent a photo of a gorgeous small-wheeled folding bike sitting in an empty bedroom. Was it her bedroom? Did all the rooms look like that in that condo of hers?

"I'll take a look at it later," I said to Dad. "Gotta go."

Dad glanced at his gold-diamond-unobtanium wristwatch. "Crap, me too."

I tiptoed out to Gray's room. As soon as I reached into his closet, I heard footsteps. I snatched up the first thing I could—a wondrous black hoodie studded with inverted silver crosses—and put it on.

The hoodie fit me heavy and loose like a soothsayer's cloak. An ancient tube of eyeliner was still in its pocket.

I crept back out into the hallway, where I would then dash downstairs before anyone could spot me—

"What the hell are you doing?" said Gray.

My head snapped up. "I don't, all my jackets, it's gonna be cold, I never go out at night?"

Gray made a sneering grin. "The year 2015 called and they want their clothes back—"

I examined Gray. "What the hell are *you* doing?"

Going from head to toe, Gray wore a dad-shirt, dad-tie, dad-slacks, and finally dad-boat shoes, all various shades of brown. He looked forty years old, and also dead.

Dad appeared, rubbing sandalwood lotion into his hands. "You look great, Gray!"

Gray's face tightened with humiliation.

Dad peered at me. "Is that a new hoodie?"

"Yesno," said me and Gray.

"Well, it'll be nice and warm for the football game," said Dad.

"Football game?" pondered Gray.

"He's going with a *gurl*," said Dad in an off-Broadway amateur-night stage whisper.

Then Dad thumped Gray's back and headed downstairs. "Let's go shake some hands, dude! Trey Fortune awaits!"

Gray held a palm down at me. "Just—shut up," he muttered.

I shut up. I could've launched any one of my dozen at-the-ready volleys against the cannibalistic blood-fever that was corporate America, but I did not. Because now Gray marched down the stairs after Dad, slow as a death march. He stopped at the door leading to the garage. He seemed to want to say something, but nixed the idea.

In the end, he opened the door and fell through with a long, slow step.

I sailed into the night. I wished I could wear my headlamp, which was obviously the smartest, most versatile choice in portable lighting. I settled instead for the primitive default reflectors, popular among most cyclists but good for nothing except feebly catching beams of homicidal oncoming cars in the moment before fatal impact.

When I reached Cirrus's condo, she was already out on the curb wearing a helmet.

"Your bike is amazing," I blurted, and immediately wished I had started with a more socially acceptable *Hi* or its popular variant, *Hey*.

She clicked on a light smartly built right in to her helmet. "It's a Blitzschnell Tango CAAD12 folding bike with hydraulic disc brakes and a shock-absorbing seat post," she said.

I wanted to tell her all about my Velociraptor® Elite. Instead, my brain became paralyzed with indecision. Could I afford to gush about such nerdery? Would it break my persona, cause suspicion?

"You think my bike is dorky," said Cirrus.

"No," I said. I wanted to say more, but found I couldn't. "It's not."

"They're all over Copenhagen," said Cirrus.

"I bet," I said.

"I baked us some ham and cheese hand pies," said Cirrus. "Do you like fontina?"

"What's a fontina?" I said.

"You'll see," said Cirrus. "Let's ride."

And now we sailed together. She wore high boots and a heavy skirt that flew like a cape. A bag of hand pies lightly bounced in a wicker cargo basket. She pedaled and shifted with an easy grace that was athletic and fashionable at the same time, something no American could ever pull off. Cirrus was cool. Cirrus could make anything seem cool, I reckoned.

"Head toward that glow way over there," I said.

Cirrus squinted. "And . . . music?"

We both leaned into a turn, then another, passing through encroaching rivers of cool night mist before reaching a cathedral of light.

The football field.

I had been here many times during the day, to laze about in the golden afternoon sun during track practice. But I had never seen this place at night. And why would I have? I always imagined football to be a sad contest full of huddle meetings and play reviews and administrata.

But football was only half about the gameplay itself. I had never seen the other half of it: the balloons, the crowds, the dozens of headlights swiveling around the vast parking lot. I had never felt the thundering beat of the drum corps announcing impending war in the distance.

It was electric.

Cirrus came to a stop with her toe en pointe. "Incredible," she gasped.

"Yep, this is football," I drawled, as nonchalantly as I could, to best mimic that bless-this-mess attitude that fans assumed when introducing their passion to someone new.

"This happens every Thursday?" said Cirrus.

"Well, they moved it because it's supposed to rain tomorrow," I said with authority, quoting what I had read earlier on the school portal. "Normally it's every Friday, every week, just like church."

I gave her a game show host's wink. Too much?

"In Australia they play rugby rain or shine," said Cirrus.

"Southern Californians melt like wicked witches in the rain," I said.

"Let's go closer," said Cirrus.

We lashed our bikes to a tree and melted into the crowd. Four pickup trucks sat back-to-back, flanking a barbecue smoking in the center tended by fans in Ruby High Ravagers regalia.

"How early do the supporters arrive?" she said.

You are the expert here, I told myself. *Be the expert.*

"They're called *fans*, and [I believe] this is called *tailgating*," I said. "People get here ~~six hours~~ very early [or so I have heard] and bring ~~nitrated meats~~ food and drink [and that atrocious 'Wagon Wheel' song on a boombox]."

Maybe it was the infectious energy in the place, because Cirrus raised a fist and shouted, "Go, Ravagers!" to the tailgaters. They instantly dropped what they were doing to shout back at us with painted faces.

"That guy has a big foam hand," said Cirrus.

We approached a snack stand marked RAVAGER NATION NACHOS PIZZA HOT DOGS SODA.

"So here's where we can get classic football food things," I said, "like nachos, pizza, hot dogs, and soda."

Cirrus wrinkled her nose. "But I made hand pies."

I leaned in and said, "The food here is crap, to be honest." Totally not honest, of course, since I'd never eaten any of it before. But right away I could tell. Just look at it.

Cirrus reached in her bag and offered me a still-warm pie, and it tasted like what I imagined merry old London in Sweeney Todd's time must have tasted like.

"This is amazing," I said.

"After four hours in the kitchen, it better be," said Cirrus.

Shouts here and there made us look up.

"Good luck, Gunner."

"Go get 'em, Gun."

Gunner came trotting out in full football gear, having peed (or whatever) in a nearby porta-potty. I could tell it was him despite the helmet because the name GUNNER was written on his blood-red jersey.

Don't jerseys typically bear last names, not first? was my thought right as Gunner's eyes locked with mine and sharpened with contempt.

"Who let *this* nerd in?" he said through his grille, and came straight toward me.

I froze.

Gunner was about to do what Gunner had done many times before in our simple, abusive relationship. He was about to clock my shoulder and send me spinning to the ground as he bulldozed past. Normally my lunch tray would be there to come down with me, but this time the hand pie would have to suffice.

It was night, I was in foreign territory—his territory—and the energy of the crowd and the lights propelled him.

Beside me, Cirrus raised her phone and snapped a picture. This was fun for her. And why wouldn't it be? She had no idea.

Gunner strode toward me with clear aim and intent. I could not let this happen. I was wearing a hoodie with protective silver crosses, for Antichrist's sake. I was a rock star.

So I began clapping and hooting. "Let's go, Gunner, c'mon! We love you, buddy!"

Cirrus, infected by my bogus enthusiasm, joined in with an awkward chant: "Go, Gun-Nur! Go, Gun-Nur!" She threw me a look that said, *Is that how you say it?*

Surrounding fans corrected us with the more properly cadenced "Go, Gunner, go! Go, Gunner, go!"

My ploy worked. Gunner quickly realized he could not strike down an innocent fan for no reason in front of everybody.

"See ya, Sunny," he blurted, clearly discombobulated. He spin-dodged me, thrilling the fans, and hustled off to the brilliant green field.

"He knows you?" said Cirrus.

I froze again, for a different reason this time. Normally, I would've turned around and run from Gunner. This was the first time I had stood my ground, and the ground felt marvelous to stand on. I fully acknowledged the irony of gaining real confidence by faking being someone else. Maybe this was why people engaged in performance. To let go of old fears.

A voice exploded above us.

"LADIES AND GENTLEMEN, BOYS AND GIRLS, PLEASE STAND FOR THE NATIONAL ANTHEM!"

The marching band wheezed their way through the desiccated Francis Scott Key relic, and the crowd groaned along with its hoary antiquated lyrics, as always omitting the third stanza threatening murder for free former slaves before erupting into a barbarian *Woo.*

"Let's get seats," I said, and led Cirrus up into the blinding bleachers.

"AND NOW, BOTH TEAMS WOULD LIKE TO OBSERVE A TOTALLY OPTIONAL NONDENOMINATIONAL MOMENT OF SILENT REFLECTION!" boomed the voice.

At that instant, everyone around us began murmuring in unison.

O God, we thank you for the privilege of playing football on this glorious night.

Please fill us with athletic resolve and blessed energy.

Grant us the grace to accept victory or defeat,

Whichever way shall fall thine judgment.

Cirrus gaped at me. "It really is like church," she whispered.

"I told you," I said, bless-this-mess. But inside, I was just as awestruck as she was. I could not fathom why so many people would worship such a tedious game with this much reverence and gravitas. And yet here we were, surrounded by them.

She touched one of the silver crosses on my arm. "You rebel heretic."

To my shock, she bowed her head, touched her forehead to mine, and giggled as the crowd prayed on.

Watch over us as we tackle and run.

Watch over the health and happiness of our loved ones young and old

As they cheer thine glory in Jesus's name, amen.

"Ra-men," I said, and looked up to see Cirrus's eyes inches from mine. Those eyes of hers. She sat up, took in the crowd. She offered me another hand pie.

"So now what?" she said.

"Oh, so now what happens is, uh," I said, stalling for time.

"PLEASE GIVE A WARM WELCOME TO THE VISITING TEAM, THE DELGADO BEACH AVENGERS!"

From the sparsely populated bleachers opposite ours came a football team that looked very much like that of Ruby High, all red-and-white as opposed to our white-and-red. Their cheerleaders looked like our cheerleaders; their coach shared the same taste in vee-neck sweaters. It might as well have been the same school, just with everything flopped in mirror image.

It was another school in the multiverse of schools, and had

the heavenly coin of fate landed heads, I would've found myself in the mirror world opposite us, rooting for Delgado Beach High.

But the coin hadn't landed heads, so I was on *this* side of the field.

The crowd on this side of the field applauded politely for our guests.

"AND NOW," cried the speakers, "HEEERE'S YOUR RUBY HIGH RAH-VAH-JURRS!"

Immediately the crowd stomped to their feet, the Ruby High marching band blasted the air with fiery brass and a fast hailstorm of ratamacues, and everyone around us began clapping and hooting.

I had a habit of ridiculing fans of sport. Teams switched players all the time. Sometimes, they even switched geographic locations. Therefore, what was a team but for uniform color combinations and logos?

But now, seeing how Cirrus batted her hands together and marveled at the aluminum trembling with thunder beneath our feet, I wondered: If being where you were when you were was but a wobble of physics, and all else was equal—Ravager or Avenger—why *not* belong?

Why not join in?

People, I realized, rooted for teams not necessarily because one was somehow fundamentally better than the other. They did it mostly just to belong.

Because it was nice to belong to something, or someone.

I glanced at Cirrus, who had glanced at me, too.

White-with-red football players erupted from a large decorated paper hymen and streamed onto the field between two lines of jittering lunatic cheerleaders. On the opposite side, red-with-white football players did the same.

The crowd instinctively steadied their applause to keep time with the music now, and I figured what the hell, and clapped along. Cirrus held her hand up so we could clap together, which was surprisingly difficult. We managed a few claps, quickly got out of sync, and wound up shoving pressed palms oddly back and forth like we were some kind of silly machine. We learned chants. We high-fived strangers. We yelled, and our cheeks became red in the deepening cold of the night.

"Go, Avengers, go!" yelled Cirrus along with the crowd. "I mean go, Ravagers, go! Sorry!"

She teetered, and I caught her with both arms.

When the Rancho Ruby High Ravagers—our side of the field—ultimately lost, Cirrus and I joined the crowd streaming down the bleachers and watched as parties dissolved into the night with murmurs and backslaps and hugs.

We'll be back, they said. *We'll get 'em next time.*

"I'm a Ravagers fan!" said Cirrus. "I loved it!"

I did too.

The ride back was flat and quiet, and the rows of dewy centenarian sycamores standing sentinel layered the sky above with all the velvet colors of night foliage: Edward greens and funeral teals and spotted charcoal. I had never quite realized how beautiful the ride home was until now.

Until Cirrus.

Her hair blew into her face, so she bicycled hands-free for a moment to deftly tie it back.

"All the Ruby High people looked so sad by the end of the game," said Cirrus.

"And for what, right?" I said, gearing up for ridicule out of sheer habit. I would've gone on, but this time I stopped myself.

"They really believed in their team," said Cirrus. "They belonged to them. It was nice to see."

My mind flicked over to an image of Milo and Jamal and back. I belonged to them. We were a team. Cirrus was new. She had no team.

~~"I could belong to you," I said.~~

~~"You could belong to me," I said.~~

~~"We could belong to each other," I said.~~

Scratch, scratch, scratch. I found I could say nothing. Cirrus filled the silence.

"So I'm settling in pretty well, thanks for asking," she said, tossing a wry smirk at me.

"Oh my god, I am inconsiderate and self-centered," I said. I squeezed my eyes. "You settling in okay there, Cirrus Soh?"

We both stood on our pedals to allow a speed hump to pass.

"Having you around makes it easier," she said.

Her words made me abnormally warm. Everything she said and did made me abnormally warm.

"Having me around makes you, uh," I said, painting myself into a syntactical corner.

Cirrus glanced at me. "You are strange," she said.

"Your mom's butt is strange," I said.

"Not that she's ever around for us to examine it," said Cirrus with a puff.

A moment appeared, and began to stretch ominously in length. I knew so little about Cirrus's home life. Imagination tended to fill voids in unpredictable ways, so I began spinning scenarios again: Her parents didn't exist, Cirrus was really a runaway, and so on.

I wanted to ask. But from the look on Cirrus's face, her parents seemed like a sensitive subject. What if I broached a subject so sore it wound up driving her away?

So I just quipped, "We're not seriously talking about your mom's butt," and when Cirrus laughed, the ominous moment snapped in two and whipped clean away.

I was lightly sweating by this point. I unzipped my hoodie, let it billow with night air.

"Whoo, got a long uphill ahead," said Cirrus, and klonked into a lower gear. "So I heard the Immortals were practicing yesterday."

I sighed, something I did whenever I got nervous. "You did?"

"Jamal told me," she said. "I think that guy is in love with me."

"Wouldn't surprise me," I said.

"I think Milo might be, too," she said.

"Wouldn't surprise me," I said.

"I would really love to hear you guys play," said Cirrus, almost coyly.

We reached her street and approached her condo. We stood and pumped our pedals until we reached it, and then we just kind of stood there on our bikes, panting.

"Can I check out what you've done with the place?" I said, shooting hot breath in the cool air.

"No," huffed Cirrus. Her eyes darted. "Sorry—it's still all boxes everywhere, nothing to see yet, but later when it's ready sure but not now is that okay?"

"Of course," I said, immediately intrigued.

Cirrus gazed at me with beautiful sheepish eyes. "Sorry."

"It's totally okay," I said. "You got boxes everywhere, I understand."

I blinked at the ironic fact that I, too, had many boxes in my room that I didn't want Cirrus to see. Only my boxes were the permanent kind.

We stood close. Cirrus's lips couldn't have been more than thirty centimeters from mine. I badly wanted to move a centimeter closer, but I could not. Every muscle in my body refused to contract, out of sheer terror. Only my lip muscles grew tight.

Cirrus stood frozen, too. Did she want to kiss me, too? Or oh god, did she not? That made no sense—wouldn't she take evasive action, then? Maybe she was just as scared as me?

We might've stayed frozen all night, if not for the voice:

"Lovely night."

These words, uttered in dreamy singsong, came from an older woman's silhouette framed in a dim amber window next door.

"It is," said Cirrus slowly.

We waited and waited, but the woman did not leave.

Cirrus leaned in and whispered, "Is she still there?"

I whispered back. "Your neighbor is terrifying."

"I think she sleepwalks," whispered Cirrus. "I think this is all a dream to her."

"Let's not wake her," I whispered.

Somehow our lips were now a hundred centimeters apart. A normal distance. The moment had passed. No longer was I hot; indeed, I was freezing now. The night mist around us had thickened into sprinkles. Those sprinkles were turning into actual rain.

"I guess I should go inside," said Cirrus.

I stomped on a pedal. "See you tomorrow," I said.

"Not if I see you first," said Cirrus, then cringed at herself. "I don't really know what that expression means."

"It means if you see me before I see you, then you'll have time to avoid me," I said.

"Well, that's horrible," said Cirrus. "I take it back. I will *see you tomorrow.*"

"Isn't that what I said in the first place?" I said.

"Bye," said Cirrus.

"Bye," I said.

"Bye," said Cirrus.

"Bye," I said.

"Go!" said Cirrus with a sweet laugh. "You're getting all wet!"

"Bye," I said, and laughed too as I pedaled away.

Later.

I lay awake in bed. The whole world was asleep, lulled by the sweeping caress of vast curtains of rain spanning all the land.

I sat up. In dim light, my room looked like some sort of ice hotel. Blocks and blocks of Arctic White airtight plastic storage containers formed walls and canyons glinting everywhere in the dark.

I suddenly felt like a hoarder. I looked around.

I absolutely am a hoarder. This room is not normal.

How had I not seen it before?

No normal American teenager lived like this. My room was not normal, because I was not normal. Even Milo and Jamal called my room *a warehouse workshop with a bed.*

A normal American teenager would've kissed Cirrus tonight.

I swiveled out from under the sheets and automatically inserted my feet into my memory foam slippers, only to violently kick them away with twin thuds. Everything felt stupid—my room, my slippers, everything. I scrambled my hair. I felt a little like I was bursting at the seams with manic energy.

Was I frustrated with myself? Yes.

Was it because I knew that I could never, ever bring Cirrus into this psychotic memory palace of a place? Partly.

Mostly, it was because of this: I just realized that I had spent my whole life thinking I was better and smarter and more clever than all the other idiots on the planet, when really I was nothing more than afraid. Meanwhile, all the other idiots on the planet were busy running around having *fun*.

I realized the one word that best described my high school self:

SHAME

In the very next moment, I also realized:

Enough.

I crept across the hallway and into Gray's room. I lay down on his perfectly made bed in the blue light. This was a normal room. This was the kind of room I wanted: a room I could bring Cirrus to, with all my stuff displayed in the usual manner—in the open, and not concealed within uniform stacks of white. A room that proudly showed who I was.

I knew that Gray's room no longer showed who he was.

Who was Gray now?

Once upon a time, Gray was Gray. Until we moved from

Arroyo Plato, and he became something else. Mom and Dad were once Mom and Dad, too. Until they weren't.

Not me. I would be as blatantly me as I could be for all to see, and to hell with the Gunners of the world. I would unpack all my white storage containers. I would even build *shelves*.

Maybe Cirrus would find this me unsettling.

Or maybe Cirrus would love this me. Maybe her love would act as a protective shield, for it was rumored that love possessed a mega-magic armor bonus.

Things could go either way.

All I could do was take that chance.

Murder

"Breakfast!"

I opened my eyes. It was morning. Around me the rain pattered on.

I clicked a sticky tongue. My mouth tasted like guano paste. My head was cold. My whole *corpus* was cold. And rheumatoid stiff.

I had slept on top of Gray's bed. At one point I had found a pillow to drool on.

The last thing I remembered was closing my eyes, lying back, and listening to "Beauty Is Truth" just one more time.

"Sun," said Gray, now stomping up the stairs.

"Oh no," I said.

I scrambled out of bed, flailing like a rough android prototype. I hit Gray's guitar still leaning against the amp, sending it to the carpet with a heavy *binggg*.

No time to pick it up. I darted out, across the hallway, and into my room to hop over storage containers and fling myself under the bedsheets.

Seconds later, a knock. Gray poked his head in. "Mom's making me tell you to come eat when she could do it just fine all by herself because I'm your big brother and I'm supposed to look after you or whatever, *god*."

"Just a sec," I said, in my best morning whimper.

After I was sure he was gone, I crept into his room to harvest the day's outfit from his cornucopia of dark and broody fashion choices. I stuffed them into a backpack for my daily visit to the old storage shed by the bike racks.

Breakfast had already been set out, all in silver and gold-rimmed porcelain in the hotel room service style Mom had always dreamed of having since forever. I shuffled to my chair, sat, and began consuming half the table.

Mom and Dad ate in silence. At the end opposite me, Gray abjectly stared into a giant bowl of rainbow cereal going soggy. He wore another button-up, another pair of khakis. He looked freshly taxidermied for a viewing.

"How did the meeting with Trey Fortune go?" I asked him, and immediately knew it was a mistake.

"I'll be downstairs," said Gray, and shot up out of his seat.

"You are *here*, Gray," barked Dad. "Be *here*. With us."

"Fsss," said Gray, and slumped back down.

"What do all winners have in common?" said Dad.

"Super-duper positive attitude," mumbled Gray.

"Plenty of people would hire Manny Dae Jr.'s oldest son in a nanosecond," said Dad. "Remember that."

"Anyway, the meeting went great," said Mom. "Trey wants

to intro him to the whole team." She scanned Gray up and down with an upturned palm, as if providing visual proof.

"That's," I said, wanting to echo Mom's *great*, but I changed tack when I saw Gray sadly sink his face nearly into his bowl. "That's, yeah!"

"You should be proud," said Mom.

"We are," said Dad.

"Absolutely," said Mom.

Gray swiveled his spoon to the other side of the bowl, then back.

"Oh, hey, Sun," said Dad to me. "Before I forget—could you?"

He handed me his phone, opened to the Inspire NV customer log-in screen.

"Honey, we have that call in forty seconds," said Mom.

"Dude, just conference me in on yours," said Dad.

"Grr," said Mom, and began tapping her tablet. She shoved Dad out of the room. "We're on, Mr. CEO, game faces."

"Yap," said Dad.

They vanished, leaving me and Gray alone. I looked at Gray. Gray looked at his cereal. He was dead still but for a single knee madly jackhammering. I thought about how I had worn Gray's Antichrist hoodie last night. It was more mine than his now.

Back to Dad's phone. Solving his log-in problem, it turned out, was a matter of flipping a content blocker plug-in to Off. I hit Reload, let the autocomplete fill in his password, and found myself successfully scrolling among forty-eight different camera views.

I tapped Driver Side Front Lower and scrubbed around. Dad was driving home from his reserved parking spot at the gleaming offices of Manny Dae Business Services. The car made its way home, entered the garage, and let Dad out. After a moment, the lights went dark and all the colors flipped into black-and-white night mode. Nothing special.

"I don't get it," I muttered.

"Get what," said Gray.

I showed Gray what I was doing. "I'm trying to find the balljiggler who keyed Dad's—"

I stopped, because Gray had stopped. He eyed the phone like it was a king cobra.

"No," blurted Gray. He lunged for the phone, splashing cereal all over himself in the process.

When I looked at the screen, I saw a ghostly figure flit past in the dark. I scrubbed back a few seconds—sure enough, a hand holding a screwdriver was digging into the side of the Inspire NV. But *inside* the garage?

Gray rose to his feet. I huddled over the phone to keep him from getting at it.

I jumped back five seconds, and held my forehead in disbelief.

There was Gray, glaring at the car with murder in his eyes.

The multicolored Os of cereal funneled themselves into a narrow white delta of milk and moseyed down a stream dripping off the rounded edge of the quartz countertop.

"Close that tab," said Gray.

"What the hell," I said.

"I just," said Gray.

"Why did you do that?" I said.

"I don't know, I don't know," said Gray. "Get me a towel or something."

"Get it yourself," I said.

Gray did, and flung it over the mess. We both watched as the cloth became dark and heavy with milk. Then Gray lunged for Dad's phone again.

"Close the tab, dude," he said.

"Dad's gonna ask about it anyway," I said, holding the phone behind me. "What then?"

Gray looked like he wanted to rip all the hair off his head.

I lowered my voice to a murmur. "Why did you do it?"

Gray searched and searched for words. It felt like a whole minute passing. I tuned my ear past the white noise of the rain and could detect Mom and Dad authoritatively babbling office-speak in the next room.

"Dad keeps saying he's proud of me for *making the hard decision to pivot home*," said Gray, eyes fixed on the sopping towel.

I furrowed my eyes. "Pivot home? As in for good?"

"I keep telling Dad that I'm gonna move back up to Hollywood," said Gray. He picked up the towel and wrung it out. "He was all, *It's just a social get-together,* when in fact it was a friggin' group interview over dinner and drinks."

"So like a job interview?" I said.

"I *am going to* move back up to Hollywood," said Gray. "No matter what."

Gray wrung out the towel, rinsed it, wrung it out again until I thought it would tear.

I was at a loss for what to say. If Gray wanted to move back to Hollywood and start up that new band he had already lined up, what the hell was stopping him?

Gray wiped the counter again even though it was already clean. "So we get back last night, and Mom and Dad are all, *It's best to keep your passion separate, because if music becomes work, it stops being your passion and turns into a job like any other job."*

"What kind of horrible advice is that?" I said, repulsed.

"Basically they're like, quit music except as a friggin' hobby," said Gray. "Just kill my dreams dead."

Gray glanced at the door, listened for voices, and continued.

"On the drive home Dad's all, *I like to define my dreams concretely, this was my dream car forever, now look at us rolling,* fsss."

"Is he trying to say a car is the same thing as a dream?" I said.

Gray chuckled with despair. "Right? Dad's been saying crap like that on repeat every minute since I got home. Every. Single. Minute."

I'd never seen him so tired. I could see him old, as old as Dad and beyond. He wrung out the towel in the sink once more.

"Let me help you with that," I said.

"I got it," said Gray. He hung the towel to drip-dry, and ground away the cereal in the garbage disposal. It looked like the spill had never happened.

Gray picked off Os still clinging to his wet shirt. He smoothed his hair. He spoke softly now. "So what's up with Milo and Jamal these days?"

"I'm sorry Mom and Dad are so annoying," I said.

Gray didn't seem to hear me. "That Cirrus seems like a sweetheart, huh? Happy for you, dude."

"Hey," I said.

"You're having tons of fun right now," said Gray. He smiled. "I can see it in your whole everything."

I wanted to smile, but when I saw Gray's own smile sag—laden with sadness—I knew his wasn't the kind of smile that was meant to be shared.

"Better go change," said Gray, and turned to leave.

He'd been back for a few days now. In that time, I hadn't heard him once play his acoustic guitar.

"Did you ever perform 'Beauty Is Truth'?" I blurted.

Gray paused, then said nothing. He drifted away to his netherworld downstairs.

I picked up Dad's phone, unlocked it using his code, which I had visually hacked (i.e., seen) long ago, and reopened the Inspire tab. I logged out. Then I logged back in, deliberately using a wrong password. I did this three times until the system dropped the big red banhammer on me.

PLEASE CONTACT CUSTOMER CARE
AT 1-888-555-5150 TO UNLOCK YOUR ACCOUNT

It would take scatterbrained Dad months to get to such an item on his to-do list. Until then, Gray would be protected from his outburst. I tried to put myself in his hideous, WASP-y boat shoes. How dejected would I have to be to key my own dad's car?

I wanted to go downstairs and hug Gray. I wanted to have him drop everything and drive me to Los Angeles. Show me all the places he ate, partied, gigged, and slept.

I glanced at the clock. Late for school. I threw on a waterproof poncho, adjusted my backpack straps, and pedaled out into the strengthening drizzle.

Originals

"Let's get this practice nonsense over with so we can work on DIY Fantasy FX," said Jamal, slinging on his bass guitar with a quick duck of his head. It had been more than a week since our first practice. We were five sessions in now, and he was finally able to wear the thing without dealing high blows to me, Milo, or the surrounding equipment.

Jamal rested both long arms on his bass neck. "Our channel has twenty new subscribers this week," he said, flashing all his fingers two times. "We gotta post a new episode, strike while the dwarven pigiron is hot."

"We will," I said.

On a nearby rolling blackboard—Mr. Tweed was one vintage cat—lyrics had begun to appear for each of our practice sessions. There was *I wanna be sedated* and *With your feet on the air and your head on the ground*. Today's was this, in Mr. Tweed's square, precise handwriting:

We could be heroes just for one day.

We of course looked these songs up and learned how to play them. They were just the right level of difficulty.

Thanks for the guidance, Mr. Tweed.

I knelt to turn on my amp and stared at its knobs in disbelief. "Someone messed with my settings!" I whined. "I had my distortion right where I wanted it!"

"Not cool," said Milo from behind his drums.

Jamal tossed a Sharpie at me. "Mark your knobs," he said. "That's what I did."

I reset my knobs and marked the respective indices. On the control plate I added

* THE IMMORTALS

"What are we playing, music master?" said Milo.

I donned my guitar. My friends stared at me for a moment in the silence. For the last few practices, we'd overcome our general incompetence to where we were able to cover the simple songs suggested by Mr. Tweed, as well as classic rock standards from bands with names like the Ramones and Nirvana and Hole.

"Well—" I said.

"Green Day!" ejaculated Milo.

"Green Day sucks my lactating nipples," said Jamal.

"No, but listen—" I said.

"Weezer?" said Milo, instantly sad.

"Weezer is Green Day Reduced Sodium," said Jamal.

"You take that back," said Milo.

"Listen—" I said again.

But Jamal was whining now. "Why does it have to be rock and roll? No one does rock and roll."

"Which is exactly why it's due for a comeback," I said. "Name one significant new rock band from the last three years."

Jamal thought. "Japandroids?"

Milo closed his eyelids with the grace of a level-twenty sage. "Japandroids formed in 2006. Fourteen years ago."

"I am so old," said Jamal.

"Yo La Tengo," said Milo, off in his own little world.

"Rock is dead, long live rock," I said absently. I imagined playing with the airlock open. I would time our first notes to coincide with Cirrus's perambulations, to ensure we fell within earshot. I would not have to approach her. She would follow the music like a scent. Just walk right in and simply be spellbound by my irresistible coolness.

"Fall Out Boy," said Jamal.

"Sleater-Kinney," said Milo.

"Ooo," we all sighed, because we were all secretly in love with Sleater-Kinney even though they were old enough to be our moms.

"Thirty Seconds to Mars," said Milo.

"That's a ding-dang Japanese RPG soundtrack," sniffed Jamal. "Best Coast."

I unzipped my backpack. "I want you guys to listen to something."

"Train," said Milo to Jamal.

Me and Jamal stared at Milo: *Train?*

"Mom piped in early 2000s adult contemporary when I was still in her tum-tum," said Milo with defiance. "All the greats: Norah Jones, Jason Mraz—"

I shook off this image of a fully grown Milo in his mother's abdomen.

This is stupid. Look at us.

"A real band wouldn't do covers," I said.

"We're not a real band," said Jamal.

"I'm talking about the *effect* we're trying to achieve here," I said. I didn't want to say the word *fake* out loud.

"Jamal has a point," said Milo. "Don't we just want her to witness us playing, so that the illusion becomes complete? What does it matter what we play?"

"It matters because a real band plays originals," I said. "Cirrus has friends in bands, I tell you. She's probably watched a million shows from backstage."

"Awesome," said Jamal. "So all we have to do is work on an amazing original song while Lady Lashblade loses interest and our ScreenJunkie channel has a final tombstone post saying, *Hey, fans, it's been a real honor over the years but—*"

"We can use this," I said.

From my backpack I produced the iPod.

Milo tilted his head to read the iPod label. "*Property of Gray Dae.*"

I turned the iPod around. "No one needs to know that."

"Including Gray?" said Jamal, wincing.

"There's a song on here he's never performed for anyone, and never will," I said. "It was sitting at the bottom of a crate. We might as well make use of it."

Jamal and Milo looked at each other, most likely wondering what they'd gotten themselves into. What *I'd* gotten *them* into.

"Just listen," I said, and hit Play.

"Beauty Is Truth" boomed and growled through studio monitors, filling the room with its ever-shifting kaleidoscope of genres and moods. I watched as it brought Jamal and Milo up, then down, then back up again on waves of energy in every hue.

When it finally reached the hard-driving four-beat of its conclusion, I opened my arms.

"Right?" I said. "Right?"

Milo kneaded his chin, lost in thought. "Your brother is a genius."

"Was," I said sadly. "I don't know about *is* anymore."

Jamal nodded. "No way in any circle of hell can we pull that off."

"Absolutely agree," said Milo. "One hundred percent incompetent."

I lunged to the blackboard and wrote so fast I broke chalk. "Look. I mapped out the chords for the first part. It's not so bad."

"You mapped the chords," said Jamal. "You came prepared."

Because I'm secretly taking this very seriously.

"G, G-sharp," said Milo.

"Chromatically up to B," said Jamal.

"Let's just pick our way through super slow," I said. "Milo, you count us in."

"A-one, and a-two," said Milo, like a USO big-band leader in the swinging 1940s, and already things felt stupid even before we'd played a single note.

We lurched into the song, if it could be called such a thing.

We were terrible. Me and Jamal seemed to be playing two totally different songs.

Milo administered blows to different drum parts with the frenzy of whack-a-mole gone pro, scrambling to keep up with what was on the recording.

Jamal's face spasmed with unsettling dork theatrics between sneers and grins as he dug deep *doinks* out of the large bass.

We did not rock. We convulsed.

I sang. My sweet, high voice pierced the air with the same golden intensity of that divine sunbeam that delivered the most immaculate of conceptions from on high, elevating our noisemaking to a cult worship service.

To make matters much, much worse, Jamal found a mic and elected to "back up" my "vocals" with off-script ululations in fake Gaelic.

I winced the hardest I have ever winced. We had slathered Gray's masterpiece with a thick layer of nerd-tella on top. I felt measurably nerdier than before.

Before Cirrus had entered my life.

"Beauty Is Truth" tumbled to an end like a nun coming to a dead stop at the bottom of a staircase with no one but diseased rats to note her passing.

"I thought we sounded convincing!" said Milo.

"Same!" said Jamal, impressed with himself. "Those were some killer time signatures you were playing."

"What is time signatures?" said Milo.

"Did I sing okay?" I said quietly. "I'm equivalent to a mezzo-soprano."

"Perfect one hundred percent on expert mode in my opinion," said Milo.

"Sounded gr-r-r-reat to me," said Jamal. "Can we work on DIY Fantasy FX now?"

Jamal and Milo, nodding maniacally.

I bit my own face. We knew nothing. We were three imbeciles complimenting each other on things we had not a single iota of basic knowledge about.

I was getting the feeling that no matter what road I took, I would always wind up back in the bramble and thicket of Land-o'-Nerd. We had to pull this off. We had to *rock*.

"Let's try it again one more time super-duper quick but this time really focusing on locking in a solid four-count backbeat?" I said, with my hands literally clasped. "The backbeat is the—"

"The foundation of traditional rock and roll, I know," said Milo.

Jamal groaned like a manatee in heat. "There goes that seat at Lady Lashblade's table at Fantastic Faire," he said.

"Hah?" I said.

"Lady Lashblade messaged us directly," said Milo. "She wants to guest review our next prop. That means she *likes* us. That means she— Uh, Sunny?"

I had been staring deep into the cone of the amp speaker. I had just discovered that I didn't know which I was more concerned with: figuring out how to dazzle Cirrus with my fake band or getting DIY Fantasy FX big enough to earn a spot at Fantastic Faire.

"Just one more time," I said. "Please. I beg you."

Jamal shouldered his bass guitar and studied my face. It must have been a pathetic sight, because he nodded. "Fine."

I clapped my hands. "Milo. Go boom-tssh, boom-boom-tssh."

After a couple of stutter-steps, Milo settled into a stable rock beat. His eyes pleaded: *How long do I have to do this?*

I pointed at Jamal, and he began: *Boon boon boon boon, ba boon boon.*

Then I joined in with my guitar, choking distorted chords short with my palm as best I could, just like Gray used to.

Jhk jhk jhk ja jhk ja jhk ja ja jhk

We limped along like a flat-tired truck full of defective appliances all trying to run. The tempo slowed and stutter-stepped as we *queenked* and *blonked* our blundering way through the chord changes drawn on the chalkboard.

I crept up to the mic and bleated out some words. Milo and Jamal looked up at the sound of my voice, then looked at each other, then kept going.

I guess that meant I sounded good?

I realized we were looking down at our own instruments, not one another, which was probably why we weren't playing in sync. So I moved to get Jamal's attention, then gave him a look—that *Geronimo!* face that I'd seen Gray give to his bandmates when it was time to switch musical gears. Jamal caught my look and passed it on to Milo.

We landed the next chord change, more or less on cue.

The look had worked.

Back in high school, Gray had called this phenomenon of nonverbal communication among players *throwing eyes.* I thrilled inside, because I now understood what he meant after all these years.

As we neared the end of the song, I threw eyes again. I raised my guitar to make doubly sure we landed the final note. When it was time, I swung its neck down.

I wouldn't say we ended the song. It was more like the song ended.

But at least it ended all *at once* like music was supposed to.

"That was awesome," cried Milo.

"We got this," said Jamal, eyes wild with adrenaline.

To be clear, we sounded bad. But I knew if we just kept at it, we'd eventually master the song.

I just knew it.

Charms

The rain in Spain falls mainly on the insane in the membrane insane in the brain, wrote Cirrus.

Cirrus!

I flipped up my face shield, shoved myself away from my workbench, and held my phone with prayer hands.

Hi! I wrote.

I have watched every last gender reveal fail video on the internet, wrote Cirrus. I think I've lost my mind to cabin fever.

I clipped my phone onto its ergonomic stand, sat erect, and typed on my butterfly keyboard.

What a coincidence, I'm losing my mind too! I wrote. The rainbow backlit mechanical key switches went *ta-KING-ta-KING* with jackhammer speed. I was able to type a hundred words per minute—a hundred ten if I was particularly excited.

Let's lose it together! I began writing.

Delete, option-delete, command-delete.

Dots pulsed. Jamal called those pulsing dots *blowing bubbles*, but I called them one of the worst user interface conventions ever designed. Worse than infinite scrolling, the Like button, or that slot-machine pull-to-refresh that always made me feel like a human guinea pig test subject pawing at the controls for either an electric shock, a dose of morphine, absolutely nothing, or a hard dry biscuit to devour while backed into a corner, scanning the edges of my iron room for hidden cameras.

Anyway if you'd like to drop everything and come rescue me from the abyss this fine rainy Saturday morning that would be fun, wrote Cirrus finally.

I flung off my face shield. Fantasy props could wait. Everything could wait.

Ok I've dropped everything to the floor, I wrote. Where?

My house? wrote Cirrus.

O, I typed.

K, I typed.

!, I typed.

Send!

I threw on the first outfit I could find—a bootleg Microsoft Zune tank top and extremely rare pair of LimeWire running shorts—before realizing I could not go to Cirrus's house looking like I had just corporate fun-runned my way through time from the early 2000s.

I crossed the hall to Gray's old bedroom, a habit at this point, and picked out what I remembered of Gray's leisure wear choices from two years ago—tight black joggers, black camo hoodie—and put them in a backpack. I packed sunglasses, too: mirrored cop things that covered half my face.

At the top of the stairs I jumped, clamped my arms around

the banister, slid silently down with my socks on the side trim rail. I loved this stupid *grand* staircase. I retracted any statements I might have made in the past—I now loved all stairs everywhere.

"Bye," I called.

No reply. I looked. Mom and Dad ate standing up at the kitchen island, hunched over their screens without a word, work-work-working on a Saturday morning. Other parents barbecued or went to the movies or pursued their ding-dang hobbies on the weekends. I had no idea what my parents' hobbies even were.

Did Mom and Dad still hold the magic, standing over their plates like they were now?

I could probably change into Gray's clothes right here, and they wouldn't even notice. But I didn't dare risk it. The last thing I needed was questions, and then a potential offhand comment to Jane or Brandon Soh.

As soon as Sunny met Cirrus, he started wearing Gray's clothes for attention.

Like mating plumage!

How adorable!

Et cetera. No.

I called to them again. "Bye?"

Mom glanced up with the blank awareness of a hypnosis victim hearing a bell. "Bye, sweetie."

"Make good choices," droned Dad without looking up.

"Already have," I said, and left.

But have I? I thought.

Since there was no old storage shed between my house

and Cirrus's, I figured the juniper lining the side entrance of the Cernoseks' house would do. Although there were so few cars (and even less foot traffic) on the spotless, wide streets of Rancho Ruby that I probably could have changed out in the open. I had gotten my whole switcheroo routine down to sixteen seconds (PR).

When I knocked on Cirrus's door, I was huffing and puffing even though I had barely expended any calories on the bike ride over.

Huffing and puffing, heart pounding.

The door opened to reveal Cirrus in a professional-looking black apron, the kind you see chefs wearing on cooking shows. She had fine white dust on her perfect nose, in her perfect hair. "I just put in Brazilian pizza."

"What's Brazilian pizza?" I said.

"We'll see," said Cirrus, with a shrug. "I gotta pee. Come meet me upstairs!"

She bounded away two steps at a time with astonishing strength and speed.

I stepped into the condo, which was already perfumed with yeast and garlic. I slipped off my shoes. My feet rested on white tile. I felt compelled to line my shoes up with the other pairs impeccably arranged there.

I peered around. My eyes blipped. I don't know what I had expected Cirrus's house would look like, but it was not this.

I knew Cirrus had lived all over the world, so I had imagined mind-boggling knickknacks and gadgets and foodstuffs the likes of which we provincial Americans could never even think to search for with our limited bumpkin query terms.

I knew her parents were away a lot for work and were also fairly *vivre-et-laisser-vivre*, so I imagined Cirrus had free rein to do things like graffiti an entire wall with award-winning artwork or set up a professional DJ stack in the living room or keep a clever family of potbellied pigs in luxurious dedicated quarters.

But there was none of that. All I could see was white.

The carpet was white, the walls were white, the ceiling was white, everything white and blank but the furniture and picture frames.

Except there was no furniture or picture frames.

There was nothing.

A television sat marooned on the floor with only a sad cable modem as its companion.

I nudged open a door. There was a bathroom. Its toilet still had the factory label marketing stickers on the ceramic tank. In the sink was a hammer, a measuring tape, and a dried-out to-go cup. The shower stall was stuffed full of flattened cardboard moving boxes.

Cirrus had gone upstairs, so up I went. More white carpet. There was what looked like a master bedroom—a naked mattress atop a box spring atop the bare floor—and there was a walk-in closet full of clear boulders of discarded bubble wrap.

Finally, I came to a door with a strangely corporate-looking nameplate nailed into its surface. *Si-ra-seu,* read a trio of letters in Korean. *Cirrus.*

I knocked. The door cracked open. I quickly performed the scan that was the tradition of teenagers the world over, searching for exclusive, bedroom-only details of her personality.

But her room was as empty as the rest of the house. She didn't even have a dresser—just stacks of folded clothes lining one wall. There was a shoebox with a tea candle melted on top. That was it.

"Hey," said Cirrus behind me.

She had removed her apron to reveal Ruby High sweats and an old cami top, and she looked radiant. She watched me with an eager sort of look.

"I love what you've done with the place," I said as goofy as I could.

"Thank you," said Cirrus with real sincerity, letting my joke whiz by. "Come in."

I came in. The slight change of perspective did not offer any additional visual information. But the room smelled wonderful. Vanilla and soap and stale musky air.

The place smelled like sleepyhead, and I instantly wanted to press my nose into her scalp and simply inhale.

What followed was the dumbest conversation ever had by two people, but for me it was the bestest.

"So what you got going on today?"

"Nothing."

"Sit, sit."

"This carpet is so soft."

"I love Saturdays."

"Are you hungry?"

"I could be."

I didn't even bother attributing who said what, because it hardly mattered. What mattered was that I was sitting in Cirrus's white room on her white carpet, whose brand-new white fibers clung to my black joggers, causing Cirrus to fuss.

"It's all over you," she said, laughing. She patted my legs with her hands.

I laughed, too. "It's like your whole house is a giant shedding pet."

Pat pat pat. Her scalp this close to my nose.

Cirrus felt different, here in her room. She moved around more, and faster. She felt more playful. She dug her fingertip into the plush carpeting and began drawing lines.

"I was thinking of putting a dresser here, a desk there, although I always study in bed," she said, busily drawing with her whole body. "Nightstand, hamper here, posters and art prints and photos up on the walls everywhere. What do you think?"

"I think that would be sweet," I said, examining her lines.

Cirrus stopped moving. "I haven't had anyone in my room for over three years."

"You just moved here three weeks ago," I said.

"No, but it's the same room wherever I go," she said. "You know?"

"No," I said, laughing.

"I just," she said, carefully now. "For the first time in a long time, I'm psyched to decorate my room. Just go wild at Bed & Bath Vortex. I wanted to invite you over yesterday, to be honest."

"Then why didn't you?" I said, admiring the perfect bevel of her right eyelid.

"I know my room is not normal," she said. "I'm pretty sure I'm not normal."

My room is not normal either, I wanted to say, but quelled the urge.

"*Normal* means 'boring' in English," I said.

"I've been ashamed of my room for so long," said Cirrus. "It's like a bad habit. Then I meet you. And you're just so *you*. I want to be more me, too."

By now you already know I began blushing and becoming hyperthermal. It was the nicest—and most dreadful—thing anyone had ever told me.

"So you sit at home cooking huge meals all by yourself on the weekends?" I said.

"It's something to do," said Cirrus. She abruptly leaned over as if doing a leg stretch and retrieved a tall square tin.

"Anyway," said Cirrus. She drew in a breath, held it, and exhaled. She held the tin between her open palms.

"This is me," she said.

ROYAL VICTORIA TOP CHOICE BISCUIT

PRODUCT OF SINGAPORE · SẢN PHẨM CỦA SINGAPORE · PRODUCTO DE SINGAPUR · 新加坡产品 · 싱가포르의 제품 · PRODUK SINGAPURA

"Hi, Cirrus," I said to the tin.

Cirrus looked nervous. She looked like she had rehearsed this tin ceremony just for me, which I found simultaneously confusing and flattering. She let out another quick breath.

She opened the tin and drew an acorn from within.

"This was from my favorite park in Japan," she said. "I don't remember what city or when, really, but I remember it was super humid and bugs were singing all around me, and it was the first time I had red bean ice cream."

"Very cool," I said, admiring the acorn. Although really, it could've been an acorn from this country, or most any other country with oak trees.

"And this," she said, "is a spare nut for that big bridge in Sydney. Harbor whatever. It's huge. That was from my first summer Christmas Down Under."

I hefted the heavy nut. It was as big as a hockey puck.

"Here's a feather from one of those birds in Hawaii," she said.

I held the feather to the light. "Which bird?"

"The details are just details," she continued. "I remember waiting for a bus. And there it was: my first double rainbow ever. Then this feather blew right into my lap."

Soon we had a collection of objects in front of us: a key-chain light, a rock, a dried leaf, a cheap plastic car. Objects so ordinary that they could've come from anywhere or nowhere. A safety pin, a carved toothpick. She had arranged them in a specific order, which I quickly realized was chronological. The sight of these little trinkets made me inexplicably sad.

"These are all my firsts from everywhere I've ever lived," she said, gazing at them.

I gazed at them, too. "All together they're like this really cool museum piece."

"I'm terrified you think this is weird," she said, not looking at me.

"I don't," I said. "It's not."

"Nothing about me is normal," she muttered. "My whole childhood was not normal."

"You forget how weird human beings can get," I said. "I don't think your weirdness measures up to even the most basic cat hoarder or compulsive coin swallower."

"No, but sometimes my charm box makes me happy," she said. "Sometimes the charms just look like a pile of crap. Because it's crap, isn't it. It's pathetic, isn't it."

I placed two fingers on her shoulder. "People fill entire houses with pathetic piles of crap to gild their lives with the illusion of meaning. Thousands of hours picking and choosing, thousands of dollars shopping. Everyone is pathetic. Everyone suspects life is meaningless, that there is nothing after death, and that all our fancy culture and history and society is just this grand illusion we choose to perpetuate every day. Your way of performing the grand illusion is just more thrifty, and space saving."

The laugh worked. She blinked up at me with a smile.

"Even when you're cynical, you make me feel better," she said. "Or maybe because you're cynical."

"Cynical detachment is my way of dealing with the futility of the universe," I said.

"Oh, Sunny Dae," she said.

Her phone buzzed with three AlloAllo alerts in a row, and she dismissed them all, silenced her device, and slid it far across the carpet.

"I have four hundred friends from twenty different countries all stuffed into my phone," said Cirrus. "But I've never shown any of them my charm box until you."

I was bursting with the urge to just tell her the truth and be done with it. Sing a song of the repentant fool on a broken lyre. But the burst burst, and left only the usual fear.

"I've spent every day since grade school terrified of everyone and everything," I said. "I've never told anyone this. Because I've been too terrified to."

This was the truest thing I'd ever told Cirrus.

She tilted her head in genuine disbelief. "But why?"

"I'm not as confident as I seem," I said.

"You got me fooled," she said with a sly smile.

From the tin she fished out a blood-red coin. Not a coin—a guitar pick.

"I stole this from your room," she said, and laid it down alongside her other charms. It became just another object among objects. "I hope you don't mind."

"It's yours," I said quickly.

"You don't need it?" she said.

"I have multiple," I said.

"Right, because when you're up there rocking out, you might drop it and then what would you do," said Cirrus. She gazed at me. "Duh."

I could tell what she was doing. She was picturing me onstage.

I felt a rising bolus of dread. "Yeah," was all I could say.

"Like at the talent show," she said.

The bolus came back up. "The talent show," I said.

"They put up posters," said Cirrus. "I just assumed, since you guys have been practicing. Probably small potatoes for a band like yours, though, ha."

She gave me the Look. It was the longest Look ever.

My eyes suddenly flooded with terror—and excitement. And lights.

Lights: beams of cyan and magenta and yellow, rising and falling. Hot air stinking of smoke and sour spilled beer of the ages. I could hear Milo's drums now thick and deep enough to shake the floor; I could see Jamal throwing himself around like a snapped cable and hammering at the heavy wound steel of a growling bass.

My chin was glued to the mesh of a mic buzzing with barely suppressed electricity as I sang. There was the weight of a guitar around my neck; my right hand sawed out a metal chain of sublime noise.

She stood in the crowd—the glowing nucleus of it all—and watched with a backhand covering a chuckle of astonishment. I dove off the stage, and floated straight into her arms.

I blinked back to reality. My pulse, I realized, was even. My voice was normal.

"We're in the show, sure," I said with the utmost cool.

"I knew it, yesss," said Cirrus. "I call front row."

"VIP backstage whatever," I said.

Cirrus beamed. Her cheeks bright as apples.

I made a mental sticky to tell Jamal and Milo that we were as of today performing in the talent show. I made another mental sticky to wear a helmet while I told them.

"Anyway," said Cirrus, quiet as a breath now. "This guitar pick is from the moment when I knew that, uh."

She tried again: "From that moment I realized that I, um, I—"

"Me too," I breathed back.

I stopped moving, and so did she. Everything stopped for a long moment.

I had never told anyone I liked them in my whole life. I always thought admitting such a thing would be the most terrifying thing possible, equivalent to lowering the chair and the whip and hoping the lion came in for a hug and not the jugular.

But right now, with everything stopped as it was, I felt no

fear at all. It was the strangest feeling—like a muscle long held had suddenly relaxed to let the hot blood thunder unimpeded. Where had the fear gone?

Right now, I felt like the chosen recipient of the most wonderful news that just had to be shared with the most urgency.

"I like you, Cirrus," I said. "A lot."

"I like you too."

We smiled. The air around us resumed. I had said the words, and they had come out so *easily.*

I could smell her sleepyhead smell; the closer I got, the more I could smell it, which drew me in closer, which made me smell it more, which drew me closer still.

Her lips, just twenty centimeters from mine.

From downstairs came a steady beeping.

"That's the pizza," said Cirrus.

"Then we better hurry," I said, and kissed her.

We moved with intense curiosity now, our fingertips very gently testing the hair, the bone behind the ear, the pulsing neck; arm muscles that went strong, then soft; those fascinating, perfectly sized gaps between each rib.

Cirrus lowered her hand to mine. She twirled the heavy ring on my finger like it was a gain knob on an amp cranking the kitchen timer beeping harder and harder until it screeched with brain-bending distortion.

I was not who Cirrus thought I was. Therefore Cirrus did not like *me*; she liked the Other Me. The one created by my lie that first night we met. Telling Cirrus I liked her—*kissing* Cirrus—only made my lie that much bigger.

At this moment I knew I was supposed to reassure myself

that my lie was only temporary, and that I could be the Real Me soon once again.

Downstairs, the kitchen timer stopped.

I realized something in this silence.

I realized that I liked the Other Me, too.

Courage

I had told Cirrus that I liked her. Cirrus had said the same thing back. That had actually happened. I floated around my room like a happy heart-shaped balloon, which, if inverted, could also look like a pair of humongous buttocks, and that was absolutely hilarious!

Cirrus and me had just become *we*.

I held a paradise-pink flyer in my hands.

RUBY HIGH TALENT SHOW—AT THE
LEGENDARY MISS MAYHEM ON SUNSET STRIP
IN HOLLYWOOD, CALIFORNIA—
NO PRESSURE LOL

"We will rock you," I said.

The cool comes later, replied the flyer, quoting Mr. Tweed.

I knew Jamal and Milo were not interested in getting *the*

cool. I already had a fake version of it—but now I wanted the real.

I wanted to be that Other Me.

I wanted to play the show.

I wanted to be up on that stage, vamping with Gatsbian heroism. I wanted a new word to define my high school self, I decided. Not SHAME, but

COURAGE

I paced the room now, clearing a white plastic storage container at every eighth step.

Why have I lived in fear for so long? Why have I never fought back?

It's not fair to expect people like us to retaliate against bullies like Gunner.

Then why didn't I just change myself? Adapt to survive?

Hey! Why should we have to change?

I feel you—but look: We changed, didn't we? And isn't life already becoming more amazing because of it?

I guess.

Wouldn't you like to see how much better things could get if we took things further?

. . .

You do!

Shut up. I do.

I spent the morning watching videos with great determination. Not LARPing videos, or maker videos, but live music performances. I watched with headphones on, under a blanket, because I did not want anyone to know what I was doing, which was *researching.*

I was researching how to be cool.

It was morning, and the texts from Jamal and Milo were already trickling in. I dismissed them all. I was busy.

As I watched, I became convinced of my hypothesis that music performance was a form of LARPing in itself. Rock performers, after all, hoisted their guitars like heavy axes; their screamsong was a kind of battle cry. Rappers swayed their arms and cast elaborate spells with cryptic finger gestures and fast rhymes. Pop stars danced love dramas, superstar DJs commanded their hordes via mass hypnosis, country crooners sold a pastiche of folktale simplicity long vanished.

There were videos on proper hair care techniques for voluminous headbanging flourishes. Videos explaining how to achieve primal screams safely by singing from the diaphragm. Videos showing the canonic list of metal stage moves: the power stance, the backswing, the pick flip, the agony of the floor solo.

I got out from under my blanket and unearthed a Gray outfit I'd hidden in a plastic container. I changed: black mesh zombie top, black wristbands, ripped jeans, Ring of Baphomet. I grasped an invisible mic stand, windmilled an arm, and raised devil horns to the sky—the rapturous satanic prayer of rock heroes throughout history.

How different was this melodramatic playacting from a role-playing game, or RPG for short, not to be confused with *rocket-propelled grenade* or *rotary pulse generator*?

It was *cool*, that was how.

Role-playing games were what you did when you were too scared to put yourself out there—and putting yourself out there was how the real cool was won.

I used to put myself out there in my own small way, back in the Arroyo Plato backyard of my youth. I was a paladin wielding a plunger, and my friends loved it. This was of course before I went into hiding with my dice and my hex graph notebooks.

I could put myself out there again.

I stopped at a sound—the doorbell, the front door, murmuring, and now two sets of footsteps hammering up the stairs.

My bedroom door opened to reveal Jamal and Milo. Jamal wore a shirt with a picture of a twenty-sided die and the words THIS IS HOW I ROLL. Milo's shirt simply had the word NERD in large collegiate capital letters. These were their favorite shirts for the weekend, when they could let it all hang out safely and without fear of judgment.

"I think we might have something," said Jamal, and brandished a stiff plastic tube about a meter in length.

Milo eyed my chest. "I can see your nipples."

"No," I said, and covered myself with an arm. "Can you?"

"Behold," said Jamal. "Esmeralda's Veil."

Jamal clicked something, igniting a concealed smoke bomb. The smoke traveled through perforations lining the tube, which he waved about to create a wide white scarf. The room filled with acrid sulfur; in moments the smoke alarm began shrieking.

"Plus six missile weapon defense," shouted Jamal.

"Turn it off," I shouted back, reaching up to yank the detector from the wall.

"We haven't figured out that part yet," said Milo in the sudden silence.

"Help me open windows," I said.

We shut the door, opened the windows, and waited for the

smoke bomb to run out of fuel. It took a good thirty seconds. The smoke cleared. A little. Not really.

"You're supposed to run ideas through the CREAPS checklist before actually building them," I said, waving my hand.

"Sorry," said Jamal. "We tried texting."

"You're the Idea Guy," said Milo. "We can't do this properly without you."

"I was busy," I said.

Jamal and Milo looked at me in my outrageous clothes. Then they looked at each other.

"I'd apologize for not making myself available," I said. "But we kissed."

"What?" said Jamal.

"Oh my god, Sunny!" cried Milo, and hugged me.

"That's amazing," said Jamal. He shrugged with resignation. "That's really, really great. Me and Milo can go figure out an off switch for this thing ourselves, I guess, mumble mumble."

Milo stopped Jamal with a hand. "Be happy. Sunny's in love."

"I'll mention that to Lady Lashblade," said Jamal, drooping now.

Milo held his hand firm. Jamal relented. "I'm happy for you."

"Also," I said with a deep breath, "I'm not going to pretend anymore."

Jamal held his forehead with surprise. "You're coming clean?"

"Listen," I said.

"That's the right thing to do," said Milo. "Even if it risks forever driving Cirrus away and branding you in school legend and lore as the resident psychotic long after you've graduated and gone."

"When I say I'm not going to pretend anymore," I said, noting that my hands were held out in my trademark hear-me-out pose, "I mean we do the talent show."

"Nooo—" said Jamal.

"We can absolutely rock the house, with just a little practice," I said.

"—ooooo—" said Jamal.

"I think all of us could stand to break out of our shells and quit being such basket cases," I said.

Jamal stopped in mid-O and peered at me. "Speak for yourself. I like my shell."

"Me too," said Milo. "I always thought *basket case* had a nice connotation, like a little bunny all cozied up in a wicker hamper."

"Then do it for *me*," I said, squeezing the air like it was a value-size bottle of mayonnaise. "Please."

Jamal folded his arms. "This persuasion feels familiar."

"Think of it as role-playing, but in real life," I said. "I get to play the paladin, but in a way that is socially acceptable, nay, celebrated!"

Milo held his chin and winged Jamal with his elbow. "It's an interesting way of looking at it."

"You're encouraging him," cried Jamal.

"Milo the drummer: the warrior of the party," I said. "Unrelenting strength and power."

"Hurr, yeah," said Milo with a grin.

"Dude," cried an incredulous Jamal.

"Jamal, hear me out," I said. "I see the bassist as a member of the rogue thief class. Stealthy. Dexterous. A little bit dangerous."

Jamal brushed his fingers on his collarbone and batted his eyelids. "You really think I'm dangerous?"

"Really," I said.

Jamal shooed his own hand away with disgust. "Ugh! Stop trying to convince me!"

Milo commented very quietly to himself, "He's got me convinced."

I waggled jazz hands. "Talent show! It'll be so so fun!"

Milo nodded. Jamal folded his arms.

"But just the talent show," said Jamal, as more of a question. "And then we go back to normal."

I maintained my Idea Guy pose. "Yes! Maybe! See how you feel!"

Jamal relented with an eyeroll.

"You guys are amazing," I said.

Jamal squeezed out a tongue-fart and held out Esmeralda's Veil. "Can we get back to this now, please?"

"Absolutely, of course, wonderful," I said.

But I never got to have a look at the thing, because from downstairs came the sound of a doorbell. I froze.

"Shh," I said.

Voices. Murmuring. Then:

"Sunny!" yelled Mom.

"Whaaaat," I lilted, eyeing Jamal and Milo with growing fear.

"Come say hi to Cirrus's parents," yelled Mom.

Strobes descended from the ceiling and bathed the room in battle station red.

"Gray's room, go go go," I said.

Jamal and Milo ran into each other, fell over a white storage container, and played hot potato with the doorknob before spilling out into the hallway.

"Why are we doing this?" said Jamal.

"Think, man," said Milo.

Jamal thought for a tenth of a second. "Oh."

"Close off that smell," I hissed, and Jamal fumbled to seal shut the door to my room.

"Sunny?" said Mom from downstairs.

The three of us sock-stumbled our way into Gray's room, where Jamal flapped his arms.

"Now what?" said Jamal.

I glanced at Jamal's shirt, and then Milo's.

THIS IS HOW I ROLL

NERD

I rummaged as fast as I could and held out two of Gray's old tee shirts. "Put these on," I whispered.

"I like my shirt," said Jamal. "It's the weekend."

"Sometimes we do things for love," hissed Milo.

I ripped off my zombie shirt—no one downstairs needed to see my nipples—and opted for one of Gray's old skull pattern tees: something I could both wear to school or onstage.

I turned to exit. I gripped the doorjamb. "When I get back, just act like we've been here all morning."

Jamal stripped off his shirt, revealing his shockingly skinny torso. "You owe us."

"I know," I said.

I spun into the hallway. I paused. I closed my eyes:

Get into character.

Normally, I would take a moment to consider all the ramifications of this thought. Get into character, meaning stash away your real persona to make room for the fake one.

But I didn't have a moment to think, because now I could see Cirrus smiling up at me from the bottom of the stairs.

Kerrang

"Hey, Sunny Dae," said Cirrus.

"Hey," I said, descending step by careful step, remembering to hold both handrails at all times for safety. Accursed stairs. I hated stairs. Again.

Cirrus looked different. Brighter. Her usual steel-eyed savvy was gone.

Next to her in the foyer stood her father, a compact man in white linen and monk's sandals and ultrawide Kobo Abe glasses, and her mother, also in linen and enrobed by a substantial necklace that looked like it was made from big red dried jujubes. Both looked at least ten years older than Mom and Dad.

"You must be Sunny," said Cirrus's father gravely and full of wonder, like a man greeting the captain of a clandestine sea voyage in the dead of night.

"Skulls," said Cirrus's mother, drawing lazy circles at my

shirt. "Symbols of death and fear to some, but to others, a reminder of the eternal life cycle, and of rebirth."

Cirrus shrugged with this sitcom face: *Here're my wacky parents!*

Mom and Dad appeared, jingling keys and checking handbags and whatnot.

"Gray's not coming up to say hi?" said Mom.

"He's sleeping *again*," said Dad, peeved. "Five bucks says he doesn't come up till dinner."

"Well, we should head out," said Mom.

Dad turned to Cirrus's father. "Can we take your Maybach? Some garbage human keyed my car."

Cirrus's father nodded. "Just beneath the smooth veneer of society lies so much rage."

"Rage," said Cirrus's mother. "Everywhere."

"We're going to that amazing camera store down on Fire Opal Street," said Mom with a happy wiggle.

"So Brandon can pick up his brand-new *Leica*," said Dad, and whistled low. "That's a twenty-thousand-dollar camera. Ta-wen-tee thousand!"

"I suppose it is a bit indulgent, birding with a medium format," said Brandon Soh.

"But you work so hard," said Jane Soh. "You deserve it."

Jane and Brandon kissed at each other.

"You absolutely deserve it," said Dad. "One hundred percent."

I could not resist wincing at Dad, who seemed to be openly lusting after not just Jane and Brandon Soh's level of success, but the ease with which they enjoyed that success. Mom and Dad had plenty of money, to be sure, but they also hustled every minute of every day. I couldn't imagine either of them relaxing long enough to even imagine taking up birding (short for *bird-watching*, which was a form of wildlife observation).

"We were hoping you could keep Cirrus entertained while we were out," said Cirrus's dad. It was a bizarre thing to say, as if Cirrus were a toddler.

"You're not doing anything right now, are you?" said Dad to me.

"Sure!" I replied nonsensically. I hung my arms at my sides, then realized how odd I probably looked, then leaned on the banister (something I never did), then folded my arms, before returning to my original pose of standing like an action figure still in its package.

Cirrus gave me a helpless look. "They flew in this morning, *without* telling me." She glanced at her parents, who seemed oblivious to the jab.

As they headed out, Mom paused to look at me. "Is that a new shirt?"

"No," I blurted with exaggerated nonchalance, before realizing that that answer would only lead to more questions. "No, but, you mean *this* shirt? Yes. I bought this."

Mom gave me a curious look. Thankfully Dad led her away before my fragile poker face could be shattered by further questions.

"Let's go check out this Maybach, dude," said Dad, oblivious with glee.

"Back in a bit," said Cirrus's father.

"Thank you for taking such good care of Cirrus, Sunny," said Cirrus's mother.

I maintained my smile in the face of such odd people. What

kind of parents left their daughter alone for two weeks to take meetings in Mexico? What kind of parents said things like *Thank you for taking care of Cirrus* to a boy her same age?

"You're welcome?" I said.

As soon as the car outside slammed shut and zoomed away, all the muscles in Cirrus's body seemed to unclench. She clasped her palms and spoke into them in bent prayer.

"They're so weird they're so weird theyresoweird," said Cirrus.

I wanted to hug her. So I did. Because now I could!

While I was at it, I told her, "I think I understand you more now that I've met your parents."

She leaned on me like an exhausted sprinter. "Let's do something normal."

"This is normal," I said, not wanting to move a single muscle.

"I could say hi to your friends, for instance," said Cirrus.

She was peering upward. At the top of the staircase I could see two half faces spying back at us like dryad imps stacked behind a tree: Jamal and Milo.

I separated from Cirrus with tremendous reluctance. "Oh, hey, guys, there you are."

"Hi, Cirrus," chorused Jamal and Milo.

"What's doing?" said Cirrus.

"Nothing," said Milo.

"Working on a song," said Jamal at the same time.

"Ooo, a song," said Cirrus, and dashed up the staircase.

I followed, silently wowing at Jamal: *Too much!*

Milo looked at me: *Song? What song?*

So did Jamal: *Why did I have to say working on a song, nooooo.*

And just like that, we were all in Gray's room: Jamal sitting on an amp, Milo on a wooden box, Cirrus on the metal desk chair, and me atop the bed, the highest point in the room, like I was on some kind of soft memory foam stage that also promoted proper spine alignment during sleep.

Cirrus rubbed her hands together like starting a fire. "Can I hear?" she said, because that was the normal thing anyone would've done.

What me and Milo and Jamal were doing was not normal at all, nor were we even close to being ready to do it. But we knew we had to perform. It would've been super strange to sit there, a band, surrounded by instruments, and refuse to play for a girl I had just yesterday declared my like for, all sealed with a kiss.

"Do you—" I said to Milo.

"So should—" said Milo to Jamal.

"What, ah—" said Jamal to me, completing our triangle of bumbling morons.

"So I already know Sunny plays guitar and sings," said Cirrus, narrowing her eyes to examine us boys. "But let me guess. Milo, you probably play . . . drums."

"How did you know?" cried Milo. "It's my disproportionate physique, isn't it."

"And you, Jamal," said Cirrus, "that means you play . . . bass."

Jamal did this weird smile where he showed all his teeth, including molars. "I mean that's pretty obvious anyone could've figured that out once you have the drums and guitar and vocals nailed down and there's only three of us so therefore the only choice left would be—"

"Intro!" I blurted. "Let's play intro? Hn?"

I had noticed Gray's iPod on his desk and remembered the song we were supposed to be mastering, "Beauty Is Truth."

"Yeeeeeaa aa aaaa aaah hhhhhh h h hhh h hh hh," said Milo, pushing his glasses up on his nose bridge.

"Cool coolcoolcoocoocoocucucucu," said Jamal.

"This is so exciting," said Cirrus, and wiggled to settle in. She was, I realized with idiot satori, our first audience ever.

I once read that a writer's greatest fear is for someone to actually read their work. An artist's greatest fear is for someone to actually view their painting. A musician's fear is for someone to actually listen to them perform. I fully understood all of this now.

I clenched my hands to stop them from vibrating. Jamal handed me a guitar, which I slung slowly around myself, stunned with panic. Jamal did the same. He held back bile like a man about to parachute into enemy fire. He flicked on my amp, then his.

My head shot up at the sound of a drum. It was Milo, batting his fingertips against his box stool. The box made a surprising number of sounds: bass kick, snare, and side toms.

I looked at him: *What the . . . ?*

"It's a cajon," said Milo. "My dad got one on a trip to Peru."

"Duh, right, my cajon," I said. "You got some serious cojones, ha ha."

"What do my testicles have to do with anything?" said Milo.

"Huh?" said Cirrus.

"Milo," I said, very quietly. "Count us in."

But before he could, Cirrus said, "What's the song called?"

"It's, uh," I said, scrambling to remember. How could I not remember?

"'Beauty Is Truth,'" whimpered Jamal through uncontrollable amounts of saliva.

"Keats," said Cirrus immediately. "Nice."

"Keats . . . I . . . like . . . too . . ." I said.

" 'Ode on a Grecian Urn,' " said Cirrus. She hugged herself. "I like the ending:

" ' "Beauty is truth, truth beauty,"—that is all

" 'Ye know on earth, and all ye need to know.' "

I was going to be sick.

I stared at Milo staring at Jamal staring back at me staring at Milo, forever infinity. A long, heavy moment came rolling through and crushed everything into splinters.

Cirrus was staring at me with puzzlement, so I gave Milo my best showman's nod.

Milo cleared his throat. "And a-one, and a-two."

At first, our intro sounded like three trash cans full of shouting goats crashing down the side of an ancient-ass pyramid at different speeds. But we stabilized soon enough. We blinked away panic and threw eyes well enough to maintain a limping momentum.

G, chromatically up to B

Boom, tssh, boom-boom, tssh

I threw eyes at Milo, then at Jamal, so that we would land the final notes. They were our most accurate notes to date. We gave one another the stunned looks of survivors.

"Wooo!" said Cirrus, clapping. "Rock and roll, baby! You wrote that?"

I blinked eight times, cleared my throat, and answered: "Yap."

"And that's just the beginning part?"

"Yap."

I glanced around. Now Milo and Jamal looked like they were going to be sick.

"You're brilliant," said Cirrus.

Me and Milo and Jamal rested on our instruments as if we knew what the hell we were doing. To make the illusion complete, I fist-bumped Milo and Jamal just like real bandmates would. The two looked like they had just outrun a torrent of Spanish bulls gone blind with the heat of Eros.

I watched as Cirrus found a Sharpie, uncapped it, and leaned over to add the letters *IM* to the Mortals flyer on the wall.

"Fixed that for you," she said. She gave me the most wonderful look. She was *proud* of me.

I grew instantly addicted to that look. I could never get enough of it.

I began taking off my guitar with the weary flourish of a warrior done with battle. "Anyway, you guys wanna hang out downstairs?"

"Wait," said Cirrus. "Doesn't your song have lyrics?"

"Yeah," I said, because it did. "But they're not ready."

"That's okay," said Cirrus, with sarcastic nonchalance. "It's not like I'm dying to hear you sing or anything. It's not like a guy singing rock and roll isn't one of the hottest things a girl could imagine."

Crap.

I looked to Jamal, but he'd already set his bass guitar back on its stand and switched off his amp. He had left mine on, though.

Thanks, Jamal.

"Still figuring out the details," I said, putting the guitar back on. It felt twice as heavy. I gave the strings a limp strum. "But in general it goes kinda like talkin' bout aa ee ooo aa oo songs unsung sound so sweet mm ah mm."

Cirrus covered her mouth with the back of her hand and giggled.

I stopped and giggled back as best I could. "What?"

"No, but your voice is just so high and sweet," said Cirrus. "I wasn't expecting a voice like that to come out of you."

I always suspected that puberty had done a half-assed job with my body. Developing certain parts while skipping others. Like my voice.

"It's a classic rock falsetto," I said, quoting Mr. Tweed. "Many a famous rock star can sound like a totally different person when he or she sings onstage."

"A totally different person," said Cirrus, intrigued.

I felt Milo looking at me: *Isn't it ironic?*

Jamal eyerolled: *Don't you think?*

The four of us sat for a moment, just staring at the little red light burning hot on the humming amp. I didn't know what I was supposed to do next. Play some more? Offer snacks?

Stare? Stare? Stare?

"What is going on here?" said an uncertain voice.

Gray stood in the doorway, looking confused. "What are you guys doing in my—"

Kerrang, went my guitar, interrupting him.

"Are you playing—"

KERRANG

I fiddled with the amp knobs with carefully feigned concern. "This gain sounds funny," I muttered, which was total nonsense. My brain was unraveling in my skull. I could not simply keep playing loud sounds to keep Gray from talking. Twice was weird enough.

"Are you supposed to be in a band now or something?" said Gray.

Gray looked like he was in the middle of getting dressed. He wore an undershirt and front-pleated charcoal khakis held up by a plain leather belt. Below, argyle socks in every shade of ash. He was a black-and-white character lost in a world of ultra-high-def color.

Gray turned his gaze. "You must be Cirrus."

"I am," said Cirrus, oblivious.

Have mercy, I pleaded silently. *Spare me.* Could Gray see it in my eyes?

"Gray," I began, but it came out as a dry croak.

Cirrus's phone buzzed. She glanced at the screen, then stood.

"Crap," said Cirrus. "My parents are back downstairs. The camera store was closed, so we're driving all the way out to Top of Topanga for some lunch thing, yay."

"Can I come?" I blurted.

Cirrus wheeled her thumbs. "You wanna?"

Oh, how I did! Just get up and run away with my beautiful girlfriend (*girlfriend!*). But on one side of me, I could feel urgency from Jamal and Milo to continue work on Esmeralda's Veil; on the other side of me, I could feel the threat of growing indignation coming from Gray.

"I should probably stay here and work on some stuff actually," I said finally.

There was an expensive-sounding car honk from downstairs.

"Text me," said Cirrus, and left.

I sat, bathing in those two heavenly words no girl had heretofore ever uttered to me.

In the following silence, Gray took five to consider the mise-en-scène before him with a hardboiled detective's eye. The ax. The dame what just scrammed. Gray's old glad rags on this sap right here, and also on Jamal and Milo. Some kind of hinky grift—with his own brother as the boss fakeloo artist?

When Gray reached the newly doctored flyer—THE IMMORTALS—his eyes narrowed.

I could see him selecting words in his mind and carefully lining them up like surgical tools.

Finally Gray simply said, "Unbelievable."

He noticed my shirt. "You—"

He noticed Milo and Jamal's shirts. "And you two—"

Milo and Jamal folded their arms in a useless attempt to hide.

Gray's confusion broke with a chuckle of amusement that quickly soured into disgust. He took a moment to sneer at all the old things in his old room. I noticed he hadn't taken a step inside. He clung to the doorway and came no farther, as if the room were a quarantine ward.

He sneered at Jamal. "You enjoying my old shirt?"

Jamal said nothing.

Gray turned to Milo. "You?"

Milo said nothing.

"Please—" I began.

"Please?" said Gray with another laugh. "As long as you're asking nicely, then yeah, go ahead and play pretend with all my old crap, you *amazing losers*! Immortals? Really?"

"You can't say anything—" I began, then stopped myself.

Gray smirked mightily. "She doesn't know."

I remained stopped.

"Holy crap," Gray said. "Of *course* she doesn't know."

I could only hold back the trembles.

"Don't worry, dude," said Gray. "Your secret is super-duper safe with me." He made a swinging exit from the doorway, leaving his grin floating behind for a long time after he left.

Promise

In the chaotic scrum of morning homeroom we debriefed one another via text message for privacy, sitting back-to-back-to-back in Triforce formation—an instinctive response designed to protect ourselves from surprise attack.

JAMAL
So Gray's gone from garden
variety dick to full-on douchtube

Welcome to my never-ending
disappointment.

MILO
I found that encounter
very stressful

JAMAL
You think?

God I think Gray wants to
blow our cover

MILO
But for what possible reason?

Just to mess with my life

JAMAL
He did say our secret is safe
with him tho

MILO
Oh Jamal, that was sarcasm.

JAMAL
Oh

MILO
Arch sarcasm.

JAMAL
So our secret isn't safe is it

I just don't know
what he's gonna do

MILO
I'm sure he won't do anything.

JAMAL
Oh god what if he does tho

MILO
I'm sure he was just bluffing,
Jamal.

But what if he wasn't

What if Gray tells my parents . . .
who will then tell Cirrus's parents . . .
who will then tell Cirrus
Oh my god

JAMAL
Who will then tell the whole
school, and then we would
be totally ducked and up shut
creek without a paddle for
sure why why why did we
agree to be in a fake band

MILO
Jamal Maurice Willow!

I will do something . . . I
got us into this mess, I will
figure this out

JAMAL
How??

I will convince Gray to
leave us alone, I promise

JAMAL
How????

MILO
Trust Sunny!

JAMAL
Trusting Sunny was the
problem to be perfectly honest
Milo Hector de la Peña

MILO

You are out of line!

JAMAL

I'm sorry Sunny

I take it back

It's ok, you are my best friends,

I feel terrible about putting you

in this situation, love you both

JAMAL

Love you too

MILO

Love you three.

Maybe we could run

CREAPS on the problem

JAMAL

lol

MILO

Everything's going to be fine.

Gray is just being an annoying

big brother, that's all.

He wasn't always annoying

JAMAL

He wasn't?

Story for another day

From before our time

Anyway

JAMAL
So Sunny uh

Mhm

JAMAL
Esmeralda's Veil?

MILO
Jamal.

JAMAL
Sorry sorry nvm

No you're right I promise I'll
work on that too . . . promise
promise promise

The bell rang.

We put our phones away. The teacher came in, made a bunch of trombone sounds, and dismissed us.

Outside, I traveled through rain-wet covered walkways, casting a tube of light and sorcery that dazzled all who beheld me. I wore a stained white Deftones shirt cut into a wide-neck; I wore a pair of Edward Zipperpants. I had discovered a studded leather cuff for my wrist. The cuff did not tell time or light up or fetch your email or anything. The cuff just *rocked.*

Did I rock?

A trio of freshman girls gave me the Look. I just sighed. If only they knew.

I was an impostor.

This morning I'd been sure I would get caught by Gray, that he would snatch my backpack, unzip it, and dump all his clothes out. But he hadn't. He was sleeping in, like every morning.

It amazed me that in this life, Gray had gotten to walk around wearing whatever he wanted, switching personas freely as needed. Meanwhile I, ever the loser, seemed to have no license to do such a thing.

Why?

What colossal acrylic lottery-ball blower machine decided that Gray should be the winner and I should be the loser? What higher order had sent down that judgment of fate? I wanted to ask a god, any god, but he was blackout drunk and had left the great wheel spinning abandoned and free for millennia now.

I flexed the leather cuff on my wrist. I wanted to punch a hole in the air. I probably could; such a move probably would look pretty cool. But was it even my move to own, if it was stolen to begin with?

I punched my palm instead, earning a Look from a boy peering out from behind a book.

I turned a corner, and walked right into Gunner.

"Now *you*?" I said. "Great."

Gunner held a tray with both hands.

"Nice pants," said Gunner through sphinctoid lips.

"Nythe panth!" cried Gunner's glistening sidekick.

Gunner gestured with whatever he was holding. "Are all those zippers for all the, like, the tiny dongs all growing all over your legs?"

In the pre-Cirrus, pre-lie era, my normal response would have been to inaudibly whisper *Go away* and flee with my eyes fixed upon the ground.

Oh, but isn't that just the perfect loser response.

Maybe we could run away from Gray, too.

And Cirrus. Don't forget her.

Yes . . . just run away into our little room and hide among our white storage containers.

Why, we could probably fit inside one of those containers if we made ourselves really small.

"Enough!" I said, and punched a hole in the air.

"Huh?" said Gunner.

I examined the thing in Gunner's hands. It was not a tray. It was a *science project.*

Gunner saw me look, then attacked again. "Your [sic] wearing a total girl shirt."

I took a step forward and squinted.

"Oh no," I said. "Is that supposed to be a cell model sculpture?"

Gunner gripped the board's edges. "You wanna flip my board? I dare you. Flip it."

"Flibbit!" said his milky translucent-skinned sidekick with a low monkey-hop.

I took a step forward. Gunner took a step back. "It looks like five different animals took turns defecating on the same doormat," I said.

"I know you want revenge," said Gunner. "For all the cafeteria trays. Go ahead, flip it, I double dildo dare you."

I waved a lazy fingertip. "No hypothesis, no research, no conclusion synthesis," I said. "This crap salad's getting an F, and you know it. Your fourth, right?"

Gunner's nostrils quivered. He looked at his work. I knew that he knew that I was right. "You shut up."

I turned to leave. "Have fun repeating junior year again."

"I know what you're doing, Sunny Dae," said Gunner.

Something about his tone made me stop and look back. Gunner was furious.

"I've known you since middle school," Gunner sneered.

My fingers twitched like a nervous gunslinger's. Where was Gunner headed?

"I know you're copying your big brother," said Gunner.

The sky flashed. Blood emptied out of my heart.

"Gyahahahaha," said his repulsive sidekick. "Luzer!"

"You're a big faker," said Gunner. He took a step, made the air rumble. Surely he could smell my spike in fear. To my endless disappointment, I cowered.

"I know why, too," said Gunner. "You're trying to be cool for *her*."

"Go away," I muttered, barely audible.

"Goway-goway-goway!" sang the sidekick.

"Okay," said Gunner, fully in control now. "I'll *go away* and tell Cirrus."

The sound of her sacred name excreting forth from Gunner's moist abhorrent lips made me wish with all my heart that I could utter *gladius sanctus!* and summon my paladin character's holy sword (special attack: « DEMONKILL ») straight from the astral plane into my open palm to slay this despicable duo *as! Well! As!* the unsatisfactory schoolwork.

Instead, Gunner smiled, turned, and began taking his leave. The sidekick scampered ahead of him off into the cold wet.

"Wait," I said.

Gunner stopped and turned as if he'd been expecting me to say exactly that word.

"Yes?" crooned Gunner, with the dark charm of a backstabbing, conniving court eunuch.

I pointed at his cell sculpture. "Is that thing due today?"

"Mhm," said Gunner.

I flopped my arms with defeat. "Can you get an extension or something?"

"I can get pretty much anything I need," said Gunner, victorious. He flung the fragile ugly sculpture into a nearby rain puddle, where it began dissolving wit each pelting drop.

"Southeast corner of Emerald Ave. and Sapphire Street," said Gunner. "Let's say Sunday afternoon."

"Can we just get this over with tomorrow?" I said.

Gunner shook his head quickly. "I got practice."

I blinked. Did this guy do anything but football?

Gunner gave his hands a big smug clap. "Bring that brain of yours, Dae."

It was now somehow Saturday night. I was back in my room.

I sat at my workbench and scowled at my white storage containers. The house was so silent I could hear myself blink.

I told Jamal and Milo I would figure out what to do about the Gray Problem. They, of course, had no idea that the Problem had expanded to include Gunner.

I, of course, had no idea what to do.

Just thinking about that problem gave me much, much angst.

I had also promised them I would work on improvements to Esmeralda's Veil. That was a much,

much, much, much, much, much, much, much easier promise to fulfill.

So I sat at my workbench and flipped my face shield down.

Esmeralda's Veil was a good idea on Jamal's part, but its biggest flaw was that it was way too noxious to pass the Safe part of the CREAPS test. I removed the stinking smoke bomb from the base of the tube and replaced it with a portable, battery-operated humidifier, one of the many compact nebulizers I kept around the house to protect my sinus tissues from allergens.

I taped the humidifier into a plastic bottle of water, flipped the switch, and watched as delicate fingers of mist began streaming from the perforations in the wand. Silent, odorless, nontoxic, easily refillable with free and abundant H_2O. For extra shiny, I lined the clear tube with an LED array strip to turn the mist blue, green, orange, and so on.

I clipped my phone to its stand, recorded a short rough to send to Jamal and Milo in the morning, and tidied up. From my tiny knight I took a tiny sword pen and wrote

Esmeralda's Veil Version 2: Success (+3 Magic Defense Bonus, +2 Evasion Bonus)

Lady Lashblade was sure to be impressed.

My feeling of satisfaction lasted only for a moment before giving way to my previous foreboding. Gray was still out there. And Gunner.

I wrote Gray's name in my notebook, then crossed it out hard with a ballpoint pen until the paper tore. I did this over and over.

~~GRAY GRAY GRAY GRAY GRAY GRAY~~

I was angry. Mainly at myself.

~~STUPID STUPID STUPID STUPID STUPID~~

All I wanted was to somehow rewind time to the part just before Gray came home. I wanted to somehow keep him in Hollywood—find him another roommate, whatever—so that I could keep being Rock Star Sunny. So that I could keep having fun, because I was having fun, in a way that I hadn't for a long time.

Why should my fun get ruined?

Gray didn't even like his old stuff anymore. Why should he care what I did with it?

Why did Gray have to be what he was—the lord of all douchetubes?

I slammed my notebook shut.

I headed downstairs.

Down, down, to where the air grew muted and musty with disuse. Gray's door was ajar. I shoved it open against thick carpet unflattened by any footstep.

Gray did not move.

I peered closer. He lay on the derelict recliner with one hand covering his eyes and frayed, gaffer-taped headphones sealed over his ears. He sighed deep and slow.

When I touched the chair with a fingertip, he wiped his eyes, which fluttered wildly against the light until they found me, focused in, and dimmed. "What," he said.

Gray had been listening to his old iPod. His eyes were poofy and red.

"What are you listening to?" I said, as bitingly as possible, which was not very much.

"Music," said Gray.

"You forgot you even had that thing," I said, wiggling my toes to muster up courage. "You're not even using it."

"What the hell are *you* using it for?" said Gray.

I stopped, searched for words like a fish gasping for air. "Nothing," I said.

Gray watched me for a long moment, and I was too paralyzed to do anything but simply let him. I wanted to say so many things, but found I couldn't.

Gray began chuckling softly. He squeezed his temples, shook his head.

"Seeing you with my guitars, and her sitting there," he said.

"Stop," I commanded.

A single laugh—a loud one—escaped his throat before he could catch it. "I'm sorry," he said, not at all sorry. "That was one of the funniest things I've ever seen."

"Shut up," was all I could come up with as a retort.

"You guys are completely stupid, you know that?"

I gritted my teeth. The only thing I could do was stand there as Gray found my predicament amusing. I wished I could stun him with Raiden's Spark for real from one hand, and then cast Esmeralda's Veil with the other so that I could abscond with the iPod while he choked on clouds of sulfur—no constitution-saving throw, automatic lose-a-turn. After that I would be long gone, and he would find himself now guarding a dungeon with no treasures left to defend.

"I miss high school," said Gray suddenly.

I released my spell-casting fists, dissipating their pent-up magic.

"I should've just gone to college," said Gray.

I knitted my fingers at my belly. Was Gray about to cry?

Gray cleared his throat and coughed a mock cough. "Questlove once formed a fake band to impress a girl," he said.

"That band became the Roots. My senior-year buddy Justin Lim formed the Mortals for the same reason."

I spoke cautiously. I was now seeing the faintest image of Back-in-the-Day Gray—the slightest tremor could tear it asunder. "He did?"

"The Mortals did not become the Roots," said Gray.

Gray picked at a hole in the recliner, realized he was only making things worse, and stuffed the brown thread back in.

"I heard Justin's getting married," said Gray. "So I guess it worked."

"Do you keep in touch with—"

"No," said Gray, stone-faced.

"Oh," I said. His laughter from just an instant ago felt like yesterday.

Gray sneered at the air. "Justin had it right," he said. "No one wants the musician, they just want the music. No girl wants to deal with gig after gig, night after night, stuck with a total loo—"

He was about to say *loser.*

Gray covered his face with his hands.

"You guys friggin' rocked," I said, and took a step closer to my big brother.

Gray lowered his hands. "We did, didn't we."

He stood. He unplugged his headphones. He picked at the back of the iPod, pick pick pick, until the gaffer tape with *Property of Gray Dae* peeled off. He balled the tape up, flung it into the other debris in the room. And he handed the iPod to me.

"Thanks," I said, and reached for it.

But Gray snatched it up. "You have to play it right," he said.

"I will," I whined, and reached again.

"Promise me you will absolutely play the hell out of 'Beauty Is Truth,'" said Gray. "I spent a lot of time on that song."

I shrugged like a marionette. "All I can say is *I'll do my best?*" I said.

Gray eyed me. "I don't like the sound of that," he said slowly. "Not one bit."

He slipped the iPod into his pocket.

"Aw come on, god, just give it, dude, what the hell," I said, increasing my pitch with each word until I sounded like I was six by the end.

"Promise me," said Gray.

"I promise, *god,*" I said.

"Where do you guys practice?"

"Music room at school."

"When are you practicing next?" said Gray.

"I dunno," I whined. "Maybe tomorrow?"

"But that's a Sunday," said Gray.

"Mr. Tweed said we could," I said.

Gray thought for a moment. "I got brunch with Dad tomorrow," he said. "When's your next practice after that?"

I stopped. "Huh?"

Gray spoke like I was a foreign exchange student who was also very slow. "Tomorrow morning. I have a brunch thing. With Dad. But your next practice. After that. We will go together. Okay?"

I blinked bemused little blinks. Was what was happening what I thought was happening?

"Okay," I said.

III

Frost holds the virus for thousands of years.
Winter eternal protects us from fear.

Blotter

The next morning, I got up and headed directly to my phone dock located safely away from the delicate tissues in my cranium, breaking my steadfast rule of not checking the infernal first thing in the morning, because doing so led to increased anxiety and unhappiness—

But things were different now.

Because on the screen was one message from very early this a.m., from Cirrus:

I'm on a boat.

And indeed, there was a photo of a boat, taken from a dock. Brandon and Jane Soh stood nearby.

Are you leaving the country? I wrote, then deleted it. Bad joke. Instead, I just went with

Wish I was there.

At the same time, Cirrus wrote, Wish you were here.

Jinx, we both wrote simultaneously. I smiled a big dumb smile.

I think your brother's a little jealous of you btw, wrote Cirrus.

Really? I wrote.

He's kind of a dork, no offense, wrote Cirrus. And meanwhile you're . . . you, heart emoji.

I slapped my thigh and twirled on one foot and hit a white plastic container, which caused me to lose my balance and fall into still more white plastic containers.

When I got back to my feet, I wrote,

Kiss emoji.

And I put my phone in my pocket, which I normally never did because of what microwaves can do to the epidermis and possibly subcutaneous tissue even through thicker fabrics. But I wanted to make sure I didn't miss a message like I had while stupidly asleep at 5:03 this morning. It was currently 11:11 a.m.

I descended toward the breakfast nook. One end of the table there was covered with folders, agreements, and invoices.

At the other end sat Mom, all by herself. Oddly, she was wearing a tee shirt and sweats and not her work clothes. I tried to remember the last time I'd seen her dressed like this. I couldn't put my finger on the right word to describe how she looked.

Relaxed.

Before her sat two bowls of red. Cold thin flour noodles with spicy gochujang sauce, topped with icy slivers of cucumber, white radish, and pear. It was the simplest meal we'd had in a while, and one we used to have often at our old place.

"It's bibim naengmyeon for brunch today, okay?" said Mom.

"Love it," I said. I was drooling already. I took my phone out of my pocket and fastidiously set it next to my chopsticks.

Mom pursed her lips like an imp thief. "Waiting for someone to call?"

I blushed. "No," I said, so unconvincingly even I was embarrassed for myself.

" 'Kay," Mom said, shrugging, and began pushing her noodles around with the forced indifference of parents of teenagers everywhere secretly aching for those days of unfiltered intimacy they had with their children back when they were small.

I pushed my noodles around, too. The noodles were winning. "Are Dad and what's-his-face out wheeling and dealing?" I said.

Mom flattened her eyes at me. "You mean Gray, your one and only brother, who you love more than anything?"

"Nurr," I said.

Mom stretched and mixed with her chopsticks, like noodle calisthenics. "Those two are doing links and drinks at the golf club with some of Trey's top subcontractors. So you're my brunch date, ha."

I blinked. "Gray doesn't drink. Neither does Dad."

"They'll hold a mocktail if it means locking in a couple new retainers," said Mom. She slurped. "Oh my god, all I want to do is carb out, I swear."

"Then I, too, shall carb out with you," I said, and slurped.

"It's gotta be the stress," said Mom.

"Everything okay?" I said.

"Just work," said Mom, glancing up at the piles of paper. "Work work work today, Sunday, every day."

"That sucks."

"It's fine," said Mom through chews. She paused. "It's funny."

"What's funny?"

"I've never had a Sunday brunch date with just me and Dad at the golf club, or lunch or dinner, for that matter," said Mom. "Only work events."

I noticed Mom wasn't wearing her usual headset. I tried to read her face. Was she sad? Wistful?

"Anyway," sang Mom, mostly to herself.

At the end of the counter I spotted something: an expensive-looking VR headset. I pointed at it, looked at Mom: *???*

Mom rolled her eyes so hard her face went slack, and then she leveled a wry gaze at me.

"From our day with the Sohs," she said. "If Cirrus's dad bought a dozen red elephants, your dad would, too."

We ate for a moment. I didn't know what to say to her. Part of me wanted to suggest we move to a cheaper house, in a cheaper neighborhood, and just coast for a good long while. I imagined we had plenty of money to do that. But then I tried to imagine Dad downsizing back to our old four-cylinder, five-door Fava hatchback from our Arroyo Plato days, and could not. American progress went one way only toward just the one eternal goal, which was always more.

Jhk jhk, went my phone.

I dropped my noodles with a splat. It was Cirrus.

I was staring at a glorious photo of a whale spouting into the sparkling green sea. It was the best photo ever taken in all of human history.

Jhk jhk, jhk jhk, jhk jhk. My phone was practically playing rock and roll. Three more photos arrived: another whale, three gray streaks of dolphins from very close up, and a diving pelican.

I took a ton of photos . . . just amazing out here, wrote Cirrus.

"Honey, please don't text at the table," said Mom. She had uttered this exact phrase at least sixteen thousand times in the last five years.

"Sorry," I said, even though I wasn't sorry at all.

"Who is it?" said Mom. She glanced over. I made no effort to hide the screen.

Mom beamed sweetly at me. "Text as much as you want," she said.

I'm only gone for the day but I miss you already, wrote Cirrus.

I miss you too, I wrote back.

I can't wait to see YOU, wrote Gunner.

Ugh! Gunner!

I unhinged my jaw and slid the remaining noodles down my gullet, then wiped my face clean with a footlong sticky tongue.

"Sunny!" said Mom with amazement and concern.

"Can I please be done now?" I said.

"What are you, seven?" said Mom.

I glanced at the phone and danced a pee-pee dance.

"Go," said Mom.

I went.

"Hey, Sun," said Mom, before I left. "It's nice to see you coming out of your shell like this. What's changed with you?"

"Nothing," I said. "Puberty 2.0."

"Huh?"

Jhk jhk, went my phone. I didn't look at it.

"Gotta go," I said.

Mom just smiled. She had no idea I was heading out to bargain for my soul.

The corner of Emerald Avenue and Sapphire Street was where Gunner had suggested we meet.

But the intersection was empty. There was nothing here, really, except one big house and another big house two hundred meters away. Beyond lay a grove of palm trees and a rocky beach keeping the indifferent sea at bay. I had reached the far southwestern edge of Rancho Ruby.

Had Gunner sent me here on a wild goose chase? I imagined him texting me another location, just to troll me.

I'm here.

Immediately he (or what I assumed was him) responded: Lock your bike to the pole and go up the orange stairs.

How did he know I had my bike? I wheeled around, looking for hidden spy cameras.

I looked about and there, indeed, was a set of orange Spanish tile stairs leading up between rows of overgrown rosemary.

Gunner was waiting for me at the top of the stairs. He stood alone before a massive tiled hacienda with an artfully weathered door studded with heavy étoile nails, the kind used to crucify Jesus on the cross that he dragged for miles under the whip of the Romans. Gunner's sidekick was not there. It was just me and him.

I stepped inside the cool dark house. I stepped into the eighteenth century. Dark wooden chests banded with black iron, coats of arms on the wall, cage sconces around every light.

Gunner had a perfectly antiqued green glass of ice water

ready for me. Was it poisoned? I touched my tongue to it. It tasted lemony. I glanced around and spotted a dispenser jug full of spa water, the kind with fruit and stuff floating in it.

"Get him a coaster," said a man in a flight suit. It looked like a flight suit. It was really sweats. The man was a dozen centimeters shorter than Gunner, but I somehow knew that didn't matter. His voice alone was bigger than both of us. His buzz cut made him look like he had white horns for hair.

"Okay, Dad," said Gunner immediately, and rushed to hand me an octagon of cork.

"You gonna introduce me or do I have to do that, too?" said Gunner's dad.

"Sunny, Dad, Dad, Sunny," said Gunner, again with an almost professional immediacy. "Sunny's here to help me with my science homework, which I acknowledge I'm lagging behind in."

Gunner's dad smiled and folded his wiry arms. "Well, good. Nice to meet you, Sunny."

I spoke with a throat suddenly gone dry. "Uh, likewise, uh."

"No *uhs* in the Schwinghammer household," said the dad.

"Affirmative?" I said.

Gunner's dad waved a hand. "Carry on. Somebody's gotta save this kid's ass."

I did not want to stay here all night. I shifted into Idea Guy overdrive mode. Time was not on our side.

"Papier-mâché takes forever and always looks like smashed-up garbage anyway," I said. "Do you have clay or even cardboard?"

"No," said Gunner. "I have Lego, though."

That could work. "How much?"

"A whole Tuffy," said Gunner.

"Then let's do this," I said, and gave a thumbs-up to Gunner's dad, who seemed satisfied enough to leave us alone.

Gunner eyed the doorway until his dad was out of sight, then looked at me with those blank eyes of his. "We better get started," he whispered.

We entered a Moorish archway and climbed stairs sunlit by narrow archer's windows. Then down a hall lined with paintings, all oils, including a sinister, unsmiling family portrait done in a dark Flemish style.

This was not what I pictured Gunner living in. If anything, I would've imagined his house as a bright business hotel bar full of televisions with football on every screen. That was not this house.

This house was messed up.

Gunner entered a room so austere it reminded me of that movie where the tormented monk flagellates himself with a cat-o'-nine-tails fashioned by his own hand.

"I'm not allowed to keep the door closed," said Gunner as I entered.

My phone buzzed in my pocket. I sighed—I'd texted Milo and Jamal that I was leaving to meet Gunner, but had forgotten to text when I actually got here.

MILO

Are you there yet?

JAMAL

If you do not update your last
known location in the next
minute we will assume you

have been incapacitated and
will call a rescue squad

I am here, I am safe

JAMAL

Still don't understand why you
can't just help this jerk over
video chat or something

MILO

We will keep pinging you
just in case.

Roger

JAMAL

Who is Roger

The only decorations in Gunner's room were six trophies, all for football, starting from the Pee Wee era all the way up.

I eyed his closet door, his dresser. I sipped my water. The water was ice cold.

I placed my glass on the coaster. "So listen," I said. "I'm happy to help you with your science stuff, okay? Just tell me what you need."

"You guys are crazy, faking at being a band," said Gunner with a sudden smile. I'd never seen him smile like that before. "You mofos are some friggin' crazy-ass mofos."

He flinched at the doorway, cautious. "I'm not allowed to swear," he whispered.

"You didn't," I said.

He relaxed. He looked at me again and slowly resumed his weird smile.

"Anyway, I don't blame you, someone like Cirrus," he said. "I'd do the same thing, too, if I could." He chuckled. Then he got sad. Then he smiled again.

It seemed like within Gunner there were multiple emotions fighting to surface. I searched his face for clues, but couldn't discern anything. Aside from being a bully skilled at catching prolate spheroids of leather, what did I really know about him?

"So I actually already got started on the cell model," said Gunner, and dragged a big new Tuffy trash can from his sparse closet. It was full of plastic bricks. Atop the bricks sat a large baseplate with something built on top: a haphazard arrangement of randomly multicolored towers that even a child would give a harsh critique session to.

"I guess you could call it a start," I said.

Gunner beamed. "Thanks, man," he said.

Gunner was different in his home. He was almost *shy*.

I set the model on a dresser, dug my hands into the Tuffy, and got to work.

"A cell is organic," I said. "You have to make the Lego curve and look rounded. Like this."

I quickly built a simple hemisphere out of thin layers that shrank as they reached the top.

Gunner held his chin like someone who had read that holding one's chin made one look smarter. "Huh."

"Also, you can't use just any color," I said. "I'd use one color per cell structure, like blue for mitochondrion, red for the nucleus."

I worked for a few minutes, sifting and snapping. I hadn't built with Lego in a while, and I found myself entering a not-unpleasant, familiar flow state. When I was finished, I realized I had replaced 99.998 percent of Gunner's original work.

"Dude," said Gunner. "That looks so rad now. We're done!"

"We're not done," I said. "Tell me what's missing."

Gunner held his chin again, then remembered he had a textbook, then went to leaf through it.

" 'Kay, so, we need the endoplastic rectum," said Gunner.

"Endoplasmic reticulum," I said. "Specifically the rough."

"And probably this Golgi thing," said Gunner.

"Apparatus," I said.

"They're so tiny and noodly," said Gunner. "Can we just leave them out?"

"Only if you want a D," I said. Both the endoplasmic reticulum and Golgi apparatus were intricate, ribbon-like structures no Lego could replicate. But I would never let such a limitation stop me. I loved limitations. Limitations set creativity free.

"Do you have ribbon, or maybe extra-wide, extra-long rubber bands?" I said.

"I have cleat shoelaces," said Gunner.

"Perfect," I said.

I instructed Gunner in how to build a matrix of axle holes, which were to be plugged at regular intervals with plentiful, easy-to-find 3M connector pegs (Lego part no. 6558) to form a small field of posts. The shoelace could then be wound around and across the posts to create an arrangement labyrinthine enough to visually convey the complexity of both organelles. We slotted in both modules and then stood back to admire our work.

"Now it looks even radder," said Gunner.

"You have to be able to say what each part does," I said. "Endoplasmic reticulum, go."

Gunner glanced out the doorway, as if his dad were there listening. "It makes lipids."

"And?"

"Cholesterol."

"Golgi, go," I said.

"Takes the molecules from the endoplasmic reticulum and makes complex testicles."

"Vesicles," I said, laughing.

"I keep thinking it's testicles," said Gunner, laughing, but he suddenly stopped and muttered darkly, "Stupid."

"Hey," I said. "Don't say that."

Gunner gave me a sheepish look.

"I tried to write up the hypothesis and conclusion stuff you said was missing," said Gunner, eyes downcast.

So Gunner had remembered that. What was more, he'd clearly *fretted* over it. I found myself wanting to lift Gunner's spirits, which blew my mind.

"Great," I said. "Let's look it over."

It was like magnetic poetry assembled by mice, but worse.

Once again, I found myself replacing 99.998 percent of Gunner's original work. I saved the file, printed it, and set it down next to the model. Done.

Gunner's eyes flicked at the door, then back. "So is it turn-in-nable now?" he murmured.

"This, young Padawan, is an A," I said.

"Really?" said Gunner.

"Really," I said.

Gunner hissed with triumph. "Yiss, I was hoping we'd finish early. Because I've been meaning to ask you about something."

Ask me about what?

Gunner glanced at the doorway again—coast clear—and motioned toward his desk. The desk was empty but for a heavy oxblood leather blotter.

Gunner lifted the blotter. He kept it propped up like a car hood, using a ruler. Under the blotter were sheets of graph paper taped together. On the graph paper was drawn a map, and on the map were little shapes cut out of paper each no bigger than my pinky fingernail labeled CL and WZ and DW and so on.

"I'm halfway through the Tomb of Horrors," whispered Gunner, "but I've been stuck at the big demon-face statue on the wall. The one with the big huge mouth, right here."

And Gunner put his big finger on a hand-drawn map.

I was stunned. "Since when the hell do you play D&D?" I blurted.

"I don't," said Gunner instantly.

I looked the map. Sure enough, it was still there.

"But you *are* playing," I said. "The Tomb of Horrors is widely acknowledged to be the most difficult module ever created by D&D inventor Gary Gygax, and you just asked me for help."

"I've been playing using single-player guides online, which isn't perfect, but," said Gunner, "I think it's pretty fun."

My mind continued to boggle along all six degrees of freedom. I glanced at the cell model, then at the paper map, then at Gunner.

Gunner hesitated, then spoke. "I heard you guys talking about the Tomb at track."

My memory fast-rewound four months, five months, almost a year. Jamal had been complaining that the Tomb of Horrors was too hard, and therefore flawed. Milo and I disagreed, and called it a masterpiece.

"You heard that?" I said now. "You *remembered* that?"

Gunner nodded. "So then last week I was in some nerd shop at some mall, and I saw it on the shelf," he said. "You and Milo and Jamal are always tight, always laughing and stuff, but then you guys also have these serious discussions, like you're really into what you're talking about. You're like brothers, man."

I wanted to smile. We *were* like brothers. But I could only stare at Gunner, to see what he would say next.

"I was all standing in that store in the mall," murmured Gunner. "I was just like, What *is it* those guys are always *talking* about?"

I was confused. "You've been mean to me ever since I moved here. Ever since the fifth grade, dude."

Gunner polished the corner of his desk with a big thumb over and over again. "I'm sorry I was so mean to you," he said.

My heart was beating strangely fast. I had always fantasized about propelling Gunner with a seventeenth-level Push spell into a fathomless crevice full of lava, but this was somehow much more electrifying:

An apology!

Gunner sniffed and ahem-ed hard. I had no idea what to say. I don't think he did, either.

"I don't have any friends I can really talk to," said Gunner finally. "With the guys, it's always training, or girls, or cars. Do you know how much we talk about friggin' training? Or girls? Or cars?"

I was struck by his melancholy. "That sucks," I found myself saying. I looked at the football trophies on his dresser. I realized they had all been turned to face the wall.

"So anyway, I just wanted to know if I should climb into the mouth, or what," he said. "I guess I *could* look it up online."

I could not believe I was saying this, but here I was. "No fun in that, though, right?"

Gunner smiled. "I figured you'd be the guy to talk to."

"Huh," I said.

"I'm really sorry, man," said Gunner.

I noticed sparse decorations tacked on the opposite wall.

FOOTBALL STAR IN TRAINING!

EXCELLENCE: DRIVEN NOT GIVEN

"Uh," I said. "Apology accepted."

IT'S NOT HOW BIG YOU ARE IT'S HOW BIG YOU PLAY

I turned to Gunner's amateurish game board and pointed to a square of paper. "This wizard here holds a clue. Literally, in their hands, as a melee weapon."

Gunner held himself tight and thought. "Artemis cautiously inserts her Staff of Light into the mouth of the demon."

"You named your wizard Artemis," I noted aloud.

"Shut up," said Gunner, and playfully shoved me way too hard onto the floor. "Sorry. I think I have a mind-body disconnect."

He helped me back into my seat. I tented my fingers and intoned my words with a resonance I hadn't used in years. "Artemis's staff finds no resistance. No effect. The weapon simply is absorbed into the darkness. What shall you do now, adventurer?"

"Artemis pulls it back out?" said Gunner.

"As Artemis slowly removes the staff, she is horrified to discover that the end of her beloved melee weapon is missing. Simply erased from existence. Adventurer?"

Gunner's whole face became an O of incredulity. "Is it a—what do you call it—Sphere of Annihilation?"

"The adventurer shows wisdom," I said.

"But that was the only staff she had!"

"Tough titty," I said. I held out a waiting hand. "Adventurer?"

We played.

After a while, Gunner snapped his head up at a sound, and he hid the board. He blipped over to the science project and feigned deep interest. It was alarming how quickly he got into character.

"You boys gittin' 'er done?" said Gunner's dad.

"Absolutely," said Gunner.

Gunner's dad peered down his nose at the work and snuffed. He nodded at his son.

"You've earned yourself a break," he said. "We got our video analysis in five." He left.

"I guess I'll walk you out," said Gunner with a twist of chagrin in his lip.

Outside, it was already night.

"I guess I'll see you later, I guess," said Gunner, and stood there on his front stoop like someone waiting to be kissed at the end of a first date.

I found myself saying it back:

"See you later."

I unlocked my phone and facepalmed at the queue of messages.

JAMAL
Are you dead? If you are dead
please confirm

MILO
Sunny Dae what is happening

And so on. I sighed and wrote back.

Everything's fine. Gunner is
not what he seems, but in a
good way. I'll tell you all about
it tomorrow. In the meantime
our cover is still intact.

JAMAL
You mean YOUR cover

MILO
We're all in this together now.
Support our friend.

JAMAL
Spent all night worried so
I'm stressed sorry

I sent them three hearts in three different colors, then threw a leg over my bike.

The night air was a fragrant mix of distant ocean brine and jasmine and plumeria coming from all around me. I rode from pool to pool of orange light coming from the streetlamps above.

Zzz, zzz, zzz went the buzzing lights overhead.

I had a thing I called the Post-Encounter Energy Scan (PEES). After hanging out with someone, you took a moment to gauge how your body felt. If you felt tired and depleted by the encounter, you should probably not expose yourself to that person again. If you felt energized, you should increase your exposure to that person.

Milo and Jamal energized me.

Cirrus energized me to the stratosphere.

After hanging out with Gunner for the first time, I had to admit: I felt energized.

I also felt depleted, because the thought of him yearning in wretched lightless solitude made my soul heavy. Wanting more from his sidekick, the football team, and that dad of his. But being too afraid to ask.

I felt depleted because Gunner, I realized, was ashamed of himself.

And finally: I felt depleted because I had shame, too. My shame was bad enough that I had turned left into Gray's room instead of right into mine that fateful night.

I looked at the houses all around me, big, bigger, and biggerer, all fronted by gardens manicured to taste, aside parked cars of varying levels of luxury. All human life seemed driven by shame—the fear of being an incorrect self. Wear the right clothes, talk the right way, like the right things, buy the right fancy toys. As if shame were an evolutionary necessary evil designed to keep the tribes of society simultaneously together and apart.

If there were no shame, would we be freer? Or just descend into chaos?

I had to get over this little shame of mine, and turn it into a light. It might take months or years. I feared it might take forever.

Nerd was an epithet of shame. People called me that because I did not wear the right clothes, talk the right way, or like the right things. *Nerd* was a catchall term for someone who failed to fit any established terms—a pejorative cousin to *whatchamacallit* for inscrutable objects or *schmutz* for unidentifiable stains.

Shame was a heavy blanket to hide under. But it was not so heavy that it could keep the energy of every undisclosed desire in your heart at bay. That energy popped out in strange ways. For Gunner, it had come out as obsessive antagonism.

And for me?

For me, that energy took the form of the Immortals.

I passed Cirrus's condo now. Her light was off.

The Immortals were fake. Cirrus, our one and only fan, was not.

Cirrus was the realest thing in my life.

Shred

Even though it was a Saturday, there were kids on campus. Kids in the lunch area, dancing in unison. Kids on the lawn, playacting. Kids in the main theater, singing. Kids everywhere, all getting their acts together for the talent show.

Three kids in the music room, plus one adult.

We had been practicing under Gray's guidance for a week now.

Even though it was a Saturday, I did not change my routine. I still had to take the heinous ten-speed. Still had to go behind the Cernoseks' junipers to change into a pair of Gray's silver-black jeans and assassin hoodie, to avoid parental suspicion. I'd brought shirts for Jamal and Milo, too: *Think of it as a dress rehearsal,* I told them.

Gray again wore corporate leisure clonewear from some breakfast meeting earlier this morning. I could smell faint traces of tomato-y alcohol on his breath. It was strange to think of him drinking, especially before noon. But that was just me, hanging on to the teetotaling Gray I knew from before.

People change.

Gunner, for instance, came over to my house.

I know.

He sat in my room and simply looked through storage container after storage container, marveling at the contents of each. We got so sucked in that we didn't even get around to playing through the Tomb of Horrors. Evening came, and I found myself inviting Gunner to stay for paella dinner. He would've, too, had it not been for another video review session with his dad.

"Next time," Gunner had said.

"Sure," I'd said, and discovered that I had meant it.

I had my first-ever conversation with Gunner's sidekick, who was named Oggy, short for August. I was quietly floored to realize I had never known the kid's name until now.

We talked about girls and cars.

Back in the music room, me and Milo and Jamal stood panting after yet another run through "Beauty Is Truth."

"Pretty good," said Gray. "You guys are at least fifty-five percent of the way to having a respectable performance. That's more than halfway, nerds."

"Please don't call us nerds," said Jamal.

"Ready, *nerds*, let's go again." Gray held up the iPod and hit the button.

We played along with Gray's recording—scrambling to match every note of every guitar, every beat of every drum. I kept my vocals in tandem with his vocals, singing with the Gray from three years ago.

As we fought our way through all seven minutes of the song, Gray watched us closely. He pointed out our cues like a conductor. He adjusted my chin to stick to the mic better.

I sang, as powerfully as I could. My voice soared high like a faerie pinpoint of light into a night sky. I trilled and rolled and added every frilly bit of rococo ornament I could remember from my boys' chorus days in middle school. I glanced at Gray, who was watching me with his palm clamped over his mouth in amazement. Pretty sure it was amazement at the time. Felt amazing to me, anyway.

Now the song was coming to an end, and I threw eyes all around to make sure we stuck the landing.

"Better," said Gray, clapping now. "Sunny, you got this rock falsetto thing going on."

"So I've heard," I said, panting.

"Rock is full of men with high, sweet voices," said Gray. "Freddie Mercury, Prince, Jeff Buckley, that guy from Muse."

"So where does that put us?" I said. "Seventy percent?"

Gray inflated his cheeks, thinking. "Sixty," he said finally, before moving on to Milo.

"You're a natural drummer," he told him. "Unselfconscious, spontaneous. But you need discipline. You need to play loose but tight. I'm giving you a click."

"Loose but tight," said Milo. "Loose but tight."

"What's a click?" said Jamal.

"No, but a *click track*, or *click*, is a cheat that turns drummers into mechanized automatons similar to the AI beats that come preloaded with GarageBand software," I said.

"*Yes, and* it's a metronome," bellowed Gray. "*Yes, and!*"

I blinked. Did I say something wrong?

"You say *No, but* a lot," said Gray.

"I do?" I said.

"Stop saying *No, but*," said Gray. "Say *Yes, and*. It's Improv 101."

"Improv," I said.

"I took a class back in Hollywood," said Gray in an offhand way that was undeniably—

"Cool," said Jamal.

"Very cool," said Milo.

"*Yes, and* keeps the momentum going," said Gray. "*No, but* shuts everything down. The former represents acceptance; the latter represents rejection."

To be clear, Gray was not being annoying. He smiled. He *glowed*. For a moment, my mind flashed back to our kitchen back in Arroyo Plato.

"*Yes, and* click tracks are very useful and valid," I tried.

Gray shot a finger at me: *That's the spirit*. Then he turned to Milo. "Use these earbuds."

Milo stuffed the earbuds into his ears. "Boop, boop, boop, beep!" he shouted.

"Obviously you guys won't have my recording to keep time with for the real show, because any chucklehead knows a real show is not supposed to be freaking karaoke," said Gray. "So lock in with Milo. Milo is the ground everyone is standing on."

Milo raised his eyebrows with meek understanding. "I am?"

"We gotta do something about this cocktail kit," said Gray. "No one plays these, except maybe Prince that one time as a joke."

I kicked a leg at Jamal. "Told you," I said.

"Eat my hole," said Jamal.

"Jamal-on-bass," said Gray.

"Yes sir," said Jamal.

"Your groove is solid, but my god, look up at the audience once in a while."

Jamal tried looking up.

"You look like you're holding in a king-size dookie," said Gray. "Give me a bass face."

By *bass face* Gray meant puckered lips and a back-and-forth head bob.

"Like this?" said Jamal.

"Yes!" said Gray. "But no overbite. You are a duck. You're a super-serious duck and you're walking, you're walking."

"Super-serious duck bass face," said Jamal.

"Actually," said Gray, approaching me, "all of you look up. Sunny, you're the friggin' front man. Look up at me."

"Like this?" I said, raising my chin as if I were at the doctor's.

"Now bring up your guitar and just kinda curse out the neck real close as you're playing," said Gray. "Just grit your teeth like this and mouth a bunch of angry stuff like, *You ugly guitar with your dumbass frets and your dumbass strings.*"

That part was easy. *Stupid rock-and-roll faker making up lies to impress a girl who do you even think you are.*

"Correct!" said Gray. "That is a proper face melt."

And he showed me a freshly taken photo on his phone to prove it.

"Ugh, no pix," I said.

"Get used to it, man," said Gray. "You will be onstage."

"Miss Mayhem, no less," said Jamal, who had a habit of saying the perfect thing to accelerate anxiety.

Gray froze at the name. "What?"

"The school rented out Miss Mayhem for the talent show," I said.

"You're kidding me," said Gray. "What in god's cruel sense of humor does that even mean, right?"

"I don't know?" I said.

Gray's eyes swam. "I *played* Miss Mayhem. Twice."

"Hey, dude," I said.

Gray returned to the room. He smiled a frown.

"Anyway," said Gray. "You'll be up there. In front of an audience. But I want you to focus on a single, certain someone. Not some flaky A&R rep or fake insta-friends. Someone important. You know who I'm talking about."

I imagined Cirrus standing before me, watching. Photographing me with her mind. What would I look like to her? Would she mostly see the top of my head as I gazed down at my shoes?

I lazily stroked a chord, then another, then another. I seemed to be unable to play any harder. I was, I realized, paralyzed by fear. Fear of taking a chance, since taking a chance meant risking ridicule, and I did not know if I was really prepared for such a risk.

"That is not rock," said Gray. He choked my strings silent and drew his face suddenly close to mine. He must've had Bloody Marys: I now detected garlic and celery. "Friggin' take it seriously. Or maybe you'd be better off taking a job as a friggin' accounting intern and sitting and nodding all day like a friggin' yes-man with the other pathetic corporate burnout losers."

I blinked. I drew my hands back. My lower lip disappeared into my mouth. Milo and Jamal looked terrified, too.

Gray released the neck of my guitar, which gasped out a quiet E-minor 11 with relief. He hung his head. He didn't have to say what he was thinking. I could tell simply from the way he found an amp to sit on. Back-in-the-Day Gray, so briefly visible, was deflating into a puddle.

I didn't know how to talk to Gray right now. So I talked *about* him.

"Gray used to shred, you know," I said. "You should've seen him onstage."

"I remember," said Jamal. "You showed us enough videos."

Milo—bless him—picked right up on my tactic. "He shredded the pants off half the planet," said Milo.

"Half the planet could just pee where they stood," said Jamal.

"You guys are weird," said Gray, finally laughing a little.

"If you gotta go, you gotta go," said Jamal, writhing with legs akimbo now.

I joined in, and so did Milo, and finally we got the laugh from Gray.

"Should we keep going?" said Gray.

I held my guitar, got into position, and nodded.

"Okay," said Gray. "I want you to channel Yngwie, or Satriani, or Reid."

"Are those . . . countries?" I said.

"Or," said Gray, thinking. "I want you to channel Tiamat. Remember that?"

"Tiamat," I said, and closed my eyes to imagine the feared five-headed goddess of all chromatic dragons. I used to go on and on to Gray about my favorite monster Tiamat, back in the days when he would still listen.

"Upon the plane of the Nine Hells you stand, releasing your evil spawn upon the sinful realms of men," said Gray, clearly struggling to recall lore so rudimentary that even baby gamers could rattle it off in their sleep. But I forgave his lack of savvy. Because it was working.

"Now Asmodeus and the ghost of Bane command you," said Gray.

I raised my guitar and played the fastest riff I could manage, spewing silent insults at my own fingertips—*stupid imbecile clown telling her Gray's room was yours*—and when I was done, I flung the neck aside like I had just sliced open a charging orc.

"*Yes, and!*" cried Gray, pointing with folded arms.

"*Yes, and* I'm a friggin' paladin," I said.

("Technically anti-paladin, since Satan is lawful evil," muttered Milo.

"Respectfully counterargue that Satan is chaotic evil because of his penchant for meting out punishment at random," said Jamal, who had been having this argument with Milo for years.)

"Power chord, now," said Gray. "Windmill it."

I wheeled my arm up and around and made my amp roar with the sonic hellfire of distortion. I ended with my tongue out and a horn salute held high.

"Cool," said Jamal.

"Hurr," said Milo.

"See how these guys' big stupid lizard brains just lit up?" yelled Gray. "*That* is rock and roll. Gentlemen, I'd say you're at sixty-one percent now."

I huffed and puffed. I remembered this feeling. Remembered it so keenly. I could hear the creaky wood floors of our craftsman house. I could see my friends—we were so little then!—sprinting down hallways through blinding shafts of sunlight. I could hear us: shouting battle cries, or casting spells in a fake tongue, or calling out for backup.

I had missed this feeling. The feeling of playing.

How many years had it been? How long had I been stuffing myself down into one of my airtight plastic containers? Trying to hide myself away?

It had felt so liberating to run around and make believe back then. It had felt so *cool.* We really did believe we were cool—the best versions of ourselves, realized by pretending to be someone else.

I wished I had stuck with it, and to hell with all the haters.

But then again, there had been so many haters, hadn't there?

Haters hating everything so much it was impossible to tell if they liked anything other than hating. Maybe that's why I had become so cynical. It was hard for me to keep any optimism once the world around me started bullying my every move.

I saw Gunner, lifting the blotter on his desk.

I huffed and puffed, still in my pose. Gray snapped a pic.

"I used to do that pose," said Gray.

"I'm a copycat," I said, with a laugh that quickly turned sour.

"Hey," said Milo. "Come on. There's no point in being hard on yourself at this stage."

"We're doing this for you," said Jamal. "You're doing great."

"There's keeping a super-duper positive attitude," said Gray. "My old bandmates could've used some of that."

Gray raised his old iPod. "Now: Let's go through it again."

$3,000

One did not go to Bed & Bath Vortex for a short period of time; there was no such thing as *popping in to grab one thing* from such a store. The building itself could comfortably fit eight soccer fields; on the roof was painted the colossal company logo, so that warships flying overhead could know of its dominion. The average documented visit to a Bed & Bath Vortex was 150 minutes long.

That was fine by me.

We strolled into the store, which was lit by thousands of fluorescent lights far above. Potpourri and rose soap filled the air.

"Sweet stench of rot," said Cirrus.

"Memento mori," I said. "Remember you too will die."

"Being aware of death is supposed to make you appreciate life more," said Cirrus. "But it doesn't look like it's working."

We pushed our way through a turnstile. I allowed her to go first, like an exemplar of romantical gentlemanliness would.

"If you forgot your twenty-percent-off coupon today, you can always visit BedBathVortex.com to sign up for a free virtual discount," said a thick voice.

We looked up to see an elderly greeter in an apron.

"You scaled the mountain of life," I said, "and on its summit was the nation's largest selection of premium domestic accessories."

The elderly greeter looked insulted. "It is better than Stalin."

I froze, then slunk away, taking an astonished Cirrus toward the mists of Humidifiers.

"It is better than the gulag," cried the greeter.

People were not always what they seemed to be.

Cirrus found an abandoned shopping cart with items still in it, considered the items, and decided to keep them. "Come on. We have to spend three thousand bucks while we're here."

"Ha ha," I said.

"No really. My mom and dad gave me three thousand bucks. To help get me *set up*."

My eyes got big. Three thousand dollars was more than what a quarter of the American working population made in a month, after taxes. "What," I said, "with like DIAMOND-encrusted soap dishes and compression stockings spun from GOLD?"

Cirrus covered her laugh with the back of her hand. "What the hell are compression stockings?"

"They're these wonderful socks, extra tight, that keep you warm without the bulk, um, increase blood circulation, and also prevent stuff like edema and thrombosis and clots."

"Thrombosis?" said Cirrus.

"Not that I would know anything about compression stockings," I said rapidly.

She regarded me with the most tender confusion—*strange boy*—and drew me into her cloud for a kiss. When I opened my eyes, it was hard to believe I was still on earth.

"Come on," sang Cirrus, resuming our stroll. "Let's spend this guilt money."

"Guilt money?" I said.

Cirrus sighed. "When my parents aren't around—meaning always—we text the same shortcut phrases: *Good morning, how are you, good night.* When they *are* around, they go all out with an all-day boat cruise. And what the hell is this—a carrying case for a single banana?"

She held up a hinged plastic case in the shape of, and for the purpose of containing, a banana.

"Great Pacific Garbage Patch," I said. "You're saying there's no in-between with them. No normalcy."

We pushed the cart out of one aisle, only to be swallowed by another.

"If I never get to experience normal life with my parents," said Cirrus, "can you still call them parents?"

"Technically yes?" I said, trying out a laugh.

"Yay," she said, betraying a flash of bitterness across her face.

I stopped, overcome with the urgent need to make her feel better.

"Do you ever tell them how you feel—?" I said.

"I have, and it's pointless," said Cirrus quickly. She snatched a packet off a nearby shelf and brandished it like Perseus with his severed head. "Normal wipes? Nay: *man* wipes."

"Society in decline," I said. "How do they respond?"

Cirrus hesitated, then put the man wipes into the cart. She slowed to a standstill. She closed her eyes.

"I think they're just not the type," she muttered.

We walked onward. Cirrus found a desk organizer, put it in the cart. Electric fan, gooseneck lamp, cork board, all in the cart.

"The type of what?" I said. "Oop—you don't want that, I promise you."

Cirrus held a big bag of pine cones, each dipped in glitter. She slowly put it back.

"The parenting type," she said.

"Hey," I said. "My parents drive me crazy, too."

"But at least they're *there*," said Cirrus, running her thumb along my cheek. "How about we talk about something else?"

"Hobbies," I said.

"Don't have any," said Cirrus. "Next question."

"But you cook," I cried. "You single-handedly invented Brazilian pizza."

"Lots of people cook," said Cirrus.

She grew quiet.

I went back, retrieved the big bag of glitter pine cones, and delicately lowered it into the cart. I made a big goofy face.

"You can have these, okay?" I said. "Maybe use them at your next yuletide or winter solstice cleansing ritual."

Cirrus finally smiled. "Anyone ever tell you you're a bit of a throwback, Sunny Dae?"

"My brother once called me fifteen going on fifty," I said. What I didn't say was that it was after he discovered me using a heating pad on my back to recover after sitting at my workbench for forty-eight hours straight.

"Is that why you choose to play olde tyme rock and roll?" said Cirrus.

"Well," I said, gearing up for one of my favorite rant topics: music.

"Jazz is stupid," I said, "because it's all doo-bee-doo-bee-doo, pop is what they resort to after waterboarding, EDM is the warning beeps before the AI apocalypse—"

"You define yourself by the things you hate," said Cirrus. "Not by the things you love."

"I do tend to do that, huh," I said.

"Me too," said Cirrus. "I agree with you, you know. All music sucks except rock."

"Rock," I said.

"Guitars and drums and rahhh." Cirrus crossed twin devil horns on her chest.

Her gesture transported me back to the school auditorium years ago, watching big brother Gray become the all-powerful God of Noise as the front man of the now-forgotten Mortals.

"Rock is the last time people had an expectation for musicians to be at least a little authentic," said Cirrus. "They wanted to know what Kurt and Courtney were like for real. They felt like when they watched Joan Jett or Zach de la Rocha or Kim Gordon, what you saw was what you got. People really thought Henry Rollins was preaching gospel."

"And yet, rock is dead," I said.

"Now everything is pop in one form or another," said Cirrus with a sad smirk. "Pop is not music. Pop is celebrity. Fabricated personas that are all style, no substance. Pop is a celebration of fakeness. Artifice is the only cultural currency left, now that the internet has erased all contextual borders. Or something. I have to think about that more."

My brother said that once, I wanted to say. *Back when he was in a rock band himself. Back when he was cool. They worshipped him. So did I.*

But of course I couldn't say such a thing, because then I would seem like a little itty bitty baby boopy schmoopy kid who was copying his big brother with a *fabricated persona.*

Which I was.

"Oyah," was all my stupid mouth could come up with. "Yappers."

"Maybe I hate pop stars because I'm like them in a way," said Cirrus. "I change whenever I move to someplace new. I do whatever it takes to fit in. It begs the question, What person isn't just a made-up thing in the first place? Is it the fakery that makes us real? Is anything real?"

I wiped my forehead, thought of what to say next, but the best I could do was

"Out of all the places you've lived, which was your favorite?"

We stood before a candy display now—we had reached the snack department already—and a row of candies sat right at my eye level:

SUPER MEGA-NERDS®

THE SOUR CANDIES YOU ALREADY LOVE, JUST BIGGER!

Don't fool yourself, Sunny, said the candies. *You are not cool. You are not a teenaged rock icon. You are a nerd. You are in fact the nerd that other nerds look up to.*

You are a super mega-nerd.

Cirrus paused. She thought.

"There's this study," she said. "They found out generally how long you have to spend with a person to make them a close friend. It's sixty hours to establish casual friendship. Another hundred to become a regular friend. After that, another two hundred hours to become a close friend."

"What stage are we?" I said.

"We're an outlier in the data set," said Cirrus.

She hugged my arm, as if to say, *And I'm proud of it.*

"It's hard enough to invest hours and hours to make just one friend," she said. "You search for a flock that might fit your feather. You hang out with them. Observe every little move. Adapt as best as you can. But even if you do hit it off, it doesn't matter. Because then you have to move away. Right as things are really getting good. And you know what's worse?"

"Having to do it all over again at a new school?" I said.

I looked at her closer. I could see faint lines in her forehead. A weariness.

Cirrus squared her eyes with mine. "What's worse is after about the fourth or fifth school. You already know how long it'll take to fit in. Let alone make a friend. It's like knowing how long a marathon's gonna be. What's worse is then deciding, eh, it's not worth the effort. Easier to be alone."

"Jesus, you're cynical," I said, in an effort to lighten the mood.

But Cirrus remained heavy. "Ever wonder what it's like to grow up without any real friends?"

"I didn't mean to call you cynical. I think I understand."

"No, but you shouldn't have to understand," said Cirrus. "No normal person should have to understand what I've had to understand. But whatever. None of that matters. Not anymore."

I swallowed. I stood staring at a value bag of cheese puffs as big as a pillow.

"Because I belong here with you," said Cirrus.

Upon hearing these words, I made a pledge deep within to do whatever it took to keep Cirrus from getting hurt.

And I kissed her.

Cirrus sent the cart away with a push. "You know, I think I'm good?"

"Really?" I said.

Cirrus smiled. "This store's got nothing."

Hand in hand, she led me toward the exit.

We left, with not a single dollar spent.

Part-A

I looked at myself in the mirror. I squashed my cheeks with my fingertips.

I was in love.

I was in love.

I stared hard at my phone in an effort to activate it using my mind powers. I firmed up my abdominals and bore down as if evacuating. *Picture her,* I told myself. *In her blank room, waking up late from a long sleep, unplugging her phone, gazing into its tiny black eye, and typing—*

Jhk jhk, went my phone.

"Yes," I said, relaxing with an exhale. My mind powers had done it.

Aaand my parents are gone again, wrote Cirrus.

Where? I wrote.

No comment, she wrote. So I decided I want to do that thing that you're supposed to do when you're in American high school and you have the house to yourself.

I nibbled my fingertips. What did she mean?

Picture me and her, I told myself, *alone in her blank room—*

Part-A! wrote Cirrus.

Huh?

Party, wrote Cirrus.

You mean par-tay, I wrote.

Oh.

You're doing great, I wrote.

I'm inviting you and Milo and Jamal of course but can you get everyone else to come? I spent all morning and there's enough of everything for everybody.

I checked my wrist. My pulse, which had surged, now flagged back down to normal. A party. Not just me and Cirrus, alone in her room. Okay.

I've been here for weeks now and never had a housewarming and I thought it would be really special to have it filled with . . . people, she wrote.

It was impossible to argue with that.

That sounds great, I said. Need help with anything?

No, I'm good!

What time should I come over tonight?

Tonight? wrote Cirrus. How about now?

Okay! I wrote.

Is it too early? I don't know what I'm doing.

You're doing great, I wrote. One moment.

I put my phone down, thought for a moment, and smiled. Cirrus wanted people for her part-A, and I knew where to acquire all of them.

Gunner appeared on screen, panting.

"Yo," said Gunner. Behind him I could see three guys—footballers—shoving padded sleds on a lawn.

"Why are you at school?" I said.

Gunner wiped sweat dripping from his nose and jogged to somewhere secluded. "Not school. Backyard. Dad's having us do leg work. How you doin', buddy?"

"You have training equipment at your house?" I said.

"You wanna meet up for some *homework* later?" said Gunner.

Normally, this sort of exchange between two strapping young men might have been considered romantic; in this case, it was game related. Such was the language of nerds.

Gunner leaned in and whispered, "I killed the gargoyle, and now I'm stuck in that place with all the doors that won't open."

I scanned my brain. "The Complex of Secret Doors."

The footballers crossed the frame in the background. I recognized them: Hunter, Trapper, and Stryker.

"We'll get to that," I said. "Listen, how many friends do you have?"

"If you mean fan-friends, then it's basically the whole junior class," said Gunner. "If you mean actual friends, there's only one. Well, two now."

Aw, Gunner.

"Think of an excuse to tell your dad," I said. "There's a party that urgently needs some love."

I enjoyed a long shower. I carefully made my selections from Gray's closet, stuffed them into one of his backpacks—a classic leather ruck studded with nickel-plated spikes—and emerged from the maw of the garage on my ten-speed to begin the downhill glide. I stopped along the way to change in the junipers.

I'd never been invited to a traditional American house party before. Such phenomena occurred solely on insipid television shows written by middle-aged hacks eager to cash in on the young adult demographic.

I had always thought house parties were breeding grounds for the next generation of idiots. But now, I found myself pedaling with eager pumps of each leg. I could see myself holding one of those red plastic cups (why always red?), playing table tennis incorrectly without a paddle, performing a handstand on a pressurized beverage container, and so on.

When I arrived at Cirrus's condo, I could only stare at what I saw.

There was a twenty-meter-long inflatable Nora the Explorer palm forest.

There were two of the biggest bounce castles I've ever seen—Ice Princess and Mulam—already spasming with revelers inside.

There was a balloon-animal-making clown who had already broken the fourth wall to share a vape and a beer with a few fellow off-duty Ruby High classmates.

There was a two-story-tall scaffold, from which a screaming girl zip-lined a hundred meters into a pit of foam cubes.

I dismounted from my bike, ducked to let two laser-tag combatants pass, and entered the house.

It was packed. How was it already packed?

In the back patio window I could see Milo and Jamal thick as thieves with Gunner, talking about something while his sidekick wended and wove between the legs of partygoers. Artemis was there, too, ignoring Gunner pretending to ignore her. But I saw him sneak glances from behind his cup.

Milo and Jamal had both come wearing Gray's shirts from before, because they knew they were coming here, and they remembered. Bless Milo and Jamal.

Gunner found me with his eyes and stabbed the air with a triumphant thumbs-up.

Cirrus emerged. She ducked and twirled her way to me for an embrace. She wore her black apron. She smelled like smoke and steak.

"I'm making Argentinian-style galbi," she said.

"That's a thing?" I said.

"It is now," she said. With one arm still hanging on to my shoulder, she turned to the party and made an announcement.

"Food will be ready in about fifteen minutes," she hollered. "Till then there's chevre, manchego, membrillo for said manchego, mild ojingeo, spicy ojingeo, stuff from my parents' liquor stash like Aperol and Ricard and makgeolli and like six bottles of clara in the fridge if you're not into makgeolli, which I get, makgeolli's definitely an acquired taste, ha!"

The whole party stopped and stared at her like she had just spoken in tongues from deep within a snake pit. Cirrus looked at me for help, so I raised her arm and yelled,

"Par-tay!"

Everyone cheered. Someone figured out how to put "All Star" by Smash Mouth on the TV-slash-stereo, and suddenly Gunner was kung-fu dancing with his ridiculous wraparound sunglasses in a circle of people in the living room.

"Hey now, you're a rock star," he said, pointing at me.

Cirrus gripped my chin. "Is the bouncy castle age-appropriate? I only realized after the rental guys came that I've never seen bouncy castles in American teen movies."

"It's highly traditional," I said. "You nailed it."

"Oh thank god," said Cirrus. "I just want to do this right."

I for one thought she was doing this right. Because I knew nothing!

"How much did all this cost?" I said.

Cirrus smiled. "About three thousand dollars."

The music switched to a house stomper, and the party accelerated to takeoff velocity. Kids everywhere were day drinking, just like Mommy and Daddy did on the weekends. The football crew showed up like marauders returning home from a voyage, and Gunner leapt to shower them with violent greeting rituals.

Everyone had to shout. It was officially a shouting party now.

"This is Sunny!" said Gunner to someone—Lancer? Driver?—and added, "This is his girlfriend, Cirrus! We're in her house!"

I beamed. I was Sunny, and this was my girlfriend, Cirrus. I looked at her and saw she was beaming just as brightly. She gripped my hand and held it tight with barely contained excitement.

"Welcome!" she cried.

Driver (Sailor?) looked at me, then at Gunner, as if to ask, *What is this guy doing here?*

"I'm making him help me with my science homework under threat of bodily harm!" said Gunner. His teammate seemed to understand.

"Say hi, stoner!" said Gunner.

Sailor (Tracker?) shook off his confusion and obeyed Gunner's command. "Hai!"

The old instinct to flee twitched in my gut, but I looked at Cirrus and acted like I belonged there. Because I did.

"Dude, there's an obstacle course!" said Tracker.

"That big thing outside!" said Gunner.

"Is that the Nora the Explorer thing?" I said.

Cirrus nodded. "I think they couldn't get the licensing."

We realized we were now standing in a surge of people—the drink table attracted them like cult worshippers—and stepped aside. One of those people was Artemis.

"I never see you at these things!" said Artemis with her halogen smile. She wiggled bedazzled fingers at Cirrus. "Oh, it's Sunny's girlfriend!"

There it was again: *girlfriend*. That made me *boyfriend*. It felt like respect, in a way. I had achieved a title that people like Artemis now officially recognized.

The music mercifully switched to a quieter electronic ballad. There was predictably no rock and roll at this party, because rock and roll was dead.

Artemis turned to look at Gunner, who had become very still.

"Obstacle course, let's go!" said Tracker to Gunner.

"Hi, Artemis Edenbaugh," mumbled Gunner, before dashing outside with Tracker.

"Uh, okay?" said Artemis.

From outside came a sudden screeching sound—pteranodons in agony—loud enough to cause the din of the party to duck momentarily.

"What the hell," I said.

"Injuries," said Cirrus with immediate concern. "Please no injuries."

We scrambled outside and quickly found the source of the anguish: a small crowd of people at the other end of the zip line.

"No no no," said Cirrus.

We ran. We shoved our way through the crowd.

In the foam pit were Jamal and Milo, holding each other.

"Arrrayayayaya!" they screamed joyfully.

"Oh for the love of sweet Jesus," cried Cirrus with a laugh.

"You guys scared the crap out of me," I said. "I got a Hershey submarine stuck in my port of call."

Everyone looked at me: *Do you?*

"You guys have to do this," said Jamal. "We figured out how to connect two harnesses for partner runs."

"Is that safe?" I said.

"No," said Milo.

Cirrus kissed my cheek. "You wanna fly?"

There was only one answer to that question.

Milo and Jamal climbed out of the pit. Milo undid his gear, then reached over to de-harness and de-helmet a dazed Jamal with the alarming efficiency of a New Zealand sheep shearer.

Together Cirrus and I climbed the scaffolding until we were at the top. There, an operator waited with a tablet.

"Thumbprints here, guys," said the operator.

We signed away our souls as well as those of our unborn.

"I recommend helping each other get strapped in," said the operator. "Many couples find it a very intimate experience."

I held the harness open as Cirrus stepped into it. I tightened the straps around her thighs, her waist, her shoulders. I had never been this close to any girl before Cirrus. Cirrus was my first. The best first any boy could ever hope for.

"Your turn," said Cirrus.

Cirrus put my harness on for me, and the operator was right. It was an extremely intimate experience.

Finally we clipped our carabiners and held each other tight.

"One," said Cirrus. She had her arm around my shoulder.

"Two," I said. I had mine around hers.

"Three!"

We shoved off.

Far below, the party bounced and screamed and vibrated. But up here it was strangely quiet. This situation probably demanded that we demonstrate our thrill with requisite performative screams and yelps, similar to when you ride a roller coaster.

I discovered long ago, however, that roller coasters were more fun—contemplative, even—when I *didn't* scream. A silent roller coaster ride gave me the illusion that I was a veteran dragon pilot expertly chaining together updrafts for speed. Aerial warlocks did not yell and whoop as they rode. The skies were simply *theirs*.

Sunny, the Ultraviolet King.

Cirrus, the Queen of Clouds.

"You are so beautiful," I said.

"You are," said Cirrus.

Did she really truly believe such a thing? That we could be beautiful together? It was hard for me to tell all that was in those eyes of hers. Too much, flashing by all too quickly as we glided through the air: admiration and affection and wonder.

And trust.

I wanted every bit of her trust. Having her trust, I knew, was the highest honor.

The cable vanished and we unfurled wings of milky translucence. Far ahead I spied a forest silent and dark but for a single will-o'-the-wisp promising to guide us through. To where?

The party grew louder; the foam crash pit was coming at us fast. That gave us a reason to finally start screaming.

"Whoaaaaa!" I said.

"Kah ha ha ha!" said Cirrus.

Without thinking we clasped each other tight. The impact smacked my helmet into Cirrus's, close enough to inhale her every exhale as we drowned in blue cubes.

Milo was right—this was not safe at all.

The moment I helped Cirrus out of the pit, someone body-slammed me to a padded column.

"So glad you're here," said Gunner with breath so strong a single stray spark could have lit it into a cone of blue flame.

"I'm glad you're here, too," I said, coughing.

Cirrus leaned in to join the scrum. "Thanks for getting the whole school to come."

"Snuthing," said Gunner. He looked around, spotted Artemis, glanced at me and Cirrus, and sighed a melancholy sigh. "Snuthing at all."

"Your apron is so cute!" Artemis screamed, and led a perplexed Cirrus away.

Cirrus glanced at me: *I guess I'm going now?*

I shrugged back: *You made a friend!*

I was chuckling, but stopped when I saw Gunner thumb his wet nose and wet red eyes over and over again. He fought away his look of open longing and palmed my shoulder. "You wanna drink, man?"

Normally I would've responded with *Alcohol is for victims,* but now was not the time. "Why not," I said.

Gunner snapped his fingers in a tight boogie. "Drinking with my homie," he sang, even though we were not actually drinking together.

A vee of footballers went lumbering by, and Gunner called out to them:

"Sss my homie Sunny!"

The jocks instinctively heard this call, noted Gunner's hierarchical supremacy, and drew close in order of rank. Normally Gunner would've had his henchmen pin me to a wall of lockers and pull my limbs off while his sidekick snapped selfies, but instead they began spontaneously supplicating.

"What's up, Sunny."

"I heard you rock the house."

"Yo, tell your girl Cirrus she knows how to throw a party."

"Sunny Dae."

They formed a ring and walked me back to the house, the Secret Service escort to my new presidency. Surrounding revelers witnessed our procession, recognized the shift in the social order, and adjusted their psychological models of the world.

Out of all the onlookers, no one looked more amazed than three specific people:

Milo, Jamal, and Oggy the sidekick.

Together they stood in unlikely audience. I shrugged at them. Milo gave a little blank wave. Jamal's face was frozen with disgusted admiration. Oggy folded tight little arms and whipped a dandelion to bits with his tail.

At the house, Gunner led his squad through the obediently parting crowd to the drink table. I hung back to swing an arm out and steal Cirrus away from Artemis and four other girls, all of whom eyed me with this strange new cartoon-like desire.

"What is happening?" I said once we were alone.

Cirrus looked around her with amazement. "The party is running itself," she breathed.

"You did it," I said.

"We did it," said Cirrus. "I just made friends. I didn't even have to try."

We pressed ourselves together as more people arrived to flood the doorway.

"Can you come see something?" I said. My chest pistoned with mischief and desire. "There was an incident."

Cirrus grimaced. "Oh god, what happened?"

"Just hurry," I said.

I hustled her upstairs. Past the master bedroom—still empty—down the hall, and into her bare bedroom. I pressed the door shut behind us.

"Sun, is everything okay?" said Cirrus, right before I kissed her.

Instantly, her hands were in my shirt, searching for my heart. They found it. They gripped me hard enough for both of us to lose balance and fall just short of the bed with a glancing blow. Her elbow landed between my anterior ribs number four and number five.

"Ow," I said, and slammed her face down onto mine for another kiss.

"Arr," growled Cirrus. She held my head with vise-like hands to taste my tongue with hers. "Harr."

Our nostrils whistled with exertion and our teeth clacked as we feverishly ate each other up with bottomless appetite. I could do this all day and it would never be enough. At the same time, it was more than I could have ever imagined. How could that possibly be?

I gasped. "I belong to you, Cirrus Soh. Okay?"

Cirrus glowed with dark wondrous light. It was as if she'd been waiting for me to say those words for a long time. "I belong to you, too, Sunny Dae."

We kissed again—slower—to permanently etch this mark in time.

A deep thud from below gave us pause. There was a cloud of laughter as the party resumed.

"Your house is gonna get trashed," I said.

"You can't trash an empty house," said Cirrus.

"Should we head back down?" I said.

"Do we have to?" said Cirrus, and kissed me again. I found my lips traveling across her cheek, down under her hair to reach the nape of her neck, then circumnavigating her torso so that I could reach the rippled plains of her shoulder blade and back. I paused to breathe. I opened my eyes.

I had tugged the scoop neck of her shirt down to reveal what to the untrained eye might seem like a very small, very symmetrical circular maze.

"You have a little tattoo," I said.

"Oh my god, that," said Cirrus, suddenly bashful. "I got it a long time ago, ha."

"It's beautiful," I said, in awe.

Cirrus laughed against the back of her hand. "Take one guess as to what it is."

I could've said *I don't know.* But I did know. I knew exactly.

It was the labyrinth set into the floor of the Chartres Cathedral, in France. I knew about it from an adventure module I ran with Milo and Jamal back in our youth, titled the Curse of the Minotaur Gothique. The entire campaign dungeon was in the form of this ornate symbol; I had spent many hours mapping its every turn and straightaway by hand.

A frisson of ecstasy vibrated all the way to my kidneys. I ran my thumb over the ink in her skin. I wanted not only to tell her what her tattoo was, but *how* I knew what it was. But there was no way I could do that.

There was a whole side of me—the real side—that I now realized wanted out of the lockbox I'd made for it.

"It's the labyrinth from the Chartres Cathedral in France," I said.

Cirrus burst with joyful surprise. "Have you been? Isn't it a-maze-ing?"

My temples flooded with blood. I thought fast.

"I just saw it in a library book once," I said.

And I also spent two months in Milo's garage exploring all of its secrets and dangers.

"Once upon a time I had these two friends," said Cirrus. "This was in Paris. Their French was only slightly better than mine, which was caveman-rudimentary. Their parents moved around just as much as mine. None of us could see the point in immersing ourselves in a culture we were gonna ghost on anyway. Out of all my schools, those two friends were my favorite. Except you, of course."

I smiled.

"We went on a field trip to the cathedral," said Cirrus. "And we ditched the rest of the class and spent hours just walking the labyrinth. It was so beautiful and meditative. There apparently used to be a Minotaur in the middle."

I was bursting to tell her that most labyrinths from that period featured Minotaurs, and that although a Minotaur was a tough bastard with a default melee bonus of +6 for both greataxe and goring attacks, it could be defeated by going heavy on spells such as Psychic Scream or Mind Sliver that would exploit the creature's weak intelligence score.

But I held everything in. I realized I hated that I had to do this, and would keep having to.

"I didn't know that," I said. I pushed my insistent heart back into place with a hard swallow.

"Well, now you do," said Cirrus.

We cleaned up in the party's aftermath later that evening. Milo and Jamal and Gunner stayed, too.

Gunner did most of the cleaning. Gunner, it turned out, was a neat freak. Only I knew where such obsessiveness came from: his spotless, dark house, his sneering father. I stepped aside and high-fived him as he moved from room to room with still-drunk determination while his sidekick slept oblivious in a corner.

Good job, Gunner.

A house with no furniture was remarkably easy to reset, even after a party, and made me want to live in a blank space like one of those minimalist enthusiasts in Tokyo.

I thought about the white plastic containers in my room. Didn't they form a minimal space of sorts?

So maybe not with the minimalism.

Milo and Jamal helped pack up the kitchen. Milo whistled maniacally—the chorus of "Beauty Is Truth"—as he wrapped leftovers, and after two straight minutes Jamal loudly ripped a sheet of aluminum foil and begged him to stop.

"Was I whistling?" said Milo.

"Yes," Cirrus and I yelled with a laugh.

Cirrus looked at me, then gently touched her gaze upon Jamal, then Milo, before wrinkling her nose: *Isn't all this great?*

I smiled back. *It really is.*

Soon the house and outside lawn were clean, the rental guys were sent off with generous tips, and it was time to head home. Milo and Jamal vanished on their bikes; I put my own ten-speed into Gunner's trunk and got ready to drive his incapacitated self home.

Cirrus mewled with joyful frustration. "Why does the night have to end?"

"Astrophysics," I said.

She didn't blow me a kiss—Cirrus wasn't that person—but she did walk backward with her eyes locked on mine long enough to fall butt-first into a plant, which was better than any blown kiss.

"Careful," said a voice. Her insomniac neighbor, staring with eyes gone white.

"Nyang," said Cirrus, creeped out. She fled behind her front door.

I drove Gunner home. Before he left, he leaned his big

meaty elbow on my shoulder, causing my bicycle wheels to buckle beneath me. His eyes were slits at this point. "You are awesome," he said. "Cirrus is awesome. You guys are awesome together."

"We are, huh," I said.

"Why'd you think you had to pretend?" he said with a petulant growl. "You din't have to pretend, silly."

I freshened my grip on the handlebars. "Because I'm stupid, Gunner."

"In that case," said Gunner, heaving himself off, "I wish I was as stupid as you."

In the night shadows of the junipers I changed into my civvies. They felt cold and baggy and uninspired. I missed Gray's clothes. This was a silly exercise, because I'd just change into my pajamas in a matter of minutes anyway, but I still did it just in case I ran into Mom and/or Dad. An ounce of prevention!

At home, I climbed upstairs, pulled the Ring of Baphomet off my finger, used it to crown my tiny desk knight as king. My phone played its two-chord rock riff—*jhk jhk*—and I found myself missing my old *Elf shot the food!* ringtone.

I was all mixed up.

I want to be with you all night, wrote Cirrus.

Me too, I wrote. I guess there's always school tomorrow

Not the same, she wrote.

Not the same at all

Are you sleepy?

Nope, I wrote.

Good, she wrote.

She blew bubbles for a moment, then sent a strange message:

WHYSOHCIRRUS HAS INVITED YOU TO

PANOPTICON LIVE

I understood immediately.

One sec, I wrote.

I slinked downstairs without a sound. I found the headset charging on the kitchen counter. I slipped the goggles on like a hat, semaphored my way through account setup using the hand wands, and defined an invisible play space in the dark living room.

Then my eyes

filled

with

sparkles.

Sylphs

I find myself floating among stars. Below me there is a cluster of dark green malachite set into an infinite sheet of pure lapis lazuli: an island alone in the night sea, lit by the single white spotlight of the quarter moon.

I float down into the forests there, where amber lights guide me. The air becomes close. Sounds of dripping rainwater and creaking wood.

We are young sylphs, still lacking wings and earthbound. Her wrapped crown of berries and lichen glows with greenish-white bioluminescence, skin a butter-pecan cream, eyes black onyx. My own hands glow a dogwood pink fading to chartreuse at the extremities. When we approach each other, our colors blend and brighten.

The fireflies of the forest light a path, which we follow. There is the puzzle of the hidden red rocks, which is easy enough to complete. There is the stone lock. We rotate it to reveal a tunnel leading to a cave of gems. More puzzles await within. She shows me how to solve them all.

At the center of the island is the tree god, who blesses us with a shower of leaves, and in twin novae of scatter-light we are reborn with long vellum wings. We can do anything now.

Sing, she says. She places me on a colossal tree stump ten thousand rings old. She multiplies herself into an audience of hundreds, each lit a different color, waiting for me to begin. I only got to hear you sing once, she says. I want to hear you sing again.

I have dozens of voices at my disposal. But I choose to be default, normal, and my voice weaves through the impenetrable forest canopy, loops a star or two, and filters its way back down. The audience glows in unison now: white and blue and green and orange.

We kiss in that awkward way avatars do: the polygons of our faces glancing off each other, never really touching. The world powers down, stripping itself of light, then texture, then the glowing wireframe underpinning it all, finally leaving only darkness.

90%

Two weeks until the talent show.

I felt light. I felt like gravity had lessened just a bit. I didn't know how else to explain my lengthening stride as I walked. The ease with which I sped my bike toward Cirrus's condo every morning with her daily call of *Let's ride!*

Every morning I jump-mounted my ten-speed, no doubt damaging soft tissues in the process, but I was starting to care less about things like that. I had neglected to wear my sleep cap twice already, for instance.

Every morning I ducked behind the Cernoseks' junipers and emerged anew, clad in, say, a torn baseball tee and plaid ska pants with chains that served no purpose other than to sparkle and clink with each step.

I was feeling a momentum that would soon push the talent show far behind me in the past, bringing me finally into a clear future where I could be me and only me.

My momentum rose in inverse proportion to Gray's

posture, which shrank with resignation as he accepted Dad's nonstop mentorship in corporate client services. Gray was normalizing. He was *accepting.*

In the hallways at school, I would see Gunner leading his squadron of meat-brains hither and yon, aimlessly patrolling. Where they once sniffed at me like hyenas, now they each gave me the nod, starting with Gunner and rippling down each wing of their delta formation:

He's cool.

Late afternoons and evenings were the trickiest, because that's when I would have to reject Cirrus even though every nerve in my body screamed to be with her.

"I want to hang out and watch you guys practice," she would say.

"I want the show to be a surprise," I would say.

That was only partly true; mostly I could not have her knowing Gray was coaching me to be a fake rock star.

"Oookaaay," she would say. And then I would watch her pedal away from me as I waved from the bike racks.

Then, at the end of each day, it would just be me, Milo, and Jamal locked in the music room waiting for Gray to arrive while the school grew quieter and quieter. Everyone else was going home to dinners and homework and television and video games; we were here to work.

We sat on the amps like they were ours, not the school's. We tuned our instruments. Milo adjusted his drums a millimeter here, a millimeter there. He had taken the cocktail kit apart and set it in a traditional rock drummer formation. We twiddled knobs to fine-tune our volume and gain and reverb and *presence.*

I did not know what that last knob did. I just liked the idea of having a control to adjust one's philosophical outlook on life.

Then we waited.

"You guys wanna go through it while we're waiting for Gray?" I said.

"Waiting for Godot," said Jamal with a sour look.

"Hey," said Milo. "I'm telling you I'm sure it's nothing to worry about."

I folded my hands over the neck of my guitar. "What."

"Jamal's being paranoid," said Milo.

"Just say it," I said.

Jamal held out his phone. "Lady Lashblade gave a like to this other wannabe prop-making clown posse."

I squinted. "LARPros? They have less than half the follower count we do. It's nothing."

"It's not nothing," said Jamal.

"Their stuff is very low quality," said Milo.

"We need to record the episode for Esmeralda's Veil stat," said Jamal. "We have to stay on the Lady's radar if we're going to get that seat next to her at Fantastic Faire."

I sighed. "We will."

"We're slipping," said Jamal.

"We are not slipping," said Milo.

I sloughed off my guitar and put an arm around Jamal. "Hey. We will get the episode done."

"When?" said Jamal. "In our sleep?"

"I know this band nonsense is eating up our time," I said. "I am sincerely sorry. I am forever grateful to both of you. Without you I would be dead. Home stretch?"

"You're impossible when you get all sincere like this," said Jamal.

The door hissed open on soundproof gaskets. Gray entered.

"Sorry-sorry, work thing ran late," said Gray.

"Work?" I said.

Gray shrugged. "I had a group interview with the entire Trey Fortune gang. Like for real this time."

"I didn't know that," I said.

"Probably because I didn't tell you," said Gray with another shrug.

"How did it go?" I said.

"Really great, actually," said Gray to the floor. "Turns out I can get excited about quarterly tax filings for small- to mid-size LLCs."

I said nothing. A *really great interview* was a far cry from coming home to regroup before returning to a new band in Hollywood. It sounded like Gray might not be going anywhere at all.

I glanced at Jamal and Milo. It was disturbingly difficult to tell whether Gray was proud of himself or suicidal.

"All that sounds wonderful," said Milo.

Gray wrestled off his blazer and yanked his tie loose. "Whatever. Let's rock."

We ran through "Beauty Is Truth" again and again. At first, we followed Gray as he guided us along with the chord changes on the chalkboard with a broken drumstick as his pointer. When we could make it through with no mistakes, Gray stopped pointing along to see if we would still manage. When we could, he erased the chalkboard altogether.

We played. We threw eyes. We landed the changes.

Gray very gently suggested that maybe Jamal did not have to sing his improvised, spontaneous backup, and this made Jamal very sad. Gray backpedaled quickly and told him that backup hoots and hollers—not Elvish—were what was called for, and Jamal was happy again.

Milo was very sad about his inability to twirl drumsticks until Gray sat him down and showed him the basics. There were three juicy spots in the song for him to spin those chopper blades, and when he managed to hit them all without dropping sticks, he became happy again, too.

It was very, very important to keep Jamal and Milo happy, and I was grateful for Gray.

Each night, we would power down and blast off a group high five above our heads, with Gray joining in as our secret fourth Immortal.

Each night I'd ask him what percentage our progress was.

"I'd say another five percent," Gray would say.

"That's it?" Jamal would cry.

"I think you're just saying that to make us work harder," Milo would grumble.

"Actually maybe only four," Gray would say, wincing ironically. After being beaten with padded timpani mallets, he would relent. "Okay, five."

Five or four, we were making steady progress.

To prove how far we'd come, Gray showed us a video he'd secretly shot from the hip last week. We looked like toddlers on a playdate playing in clueless parallel. We didn't look like that anymore. The latest video proved we were well aware of one another and communicating like an actual band.

To prove how far we still had to go, Gray showed us a video

of himself performing with the Mortals taken years ago. It wasn't "Beauty Is Truth," but it got the point across. Gray *performed.* By contrast, we were still just knocking out notes with all the grace of dockworkers.

Each night, Team DIY Fantasy FX would promise ourselves we'd go set up at Jamal's after band practice to put together the Esmeralda's Veil episode, but each time, we'd find we were just too exhausted. There simply weren't enough bars left in our batteries.

Before bed, Jamal would report on his obsession with those LARPros interlopers.

They are still idle, no new episodes, no updates, he would write. But for how long?

Friday came. We'd been practicing for more than four weeks now.

"How ready are we?" I asked.

"Let me see your hands," Gray said. Jamal's fingertips were nicely callused, as were mine. The insides of Milo's index fingers were sandpapery now from his basher grip on the sticks.

"There goes my hand modeling career," said Milo.

Jamal batted our hands away from Gray and gripped his shoulder. "How ready are we? Spit it out, man!"

Gray sighed, blew out his cheeks like he did every night. "Eighty percent."

"That's like a B!" said Milo.

"I will take a B!" said Jamal. "Does that mean we can stop early?"

Gray made a reluctant face: *No.* When Jamal and Milo turned to look at me, I was making the same face.

"Come on!" said Jamal.

"Just a little more," I said.

"Well, it's Friday, and I'm starving, so I'll smell you guys later," said Jamal.

"I'm gonna go to bed," said Milo with a yawn.

"It's barely eight," I said.

"Said the boy in love," said Milo.

"Bring it in," said Gray. "Excellent work today. You remind me of me when I was your age."

"Stop being momentous," said Jamal.

We brought our hands together, lowered them, and thrust them skyward with the help of our voices uttering in unison:

"To metal."

Four of us, four devil horns now held high.

At home, Gray ran interference with Mom and Dad while I scampered upstairs to change back into my Sunny-garb. I flopped onto my bed, exhausted.

My phone buzzed, and my heart flipped.

Come down and hang out man, wrote Gray.

I stared at the phone. Gray was inviting me to his basement lair.

Ok, I wrote.

I headed down, and the air grew thick with the smell of food as I approached the game room door.

"Just made some frozen samosa things," said Gray.

There was a small fridge in the basement now, and a microwave. The piles of clothes were put away; the luggage was gone. A little candle waved hi from the room's single windowsill. The place looked tidy, bordering on cozy.

I sat on the plush carpet—freshly vacuumed into neat Ws—and dug my fingers in.

My phone buzzed. I looked. Everything went soupy as blood suddenly pounded in my ears.

Guess what came in the mail today, wrote Cirrus.

There was a photo of a cardboard box bursting with brand-new black cloth.

Shirts.

Shirts bearing red letters artfully formed from razor slashes:

THE IMMORTALS 2020

ONE NIGHT ONLY

SUNSET STRIP, HOLLYWOOD

There was even a logo: the ring of Satan.

I ordered a hundred, wrote Cirrus.

A hundred tee shirts. A hundred people wearing a hundred tee shirts. A night at Miss Mayhem in front of an audience of a hundred people wearing a hundred tee shirts. Me onstage with a mic performing at night at Miss Mayhem in front of an audience of a hundred people wearing a hundred—

"You all right, dude?" said Gray.

"Everything's fine," I said.

You are amazing, I wrote, flubbing every word along the way. *Thank you.*

I'm your number one fan! wrote Cirrus.

I could not think of what else to write, so I sent a few emojis panic-chosen at random. Emojis were the makeshift poetry spackled in the gaps between words, and if you didn't look too hard, you didn't even notice the seams.

"You sure?" said Gray.

"Nn," I said.

"So I lied earlier," said Gray. "You're almost at ninety percent. Don't tell the guys, shh."

"Shut up," I said. "Really?"

"It's kinda true that rock is mostly three chords and an attitude," said Gray. "Most anyone can get the chords right. What they don't get is the last ten percent. That's the attitude part, or *showmanship*. That's what we work on next."

"Uh," I said.

"We have to," said Gray through a hot samosa. "Think about it: We really only have three more practices left. We gotta cram in some style."

Gray abruptly straddled the recliner and clawed an air guitar before him while whipping his necktie around in wild ellipses. I could almost see the flames of hell licking at the pale skin of his exposed Adam's apple as he cackled before the burning sea of the damned.

"Like that," he said, flopping back into his chair.

I sucked in my lips. "Cannot. Do not have skill."

"You do," said Gray. "You will. Because you guys already have the discipline to *do the work*. It's good habits from all your nerd prop making. It's inspiring."

"You're saying *you're* inspired by *me*?" I said.

"I keep coming back to coach you guys, nn?" said Gray.

I dared myself to say it: "It's been nice to see you in your natural habitat."

Gray smiled, but there was some sadness there.

"To provide a belated answer to your question," said Gray, "what happened in LA was people . . . producers . . . kept telling me I wasn't *authentic* enough. Which is their flaky Hollywood way of saying I wasn't good enough."

I nodded. I lowered my head. People never said what they actually meant, in my experience. "Why didn't you stay there and keep trying?"

"I ran out of money."

I understood. It killed me that people had to cancel their dreams for endless toil, unless of course we somehow managed to pull ourselves out of these late-stage capitalist dark ages and into a *Star Trek (TNG)* future blessed with a universal basic income and sweet jumpsuits.

"Why didn't you just ask Mom and Dad for more money?" I said.

Gray shot me a look before he caught himself. He jabbed his fingertips at his heart. "LA was all me. I needed to know if I could do it. Me."

I understood this as well. Imagine Mom and Dad funding DIY Fantasy FX—and now imagine all the *advising* that would come with such an investment. The thought was so preposterous I almost laughed out loud.

"Anyway," said Gray to the floor, "I'm gonna take that Trey Fortune job. I'm staying here in Rancho Ruby. I'm not going back to Hollywood."

"Hey," I said. "What if you tried again? What if—"

Gray shook his head. "It's better this way, trust me."

"Okay," I said.

For a moment we just sat. Gray handed me a samosa.

I took a bite and made a face: *Pretty darn tasty!*

We ate without saying much of anything. Gray thumbed his phone. He noticed something, peered at it, and chuffed. An idea seemed to occur to him.

"You know what," said Gray. "I think I will go back to Hollywood."

My eyes got big. "What?"

"Not for me," said Gray. He stood.

"Huh?" I said.

Gray tossed me a samosa for the road. "We're going to Hollywood for *you*."

Pathetic

The Inspire NV crested a hill and sailed into a black ocean glittering with pinpoints of gold and red and green.

"Angel City, baby," said Gray.

Los Angeles.

Everything Rancho Ruby was not.

A grimy endless tumble of sagging dingbat apartments next to gleaming taco trucks next to million-dollar condos, all flanked by mile-long rivers of homeless encampments. Everyone driving too fast and playing music too loud and wearing too little, boys and girls and everyone in between. As we glided along, the maze of downtown's deserted skyscrapers helplessly gave way to the vast autonomous regions of Koreatown and the Byzantine Latino Quarter, which in turn gave way to the inscrutably hip drag strips of Third Street, Beverly, Melrose, Fairfax, and so on, with all their cryptic signs and signifiers.

I loved LA. I was terrified by LA.

Gray reached out to close the mouth that I'd left hanging open in awe. "You'll catch flies," he said.

I smiled. It was ten o'clock, and me and my big brother were going to Hollywood on a Friday night. There was no other word to describe this except *cool.*

Gray thought so, too. "It's so friggin' cool here. I can't stand it."

I nodded. "It's a total city planning nightmare built upon greed and excess."

"You're so cynical," said Gray.

"No, but, I'm just being honest," I said.

"Don't get any of your cynical honesty on me," said Gray. He smiled. "And stop saying *No, but.*"

We watched the city kaleidoscope by: diner, dealership, temple, taqueria.

Finally Gray parked. He lifted the gull wing open and stepped out into the hot night. I peered outside. A modest line of young Gothic enthusiasts stood before the infamous Miss Mayhem stage, under an incandescent marquee bearing the name of the band Gray had noticed on his phone back at the house: THE REPUGNANTS.

Dazzled, I set foot onto the exotic shore of Sunset Boulevard.

Gray led me to the front of the line and received an immediate dap and hug from the bouncer there.

"So you're back?" said the bouncer.

"Long story," said Gray. "Good to see you, man."

The bouncer gave him another hug and unhooked the velvet rope. He pointed the brass end at me. "Please don't let me catch you drinking, little brother."

Gray led me into the velvet-hued cavern and headed straight for the empty bar, where he got a beer for himself and a club soda—the classic choice of sober gentlemen throughout history—for me. The club was half empty; we easily scored a high-top in the darkness at the back of the room.

Gray lifted his glass. "To memories. Memories, *god*."

"When did you play here last?" I said.

Gray gulped, then pointed with his beer. "You're gonna be up there soon."

I gulped, too, but out of rising terror. "I'm realizing that."

"You need proper orientation before your big night—that's why I brought you here," said Gray. "And you're gonna learn a thing or two about showmanship from this band. They're pretty wild."

"Wild how?" I said.

Gray just smiled, somehow psychically triggering an eruption of sound. The show had started. Then he settled in and watched—*studied*.

Up close, I could see how Gray's eyes danced; how they caught every dot of light from the stage; how they noticed even the smallest twitch of the guitarist's fingers there.

"System of a Down meets LCD Soundsystem," said Gray right into my ear, like a secret. "Disco dressed up as metal, very, very smart."

I could hear it now. "No, but, they've got everyone fooled."

"It's not a trick," said Gray.

"So more like a schtick."

"Stop judge, judge, judging," said Gray, exasperated. "Just *watch*."

I shook my head at myself. What Gray was saying was *Stop thinking. Start being.*

So I watched. The lead singer, his eye sockets blacked out

with makeup, groaned and howled into the mic. He sawed away at his guitar. He pointed at the crowd. The crowd pointed back.

At one point, he slung his guitar behind him and flung the mic in tall arcs, like chain whip tricks just above the heads of the audience. He reeled it in just in time for the next verse. Then he summoned his guitar back around his torso and led the band charging in to thirty seconds of solid headbanging that commanded all before him to do the same.

"How is he doing this?" I said.

Gray leaned in. "They believe in him. Once people believe, their minds open up to just experience everything."

Gray kept me close to give me a steady stream of commentary. The performance wasn't just about the clothes or the moves. It was something ineffable.

"These guys are freaking cool," I said. "It's not great music, but—"

Gray looked at me. *But?*

"But it's fun," I said. "Fun is the point."

"That's the spirit," said Gray with a grin.

Gray hustled off for more drinks—to beat the intermission rush—and in the subsequent lull we drank in relative quiet while the audience queued up at the bar or the bathroom or the entrance to smoke outside. I watched as a woman air-guitared to her friend, who headbanged in response; after a few seconds of this they reached some kind of accord sealed with devil horns.

It was the stupidest, most beautiful conversation ever.

Gray watched them, too, with a wistful look.

"What was your band called?" I said. "When you played here last?"

"Nausea," said Gray, still watching. "Most people don't know this about these clubs on Sunset, but unless you're Radiohead, you have to pay to play," said Gray. "Your band buys a wad of tickets up front; then it's up to you to sell the tickets to recoup your costs."

"How spectacularly exploitative," I said.

"We were sick of the scene," said Gray. "We did not recoup our costs."

Gray sucked a bitter gap between his teeth, then found the energy to smile again.

"What was your music like?" I said.

Gray looked bemused. "Like young Trent Reznor meets old Trent Reznor."

"Does every band base themselves on another band?" I said. "Is any band truly unique?"

"The only way to learn who you are is by copying someone else first," said Gray.

"That makes no sense," I said.

"It doesn't," said Gray with a big open laugh. "But also it does."

I could've asked Gray questions all night. Maybe it was because we were outside of familiar Rancho Ruby. Maybe it was seeing Gray where I'd always only imagined him, deep in the gullet of Los Angeles, witnessing with my own eyes how he was so at home here in the dank, sour dark of a rock club.

"Was the plan to get signed to a big label?" I said.

"You know?" said Gray, searching for words. "I didn't even care about playing stadiums or becoming famous. I just wanted to make music and have a place to live and be happy on my *own terms*. Like, be my own boss, not get stuck in a suit like—"

Gray paused. He took a sip. "Like Mom and Dad."

He was growing heavy, so I changed the subject. "Why music, specifically?" I said. *Why not, say, fantasy props?*

"Why music," said Gray.

"Nn," I said, and sipped more of my club soda, which was quickly becoming my favorite beverage ever. Onstage, the Repugnants were getting set up again. The crowd began to stir with hoots and chirps.

Gray thought. "You can really be yourself onstage. If you don't like that self, you can try on some other one. It's really freeing. But also limiting, but in a good way? Plus dangerous, but at the same time weirdly safe. I'm not explaining things well."

"You're really not," I said, with a laughing sputter.

"Why do *you* make your videos?" said Gray.

My belly quivered. *Because I've been bullied. Because it's easier to hide behind a computer screen.*

Because my big brother hasn't been there to protect me.

"Because," I said finally, "like the rest of humanity I'm just another pathetic soul scrounging for likes in a world deadened to all sensation?"

It was a cop-out answer: one of my cynic's prefab proverbs.

My cynicism, I realized, was my way of removing myself from the equation so that I could not get hurt.

The band began a slow dirge—a wall of sonic sorrow.

Gray had to shout. "Everybody's a pathetic soul. But when you put yourself out there, and the audience responds, we're no longer pathetic. I think that's why you make your videos. That's why I did music."

I blurted out an awkward laugh, because I had never heard Gray talk like this before.

Gray continued in a kind of dream. "Our audiences would respond to our performances, and it was this amazing feeling of, like, *I see you.*"

"I see you," I said.

"I really see you," said Gray. His aura grew so thick, I could smell stargazers.

"Cool," I said, using the word as nonchalantly as possible.

"You'll see once you're up there," said Gray. "It's the best high. Better than any drug."

I regarded Gray for a moment. No matter how old you got, your eyes stayed the same.

Me and my brother turned to watch the band together, without a word.

Eucalyptus

I woke from another one of my dreams. This time, I was paddling to keep afloat a raft made out of a giant crispy marshmallow square. The faster I paddled, the faster the square dissolved. Meanwhile, a nimble mermaid flashing scales of silver-black named Cirrus peered at me from the water and asked me why I even needed a raft in the first place since I could just swim with her.

It was a super-obvious dream.

Come over, wrote Cirrus. I sprang out of bed and got dressed.

But at Gray's closet, I stopped. I felt tired. Tired of changing in the dirt by the junipers, doing laundry in secret, putting clothes back where I found them, leaving no trace for Mom or Dad to find.

After the talent show, I wouldn't be able to just go back to being Old Sunny, like flipping a switch. I would have to keep up the disguise for a while. I would have to gently dial things back from Rock Star to Super Mega-Nerd, where they originally belonged.

Which was ridiculous, because I wasn't even that person anymore. I was more confident. Even my body moved differently. I wasn't sure if I still even liked all the old things in my closet: the criminal cargo shorts, those dot-com-era tees that were really an exercise in obtuseness born of insecurity. Honestly, who on earth knew or cared about Boo.com?

No one did, and that's what made that shirt so safe to wear. It was a way to make a statement without risking ridicule.

I left Gray's closet and went back to my room.

I chose normal jeans and a simple red tee bearing the ampersand from D&D, done with an ornamental dragon head. It was understated. It could be anything, a pretty letterform.

But it was me.

I really wanted to start being me.

I packed a bag with a blanket and food—adorable mini-gimbap rolls and sodas and cheese doodles and teeny-weeny probiotic yogurt drinks—and gave my Velociraptor® Elite a wistful caress before rolling out instead on the creaking ten-speed.

I would glide on elliptical platforms once again, soon.

Cirrus kissed me at her front door. Amazing how we could do that, right out in the beautiful sunlight. Only the sound of Cirrus's mom's voice made me leap back.

"Hello, Sunny," said Cirrus's mom.

"AAAaa-hi," I said.

"I noticed the house is conspicuously clean," said Cirrus's dad, who had slid eerily into the door frame like a shooting gallery target. He held an eyebrow raised behind his transparent

Bong Joon Hos, and it was not clear to me if his brow was playfully conspiratorial or accusatory.

Adults.

"Welcome back from . . . ?" I said.

"We're not really here," said Cirrus's mom. She touched a necklace made of golden toothpicks. "Just a few days of meetings, then it's off to the Middle Kingdom."

"You mean Middle-earth?" I chirped.

"I mean China," said Cirrus's dad, as my attempted joke cleared the top of his head with meters to spare.

"I should put on my bike helmet," said Cirrus, reaching for a hook.

Cirrus's mom examined her daughter sideways. "This American obsession with helmets."

The two went back inside.

Cirrus strapped on her helmet tight so she could slam her head safely into the steel doorjamb three, four times, more, had we not noticed her neighbor's unsettling eye and fled.

We journeyed forth on wide, quiet roads filled with sparkling trees and jasmine and birds cheeping high and low. The sun warmed our skin without burning it. The air perfectly humid, never sticky. The sky with just the right amount of clouds.

Cirrus beamed at the road before her. "This right here is why you live in Southern California."

"Who needs their daily thousand-IU vitamin D supplements when you have this?" I said.

"Sad old people who never venture outside," said Cirrus.

"Ha ha ha," I said, making a mental sticky to get rid of my collection of vitamin, cod liver oil, and gut flora supplements as soon as I returned home.

"Did I mention I'm starting track?" said Cirrus.

My mind boggled. "You run?"

"Oh my god no," said Cirrus. "Artemis roped me into joining. I'm kind of weirdly looking forward to it. My uniform is very officially official. Go, Ravagers."

"Welcome to the team," I said, grinning like a fool on my bike in the sun with my beautiful girlfriend.

"Where are you taking me?" said Cirrus.

"You'll see," I said.

I remembered the way through pure muscle memory. Hop the curb at the horizontal fire hydrant. Take the wide drainage ditch down past the embankment of multicolored succulents. At the five-armed intersection, take the one marked Pyrite. Dismount at the fire road, walk around the chain barrier, and—

"We're here," I said.

Cirrus held on to her helmet and inhaled deeply. "What is that?"

"Eucalyptus," I said.

The eucalyptus grove was the same but for a plastic hubcap that had found its way in from the road. I picked up the offensive garbage and placed it on the curb for street sweepers to later consume.

I hadn't been here in years. Not since my last attempt at gaming in public, right before Gunner stole Gray the Paladin from my locker and rasped the figurine down to a nub.

I led her to a spot—a tree stump, where Jamal and Milo and I once sat—and spread the blanket. We ate. The wind picked up, but the surrounding thicket protected us from flying dust and leaves. It was like picnicking on the floor of a cathedral ruin sparkling with sunbeams.

"I haven't been here in forever," I said. I popped a gimbap into Cirrus's mouth and watched her chew.

"Was this, like, your spot?" said Cirrus.

It could've been, if only they'd have let me be.

All that was too much to explain, so when I spotted movement in the distance, I was grateful for the distraction.

"Look," I said.

Cirrus turned. Six children, each around age ten, ran about wielding tree branches, which they used to spray each other with imaginary elemental attacks.

i got you

no because mine is fire and fire melts ice

lightning cancels fire

no it doesn't

and so on.

"They're so cute," said Cirrus.

"Nn," I said.

We snuggled in closer. We kissed. The sky above fluttered and rasped like the world's most elaborate paper chandelier.

"Ew!" said a voice.

A girl stared at us. She wore mirrored swim goggles and a Frisbee as a chest plate.

"Hey there," said Cirrus.

The girl aimed a toddler-size tennis racket at us. "Avada kedavra!" she screamed, and ran away to join the rest of her group.

I watched the children play. *I'll make that one Jamal,* I thought. *That one is Milo. That one can be me, that one can be Cirrus.*

"Kind of makes me want to be a kid again," I said.

"Kind of does," said Cirrus.

All at once Cirrus took a pause. She became lost in a tiny cluster of eggs on the backside of a dead leaf.

"What is it?" I said.

"My parents," said Cirrus. "They keep going on and on about some big project going on in China."

I killed inside at the word *China*. All I could say was "Okay."

"Another mall, the world's biggest this time, but apparently still not big enough," said Cirrus. She found a twig and bent it.

My heart fought against blood suddenly turned thick as syrup. "But you haven't even been here two months. I thought that project in LA was supposed to last for a long time."

I thought we were supposed to be together for a long time.

"It's on hold because of city budget red tape or something," said Cirrus. "Dunn matter."

"Wait—" I said. "So—"

Cirrus snapped the twig, flung it away, and grinned. "Wanna know what I told them?"

I could not help but admire her smile. She had two beautifully crooked incisors.

"I told them that if they just waited a year for me to finish out high school, they could move wherever they wanted without having to bother anymore with the whole parenting thing," said Cirrus.

I covered my mouth and hooted. "Dude."

"You should've seen how guilty they looked," said Cirrus.

I tried to picture her parents with any kind of emotion aside from detached inquisitiveness, and failed. But I didn't care. Because what Cirrus was saying was—

"I'm not going anywhere," said Cirrus. She buried her

forehead in my neck. "I've been wanting to say something to my parents for years. Know why I finally did?"

She lifted her gaze to meet mine. I thrilled inside at the sight.

"Why?" I said.

"It's not because of this place," said Cirrus. "I've seen better places."

"Uh-huh," I said, smiling now.

"It's just that I met this guy," said Cirrus. "Real dark and broody rock-and-roller type."

I killed inside again. I thrilled, I killed, thrillkill.

"So Rancho Ruby's not so bad," said Cirrus.

"Could be a lot worse," I said.

I kissed her, and she kissed me back, tighter and tighter, neither of us having any clue just how much worse.

"I love you, Sunny Dae," said Cirrus.

"I love you, Cirrus Soh," I said.

And for the rest of the day, neither of us went anywhere except right where we already were.

Ready

You didn't see my email, did you," whispered Jamal.

Around us, imbeciles sprinted and hurdled in the purposeless Sisyphean contest known as track.

I removed my cleat spikes using a hand tool, then blew sharply to eject red clay debris. I hated dirty cleats; I found the best way to keep them clean was to avoid running whenever possible.

"Email," I said, "is the awkward transitional technology between snail mail—"

Jamal hissed me silent, like one does to a bad cat. "I wrote Lady Lashblade late last night. I thanked her for her support. I wrote a freaking torch song for her."

"You should see this email," Milo susurrated, like a spy.

I dropped my hand tool. "You *wrote* to her?"

"I had to do something," said Jamal. He counted on his fingers. "It's Tuesday, and last night I wasn't around because of that stupid dinner with my stupid uncle, and now tonight Milo's not gonna be around."

"I have a quinceañera for my cousin all the way in Topanga," said Milo. "Shoot me."

"What did your email say?" I said to Jamal.

"And all the after-school time this week's been eaten up by band practice!" said Jamal, ducking his voice as two jocks passed. "Then we have the show on Wednesday!" he hissed. "The whole week's been fubared for DIY Fantasy FX!"

"Jamal," I whispered. "What did your email say?"

"I asked if she could guest star on an upcoming episode," said Jamal.

"He showed her your video of Esmeralda's Veil," said Milo.

"And then what?" I said.

"She loved it!" whisper-shouted Jamal. "She wanted a date and time from us! So I just freaking made the executive decision and said Thursday!"

"The day after the talent show," said Milo, arms folded.

There was no school Thursday, to allow for what the faculty called a *staff work day*, otherwise informally known as a *staff recovery day*, otherwise even more informally known as a *hangover day*.

"We are locked in," said Jamal. "I'm forcing our own hand."

The three of us sat in silence while Jamal fumed.

"But wait—isn't this a good thing?" I said finally. "This is amazing. I can't believe you had the guts to reach out to Lady Lashblade herself."

Jamal, realizing there was actually nothing to be angry about, reluctantly began to calm down. "I did," he said. "Because I am amazing."

"Lady Lashblade?" hissed Gunner, jogging toward us.

I high-fived him, realized he had just transferred a few

milligrams of his sweat onto my palm, and wiped my hand on the grass before giving Jamal a hug. "Thank you for picking up my slack and taking charge. What's there to be mad about?"

"I think Jamal just wants some validation," said Milo.

"Yap," said Gunner with dual pistol fingers. He jogged away backward.

Jamal softened. "I miss doing our stuff. Our *real* stuff."

"I got you," I said. I touched his shoulder. "Thursday will be spectacular."

"We nail that, she can't *not* invite us to the Faire," said Milo. "Everything's getting better and better, I can feel it."

I could, too. I ran an open hand over the ground covered in green, and when I pinched my fingers closed, I saw I had found not a four-leaf, but a five-leaf clover.

I held up the tiny miracle to the warm afternoon light, where its leaves glowed with a lime translucence. I asked its forgiveness for murdering it and its brethren. All of time slowed down as I beheld this very special specimen: the trees in midsway, the clouds now halted, the wind just a trace of a breath.

I watched as Jamal and Milo gave each other the slowest high five ever. They swung their arms mightily as if underwater.

I blinked one blink, then another. In the distance appeared the girls' track team, all agonizing over where to sit on the opposite end of the field. Cirrus emerged, her arms limp and exhausted. She plopped down where she was. She sat alone. She picked at the clover. Held it up.

I knew exactly what kind she got.

There was a low, syrupy yell from Ms. Coach Oldtimer, the female fraternal twin to Coach Oldtimer, and Cirrus heaved herself up to run a hundred-meter dash alongside Artemis and six identical blondes.

Boosh, went the starting gun in slow motion. Exploding lazily against the amber sky. The girls: statues en pointe as they accelerated millimeter by millimeter off their blocks. Cirrus, moving a little later than everyone, a little slower than everyone,

her tee shirt the newest,
her shorts the newest,
herself the newest,
feet slapping clay while the others gazelled,
evanescing upon spiked hooves that propelled,
while she stomped to a stop with her arms all a-flail,
now Artemis crashing right into her tail,
both girls grasping their knees
and gasping *oh please,*
screaming with laughter as they readied their fingers,
cocking and shooting like merry gunslingers:
two fingers—middle finger—
two fingers—middle finger—
and, as if she heard my heart cheering her on,
turning her gaze to meet mine from far yon
and flip her final, most colorful bird—
for me, a boy so happy it was perfectly absurd.

"Show me windmill," said Gray.

I windmilled.

"Good, but not so hard that you'd break your strings," said Gray. "Now show me machine gun."

I raised my guitar and decimated the imaginary audience with four fast left-hand trigger fingers.

"Headbang," said Gray.

"Fist of Lucifer," said Gray.

We were in the music room at school. Milo and Jamal sat and watched, smiling dorkily at me through their upper teeth. As if that wasn't bad enough, Gray was shooting video.

"Finish with a Statue of Liberty," said Gray.

I did and held the pose, panting. I had worked up a light sweat. Gray hopped down from his perch atop a swivel stool.

"That's it, great job," said Gray.

"Years of role-playing!" I said.

"Critical hit, baby!" said Milo.

"Sword of Damocles!" said Jamal.

"Didn't that hang by a single horsehair?" said Milo. "Something about with great fortune comes great risk?"

"Sword of Sages?" said Jamal.

"Zelda," grunted Gunner, nodding earnestly.

"Bunch . . . of . . . nerds," muttered Gray with awe.

I glanced at Gunner, who seemed to take this as a high compliment.

Gray took a swig from his big water bottle, and when he belched, I could smell beer.

"You're not supposed to have that in here," I said.

"Come on," said Gray. "I look forward to this all day."

I blinked. "You do?"

"Final practice, you guys," said Gray. "Let's get it."

We ran through the song. We no longer thought about hitting the right notes. Now was the last chance to earn what Gray called *style points*.

Jamal was too stiff to really do much of anything, so he settled on a somewhat convincing figure-eight headbang over the neck of his bass.

Milo could twirl both his sticks now, and still land them in time to the music.

And I could windmill, machine gun, headbang, and Fist of Lucifer.

At one point I spied Mr. Tweed spying us through the door glass with snarled lips and finger horns. Gray slid his "water" bottle behind him, out of Mr. Tweed's view. Not that Mr. Tweed noticed or would even care. After today we would most likely never practice in here again.

We played steady and hard, like an unstoppable windowless steel train traveling straight through the fires of hell. We were not just making music. We were putting on a show.

Throughout it all, Gunner maintained the sound levels and made sure cables were routed safely. Gunner had swung by to wish me luck, took one look at the mess of our setup, and swooped in *tsking* to tidy things up.

I threw eyes at Milo, and he instantly knew it was time to play forte, then double forte, then dig hard into the last measures. Jamal spread his long high-jumper legs to form a power triangle. He threw out a kick high enough to ignite the upturned fist of my final Statue of Liberty.

We all turned to Gray to hear him call out his percentage. For a moment he said nothing. Then he simply shook his head.

"Always wondered if my song would actually work," said Gray softly. "Beauty is truth, is beauty, is truth."

I exchanged glances with Milo, Jamal, and also Gunner—our first and last roadie.

"Well?" I said.

"It does," said Gray. He laughed a laugh stained blue with memory. "Better than I imagined."

Gray went to each of us and jiggled our weary shoulders. The five of us brought it in for a final band salute: *To metal.*

"My beautiful nerds," said Gray, "you are at one hundred percent. You are ready."

IV

Kids think they vanish when their eyes are closed.
Everyone else knows that they are exposed.

Sunset

Did I sleep?

I couldn't tell.

All night I rested on the uncomfortable sharp edge dividing consciousness and unconsciousness, afraid to move for fear of falling.

If I slept at all, my dreams were the meta kind—dreams wondering if I were really asleep, dreams about dreaming.

It was the day of the talent show.

I woke up late. I'm pretty sure half the school did, since so many of us were slated to be at Miss Mayhem's in Los Angeles all day for sound checks and last-minute stage blocking and whatnot. Classes were in disarray because so many people were missing.

It's one big study hall today, wrote Cirrus. Just people passing the time. I miss you.

I miss you too, I wrote.

Are you nervous?

Nope, I wrote.

Duh, it's not like this is your first show.

I stared at that last line, not sure how to respond.

See you tonight, I wrote finally.

Milo came over in his mom's bulbous minivan, which we loaded up with guitars and whatnot. I brought a toolbox containing Gray's old stage makeup. Out of the corner of my eye I saw Mom and Dad staring out the window with utter bafflement. They had no idea what was happening.

I waved to them, and they waved back.

Milo and I drove to pick up Jamal, who met us with armloads of snacks.

"It's just a forty-minute drive," said Milo.

"Road trip," cried Jamal, ignoring Milo.

"I guess let's do this," I said.

We wound through the spaghetti streets of Rancho Ruby, passing Cirrus's condo, passing the school. We ascended onto the freeway.

We were three fake bandmates in a van. Anyone regarding us would think we looked cool. If we looked cool and acted cool, did that make us cool?

The equipment squeaked in the back. We were listening to "Beauty Is Truth" just a couple times, at my insistence, to cement it in the backs of our minds.

In a vintage GeoCities hip bag I had brought ibuprofen, adhesive bandages, antacid tablets, cough drops, baby wipes, spare change, a key-chain flashlight, a hand-crank radio, earplugs, potable water, MREs, and so on—everything you need for a disaster preparedness kit, just in case.

The van crested a hill, and Los Angeles sat waiting in the smog: a jagged citadel of dirty gray steel in the hot sun like the last bastion of civilization in a world baked lifeless after decades of catastrophic global warming.

My god, Los Angeles was an ugly city.

But my god, Los Angeles was still cool as hell.

We approached slowly, like a scout ship being pulled into a galactic destroyer by tractor beam.

"Take the next exit for Vermont Avenue," said Milo's mom's minivan.

We did. Jamal and I pressed against the window to behold the city's wonders: a raven-haired model aglide on a single-wheel scooter; a naked man bathing himself with a brand-new Super Soaker; a United States Post Office Lamborghini; five soaring palm trees, painted tip to root with pure white. Murals swirled by on every wall. We rolled down the windows and smelled everything we could, like dogs do, and detected pupusas and longanzina and anise and curry.

"Take the next left onto Sunset Boulevard," said the van.

The cynic would say Sunset was like any other street in this godforsaken post-apocalyptic wonderland. But it wasn't. It was a twenty-some-odd-mile-long serpent behemoth whose head had no idea what its tail was doing.

At one end was a cozy neighborhood art park, then a gleaming hospital complex, then a storied media studio district, then the world headquarters for a global cult. The grimy ironic hipsters came next, then the street artists with their dyed fingertips, then the string of guitar shops populated by off-duty rockers in black afternoon denim.

After that came the Sunset Strip known all over the world. Music club after music club, where stars rose and fell and, yes, literally died at its curbs. The Strip was where the Sunset Boulevard of the mind ended. In reality, Sunset continued on all the way to the sea, passing through fiercely manicured, fiercely white Beverly Hills and Bel Air—those intensely boring, parasitic enclaves solely obsessed with sucking as much wealth out of surrounding Los Angeles as possible. No one cared about that part of Sunset.

Who would, when Miss Mayhem was right there in front of you?

"Long live rock and roll," said the minivan.

I stared at Los Angeles baking below me. Everyone liked to call Angelenos *fake*, because they would do and say anything to make their dreams of stardom come true. According to the internet, Andy Warhol once said, "I love Los Angeles. I love Hollywood. They're beautiful. Everybody's plastic, but I love plastic. I want to be plastic."

Andy Warhol, embracing the fake. A pop artist through and through.

As for the rest of us, didn't we all fake it? Just a little bit, every day, at school, at work?

Wasn't it more unreasonable to expect someone to be perfectly honest and unwavering and unaccommodating every waking moment of their lives?

Was I asking myself all this stuff just to try to make myself feel better?

"Let's load out," I cried, and leapt into the heat.

I squinted up at the marquee.

RANCHO RUBY SENIOR HIGH SCHOOL PRESENTS
THE 8TH ANNUAL TALENT SHOW EXTRAVAGANZA
AND GALA FUNDRAISER

I carried equipment up the stairs—curséd stairs, just perfect—which led to a "greenroom" backstage scarred with the autographs of thousands of rockers throughout time, all circling an ornate framed silver print of the eponymous Miss Mayhem herself.

I had to look. It took me a few minutes of careful searching. But then I found it, written small in Gray's hand:

THE MORTALS 2017

"May we play the hell out of the talent show tonight," I prayed to Miss Mayhem.

"Sure, whatever," said Miss Mayhem. "Your school prepaid all their tickets."

I stuck my tongue out at the portrait.

Jamal and Milo brought the last of the stuff up. Other kids followed. Soon the greenroom became crowded.

"All right, listen up," said a familiar voice, and Mr. Tweed emerged from behind a curtain. "First we're gonna set up our stage props and equipment, with the least complicated acts in the front—Juggalo Acrobats, that's you—and the most complicated in the back. That's you, Immortals."

I looked at Jamal and Milo. Things were getting really real really fast.

"Then it's time for sound checks, 'kay?" said Mr. Tweed.

"Once we get your levels set, remain onstage and let Gunner tape and mark your mic with your name."

Gunner appeared. He wore an Immortals tee shirt. The sight of it made my brain momentarily brown out.

"What are you doing here?" I said.

"Ditching school—*and* football practice!" said Gunner with glee. "My dad's gonna be so mad!"

"After your sound check is done," said Mr. Tweed, "you're free to get lunch or hunt for celebrities or whatever. It's back in the greenroom by three, makeup at three thirty, curtains at four. Any fundraising merch goes on the table downstairs. Everybody ready to put on a show?"

We clapped. Everyone pitched in, each helping the other set up their equipment, spike the stage with fluorescent tape, and so on. We handed around snacks while Gunner manned the sound booth, barking orders to move a light or adjust a mic. He was good at this. I idly wondered if he'd be useful for future DIY Fantasy FX videos.

Finally there was a lull. Everyone was sitting around, hanging out with their legs dangling off the black stage, taking selfies, buzzing with anticipation.

"Immortals, to the stage for sound check," cried Mr. Tweed from the theater.

I jumped to my feet, bumping off a column to bump right into another.

Jamal and Milo took their stations. As soon as I joined them, Gunner plugged us in and sprinted back to the board to adjust our levels.

"Immortals are good to go," said Gunner over the speakers.

All around us were kids and parents and teachers, all

carrying stuff or taping things down or whatever across the empty audience pit, which seemed just really too huge, like an airplane hangar, really.

They all glanced at me as they hustled by, with this look that said, *Oh, so that's the show's finale, and Sunny's the front man.*

I grimaced at Milo and Jamal. They grimaced back. Then we launched into the intro.

Jamal played on an impeccable Orange with unlimited tightness and tone. Milo finally sat before a real drum set, a beast that could move huge quantities of percussive air—much better than that gangly cocktail kit that looked like a vaporator from the Skywalker farm.

And me? I had a mic on a stand with a scarf. I had a floor monitor to lean up on, and acres of stage upon which to earn *style points.* I had a Marshall stack towering behind me, a blind and all-powerful moai waiting to unleash its ancient scream.

We played. We opened the doors of hell, just a crack, just a fiery slit of orange with screams coming from within. I leaned up to the mic—I preferred it just a few centimeters out of reach—and screamed those first lines penned by Gray so long ago:

> *You fade out, I reach in*
> *Crack the floor, fall within*

After sixteen bars, I slit my throat with the edge of my hand to stop Milo and Jamal. From the back of the club I saw Gunner underlit by the orange lights of the mixing board. He looked demonic, but friendly, a friendly demon, and gave us a thumbs-up.

"Levels are good," boomed Gunner.

The crowd around us gave a house cheer.

Mr. Tweed hopped up onto the stage and bellowed into a mic, "Whoo, Sunny and his Immortals bringing it!" he said. "And that was just a teaser!"

The whole room looked at me. I could only wave back, like a motorized mannequin beckoning customers from the side of the road.

In the greenroom, Jamal and Milo massaged what muscles they could find in my shoulders.

"You got this," said Jamal. "Think about your reward. Clean slate with Cirrus. Livestream with Lady Lashblade tomorrow. Back on track."

"Are you shaking?" said Milo.

"I got this," I said. "I got this Igotthis igotthis."

"You kinda have to," said Jamal.

I breathed in and out. "Okay."

I sat at the dressing room mirror and began streaking my face with tears as dark as ash. Jamal and Milo joined me, and we regarded our collective reflection.

"We look like an old-skool album cover," said Jamal with delight.

We sat and stared at one another, the most nervous goth metalheads ever. I waited a few minutes until we had the room to ourselves; then I took a marker from my disaster preparedness kit, found the spot on the wall, and added the words:

THE IMMORTALS 2020

Then I wordlessly motioned for Jamal and Milo to crowd in for a selfie.

We crowded around the screen to examine the resulting photo.

"We look great," I said.

"We look like we need buckets to barf into," said Jamal.

"They have buckets in the loading dock," said Milo.

There was a commotion, and distant applause. I crouched and peeked out beyond the stage, where Mr. Tweed was. He murmured this and that to a small crowd.

"They're here already?" I wondered.

Milo crowded in. "Who?"

"*People,*" said Jamal, kneeling at my side.

Dad was there, standing oddly stock-still even as Mom held his arm and danced to the pre-show music coming from the speakers. She punched him playfully, and he snapped out of whatever daze he was in to give her a forced smile.

Next to them stood Jane and Brandon Soh, observing the stage through little brass field binoculars. They looked like they had just stepped off a steam-powered drill transport that had arrived moments ago from the secret civilization at the center of the earth.

Thirty more people filled the floor out of nowhere, and suddenly the club went dark but for the pastels of the stage lights.

"Welcome to the eighth annual Rancho Ruby Senior High School talent show extravaganza and gala fundraiser!" said Mr. Tweed.

The audience erupted.

"I didn't think we'd be starting so soon," I said.

"We're right on time, actually," said Milo.

"Feels really soon," I said. "Doesn't it feel super soon?"

The three of us held one another as if we were riding out a bombing raid.

"First act's up, here we go," said Jamal. "These guys rap *and* juggle at the same time."

One by one, the acts went up and did their thing.

We watched. We waited.

Next came the celebrity impersonator. Then the comedy skit. The tap-dancing magician. The acoustic duo. Each act had their little legions of fans, and they all bowed to the rabid kind of applause only friends and family could provide.

Finally Mr. Tweed took the stage again, with a show host's languid ease, and murmured words into the mic. A yelp came from the audience. I didn't have to look to know it was Cirrus's voice.

Mr. Tweed said more words, like *These guys have been working at it for weeks* and *If you think rock is dead, then think again,* but I pretended not to hear them. I looked over and watched Jamal and Milo slapping each other around to get psyched up.

"Get in here," said Jamal, extending a hand.

"Let's rock," said Milo, extending his. He looked at me. "Say it."

"Last time," said Jamal.

I extended my hand, too. We saluted the air on three.

"To metal," I said.

Losers

I stepped onto the stage.

Stepping onto the stage felt like stepping into a dream box painted black on all sides.

The multicolored lights, the buzzing mic.

The crowd, clapping soundlessly now.

And Cirrus, standing in the middle with the back of her hand covering an uncontrollable smile.

Hadn't I seen all this before in my head?

Yes, and now it was all there before me. It was all real.

There was no shouting *How you doing tonight, Hollyweird!* or anything like that. I barely remember the mic. I didn't think I'd thrown eyes at Milo to count us in, but I guess I had, because suddenly he just was, and now we were playing the intro.

Gee, GEE, GEE, chromatically up to BEE

Like a car heading straight for a cliff, we reached the part where I had to touch my chin to the mesh of the mic and sing.

You fade out, I reach in
Crack the floor, fall within

Did I move my lips?

I did.

Did I sing up into the mic? Did I curl my lips in a snarl now?

I did, I did, I did.

I was doing it. It was happening. If I stopped, the whole thing would stop—a terrifying thought. So I did not stop. I went louder and harder, because this was it. After this, I was done. There was a light at the end of this tunnel, and as I exited through the other end, I wanted to make sure to scorch the sides with green flame—the hottest kind.

The audience screamed with joy. I eyed Cirrus—she and a group of about ten classmates were jumping up and down in their black Immortals tee shirts, including Oggy. Cirrus excitedly pointed at me, then herself: *That is my boyfriend!*

I caught sight of Mom. She beamed at me in a stupefied daze. Next to her were Cirrus's parents, moving their arms in steady reciprocal fashion like a couple of motorized good-luck cats. I saw Mom cup Dad's ear, shout into it. What did she say?

First Gray, now Sunny?

Did you have any idea?

Dad shrugged excitedly—*I have no idea what is happening!*—and cupped his hands to yell my name. I couldn't hear it, but I didn't mind.

I threw a side glance and saw Gray, too, standing in the underlit glow of the stage wings. He held on to a truss and raised his beer in a swaying toast at me.

We ripped through each chapter of the song: the first chorus, the EDM breakdown performed on our non-EDM instruments, all of it. I windmilled, machine gunned, even found a moment or two to chain whip the mic like I was a Repugnant. Milo twirled his dual sticks and landed them each time except for one barely noticeable slip-up; he recovered seamlessly thanks to two drumstick wells placed to the left and right of his snare. Jamal headbanged so hard I was worried his head would bend clean off.

I drew my guitar up and face-melted: *Love you so much Cirrus after tonight it's just you and me and I will show you all of my hidden pieces no matter how weird they are without shame or fear.*

When we made it to the a capella part, everyone's phones shot up as if on cue.

Little confetti rectangles of light glowing white and blue and green and orange.

It was beautiful.

The truth is you're beautiful when you lie
The truth is you're beautiful when you lie
The truth is—

"You're beautiful when you lie," screeched Gray.

What was happening?

I looked up at Gunner at the sound board in the distance, and he stood with an arm pointing toward stage right. I stayed pinned to the mic and threw a glance.

Gray had stepped onto the stage and hijacked Jamal's mic.

"The truth is you're beautiful when you lie," sang Gray.

The crowd applauded, to my horror.

And why wouldn't they? This was all part of the act, for all they knew. He was handsome! He could sing! Perhaps he was a minor celebrity making a cameo appearance!

Gray swung from Jamal's mic toward mine like a drunk navigating a moving subway car, because Gray was drunk, very, very drunk, and he embraced me in his cloud of beer breath to share my mic.

"The truth is you're beautiful when you lie," we sang.

I had to sing. I couldn't just stop singing.

I didn't dare look at Cirrus. I'm sure she was cheering, too. How sweet that Sunny the rock star had invited his corporate workaday brother onto the stage like this!

Gray leaned on me, playfully at first, then with all his weight as he lost his balance.

We fell extremely slowly.

Our fall took long enough to give me time to realize that I was passing through some sort of point of no return, like a one-way portal into another, worse dimension. Through the still-open portal I could see myself finishing "Beauty Is Truth" with the perfect butt-kicker landing of the true lead guitar rock performer; I could see the audience exploding; I could see Cirrus, the glowing nucleus of it all.

The portal shrank down into a spark that died the instant it touched the floor.

Jamal and Milo stood frozen solid. Mr. Tweed quick-stepped onto the stage.

"Are you guys all right?" he said quietly.

Mr. Tweed helped me up, then Gray. "Been a minute, Gray Dae," he said.

The audience began to murmur.

Because I could not help myself, I glanced at Cirrus. She

crossed her mouth tight with both hands, like one does when witnessing an accident.

Gray wobbled—his phantom subway car taking an S curve—and popped hard into the mic to fill the air with an unearthly *om* of feedback.

Gray held the mic away until the howl died down, then breathed into it. "Sorry 'bout that ever-body."

Was this really happening? My brain was numb with confusion.

"Guys," slurred Gray, "let's pick it up from the last measure before the appa kella, capa pella, a capella, *god!*"

Mr. Tweed clapped his hands at us. "Let's be done now, good job, guys."

I watched as he motioned for Gunner to kill the spotlights dead. We stood in the dark now as the crowd softly babbled on.

Let's be done?

How was I suddenly done now? What was I supposed to do with all this adrenaline still racing through my body? Where was all this hot blood supposed to go?

We could not be done. It wasn't fair.

We were supposed to have a moment, and now we didn't. Because Gray took it.

"What the hell," I said.

Milo whispered something at me in the dark, but I ignored it. I was talking to Gray.

"What, you guys were sounding kinda thin," said Gray. "I's just tryna help."

"This was supposed to be mine," I shot.

Gray shot back right away. "But it's my song."

We rallied with increasing speed. "But—"

"I just let you borrow it," said Gray. "It's *my* song, and I know how to play it."

"You guys," said Milo.

"Off the stage, please," said Mr. Tweed.

"You've never ever ever performed!" said Gray. "You wouldn't even be here if it wasn't for me!"

"Fellas," said Mr. Tweed.

But I barely heard him. My hands throbbed with ebbing energy. I could feel the makeup on my face, and it didn't feel cool at all anymore. It felt stupid.

"You thought we couldn't pull this off," I hissed, "because we're just a bunch of pathetic nerds faking it to be cool."

"I's just tryna help," said Gray.

"Help prove that we're losers?" I said. "Because good job. We were already losers before, and we're even bigger losers now."

"You still get to be the front man," said Gray. "Okay?"

There were so many comebacks I would think of later. Sharp, shameless, profane, profound. But right now I couldn't think of any. All I could say was

"Thanks a lot, *Gray*."

Finally a strong hand grabbed me. I turned.

"They can *hear* you," yelled Milo.

He stabbed a finger at the mic in front of me, and its little green light. Green meant *on*.

"And don't you *dare* call us losers," Milo added. He threw his sticks aside and grabbed Jamal, who flung his bass down with disgust.

I stared with terror at my friends. My insides turned to ice that crashed apart in beautiful sparkling sheets.

I'd only ever seen Milo get mad—like truly mad—twice in

our entire friendship. It was terrifying and exciting to behold, because Milo mad could cause serious physical damage unless he removed himself from the situation. Which was what Milo was doing right now.

I had just hurt Milo.

I had just hurt Jamal, too.

Someone—a volunteer mom with a headset—scooted us stage left with outstretched arms. "And we're offstage," she said.

The spotlight turned back on behind me.

"That's one way to end a talent show," said Mr. Tweed into what once was my mic. "Everyone give it up for the Immortals!"

Another spotlight followed me as I was escorted away, and in its rainbow glare I could discern a cringing audience clapping dutifully through their bafflement. I could discern Cirrus simply clutching fistfuls of hair in a kind of confused paralysis. On her shirt I could discern words that were losing meaning by the second:

THE IMMORTALS 2020

ONE NIGHT ONLY

SUNSET STRIP, HOLLYWOOD

Then I saw her vanish.

Pity

I came to a skidding halt outside. Around me, Sunset Boulevard busily went about being its famous self: drunks careening, rockers smoking, tourists poised with their cameras.

I spotted Cirrus as she dashed around the corner of the club. I could hear my heart beating everywhere. I ran, turned, and almost collided with her.

Cirrus had turned her shirt inside out. She stood before me like she could melt me down into gristle with just her mind.

Angel City howled its nightsong all around us.

"Tell me what I just saw is not what I think I just saw," said Cirrus.

I had no idea how to do that, so I found myself saying precisely nothing.

"Have I been made the fool?" said Cirrus.

Again, nothing.

Cirrus's eyes widened. "This *whole time*?"

Finally my mouth began to move. I wiped sweat from my

forehead, my eyes, and saw my hands come away black with makeup. I probably looked like a mess of fingerpaint now.

I held my hands out in the weakest version of hear-me-out ever. "I didn't want you to think—to think—"

"To think what?" said Cirrus.

"That I was a loser, so—"

"Why would I ever think that?" said Cirrus, angling her head with outrage.

"So I did what I . . . *did*," I said, eyes dancing hard enough to make me dizzy. "And then I had to keep doing it, because otherwise, I don't know. And I'm sorry, can I just say that? I'm so, so sorry?"

A limo went by, and two good friends leaned out the window and screamed at the world with joy. Everything was probably perfect in that limo.

Or it wasn't, and everyone was just faking having a great time.

"Right now," said Cirrus through gritted teeth, "all I can think is *What else is this guy lying about?*"

"This is it," I said. I couldn't believe I was saying such stupid words. But I kept going. "This is the only thing, I swear."

Cirrus chewed her cheek. "What the hell am I doing here?" she muttered, inadvertently quoting Radiohead. "Why am I here, why do I even bother being anywhere?"

My hands grew heavy, but I held them up. "You have every right to—"

"You're damn right I do," cried Cirrus. "You lied for months. *Months!*"

She kicked a chain-link fence.

"If I put on my little Sherlock hat," she said, "I can deduce that you lied within the first ten minutes that night when we first met. I'm right, aren't I?"

I said nothing.

"And wait—Jamal and Milo, too?" said Cirrus.

Again, I said nothing.

"Oh no no no," said Cirrus, in shock at my nonanswer answer. "Every stupid place I go, I have to figure out what the hell is going on, because every time, I go in knowing nothing. Knowing no *one*. That means I must be being made a fool right now, because I really thought for sure I had it right this time around. You asked me all those questions like you really wanted to know the answers. I'd *never* had that before."

Her face crinkled as she sneered at her own oncoming tears. She gave the fence another kick.

"And then I told my parents I wanted to stay," said Cirrus. "Because I have this super-great boyfriend who I super-much love, and these super friends, and a super life. But none of it was super, because none of it was real. It was all super fake."

A fresh horror dawned on Cirrus's face as she opened her eyes wide enough to set her twin black irises jittering.

"Gunner was in on it, too, right in my own house," said Cirrus. "Plus his sidekick. The whole *school*."

"It wasn't the whole school," I said.

"That makes everything better," said Cirrus.

I made those hands you make when a lion is about to charge. "It was my idea," I said.

"I sat there grinning like an idiot," said Cirrus. She held her chin, fascinated. "Just happy to be there."

"I made them do it," I said. "They've got nothing to do with my mistakes."

"I showed you my tin," said Cirrus to herself, as if in a dream. "That guitar pick should go, shouldn't it."

"This is super real, I promise," I said. But I could feel her slipping away from me.

"I don't know who you are," Cirrus finally concluded.

I took a deep breath. This was my last chance to make a statement.

"I did this because you were so cool and you traveled the world and knew everything and I'm a loser who hides away in his room with a bunch of childish nerd toys and I wanted to impress you," I said.

"Sunny," said Cirrus, crumbling a little now. "You *did* impress me."

I stepped into a beam of sodium vapor lights to expose my streaked and ruined face. "Did I, though?"

Cirrus reached out to me, stopped, and hugged herself instead. "In the first sixty seconds." Her face had reached its melting point and now dripped with bitter tears.

I held my hands out. "What I mean is, was it Real Sunny who impressed you? Or Fake Sunny?"

Cirrus let her arms fall. "It was you, Sunny. Don't turn this around."

"All I'm saying is you really, really liked Fake Sunny," I said. "And I liked *being* Fake Sunny. But the whole time I was petrified, because in the back of my mind I was wondering if you would've liked Real Sunny, warts and all."

Cirrus stared hard at me, her face a mixture of anger and confusion, but also pity. "What are you saying?" she said.

"I am a super-huge mega-nerd," I said. "I have been uncool ever since middle school. I have been bullied ever since middle school. I like to dress up and pretend I am living a fantasy adventure. I spend my weekends making fake magic weapons. What I'm saying is, would you have liked that Sunny?"

"Of course I would've," said Cirrus, but her pensive squint told me she couldn't know for sure.

She would never know for sure.

Because I'd been Fake Sunny for so long that Real Sunny no longer existed in his original, pre-Cirrus form.

And now it was all moot anyway.

Around us, the lights of Sunset bloomed cyan and tangerine and magnesium. A rowdy cheer rose from the street and was drowned out by a fleet of rumbling Harleys.

"Heyyyy," said a voice. "There you are."

Gray came toward us with the careful catwalk of the inebriated. He found a pole to lean on.

"Look," said Gray to Cirrus. "If you wanna blame someone, blame me, 'kay?"

Cirrus could only stare, and I couldn't blame her.

Go away, Gray, I willed, but it didn't work.

Neon blinked red overhead, and Gray smiled at it.

"I'm the fake one here," said Gray. "Not Sun. My little brother, Sunny Dae, played the one song big brother Gray Dae never had the guts to perform in public. 'Cause I'm a no-good piece of crap failure."

"Go away, Gray," I said, aloud this time.

"I mean, he might've started out by faking it," said Gray. "But he turned out to be the real deal. All for you. I feel like most girls would think that's kinda sweet. Whoo, gotta sit."

Gray slid down to the ground.

I watched as Cirrus's eyes puzzled between these two brothers before her.

More motorcycles shattered the sky: *dr-r-room!*

"It was nice knowing you," said Cirrus, and walked away.

Cirrus was gone.

"You'll get her back," said Gray.

"No I won't," I said, and kicked a rattling fence.

"This too shall pass," said Gray.

"I hate you," I said.

"I hate me too," said Gray.

"This isn't about you," I said.

"You have no idea," said Gray, which might've made some kind of sense in his drunken mind but to me sounded infuriatingly nonsensical.

Gray teetered back to his feet and stood. I suddenly wanted to fight him. I of course had no idea how to fight—all I knew was fire attacks and sword slashes and magic missiles, all fake as hell—and only managed a pathetic shove with both hands, easily batted aside.

"Cut it out," said Gray.

"I used to think you were cool," I said, as the sky around us turned dark green. "You're not cool. You're a loser."

Gray simply acknowledged my words. He scowled at the city glittering below us. "I wasted three years of my life in this dump. Do you know I was scheduled to pitch one of the biggest A&R execs in LA, and I stood her up because I overslept? That was it. I was done."

Dr-room-dum-dum-dum!

I could only stare at him. He had just crashed my show, and now he was throwing himself a pity party?

"All I had to do was let you make it through tonight," said Gray. "And I screwed that up, too."

He chuffed to himself. Chuffed!

"I'm going," I said. "Feel free to hang out on this amazing sidewalk for all eternity."

Gray threw me a testy look. "You'll get her back, *god!* Or you won't, and you'll be fine! *So* many second chances out there, you don't even know. It's not like it's the music industry. This is nothing, trust me."

Something about the words *trust me* made me stop. When Paladin Gray had gotten erased down to nothing, the real Gray had not come to my defense. The real Gray was already long gone.

When I shoved him this time, Gray was unprepared. I tripped over a pipe jutting from the concrete; Gray hit the ground backward.

I caught my balance just in time to see Gray do a rolling tumble into the rightmost lane of the rushing river of white and red lights that was Sunset Boulevard. He found his feet, looked right, and held up a polite hand as tires shrieked.

Then he was taken down.

Cool

I watched the black and white and red swirl down the drain. It took three good washings before the makeup was completely gone. Then I rinsed the sink, rinsed it again, and again, and again.

"I think it's clean," said a voice.

I looked up and saw Dad.

"You all right?" said Dad.

I gave a grim nod: *No.*

The restroom door opened, and a nurse walked in.

"They said it's a mild concussion," said Dad. "But they want to keep him until the hematoma goes down. *Hematoma* means the bump on his head."

"That is correct," said the nurse, before entering a stall.

Out in the hospital hallway, Dad found a carpeted bench by the vending machines and sat me down.

"You wanna talk about it?" he said.

I shook my head.

"Do you even know how to talk anymore?" said Dad, attempting humor.

"Yes," I said.

"You know," said Dad, "I used to look up to my older brother. Like, a lot."

"Not like this, I bet," I said. I squeezed my cheeks hard enough to pull my face off.

"You made a mistake," said Dad. "But you're gonna be okay."

I curled a lip with resignation. I could not see how I was going to be okay.

"Let's get you a snack," said Dad, and began fussing with the machine.

I took out my phone and stared at its black glass. It was late. I didn't know who to talk to. Gunner, maybe? Certainly not Milo, or Jamal, or of course Cirrus, or even Mr. Tweed. I felt like my whole world had had quite enough of me for one night. What would I even say besides? *I feel terrible that I accidentally pushed my brother into oncoming traffic?*

Mom appeared, motioned for Dad to go in. Only one person was allowed in the ER curtain cubicle at a time.

"How much did Gray have to drink?" said Mom. "Do you know?"

"No," I said.

"And since when did he start drinking?" said Mom.

If you looked up from your laptop now and then, you would know.

Mom offered me a thousand-kilocalorie snack bar the size of a deck of cards—a dystopian triumph of legions of misanthropic food engineers—and I politely refused it.

"I thought I could be him," I said. "It was such a stupid thing to think. Because even *he* can't be him. And now look what I caused."

Mom took me under her chin. "This is not your fault. I promise."

"I called him a loser," I said with a sob. "Right before I pushed him."

Her phone buzzed, and Mom took a peek. "Get up," she said. "Dad says they moved him to a private room. We can go in."

I wiped my eyes.

"This is not your fault," said Mom again.

I shut the door. This was Rancho Ruby, so all the hospital rooms had couches and sinks and views of the Pacific. Out of habit I began formulating a rant about our failing, deeply inequitable *Pay up or die* health care "system" (if it could even be called that), but stopped when I caught sight of Gray.

Gray slept. His hair lay crushed to one side, like a hog-bristle brush slashed diagonally. He was all tubes and wires: lines coming out of both arms, wires coming from his chest and fingertips.

"Did you not know he'd given up on music?" I said. "That he was basically depressed?"

"No," said Dad. "I did not know that."

My face twitched. What were we doing as a family, if we were not even aware of such fundamental things about one another?

I lost it. "What the hell is wrong with you guys?"

"Sun," said Mom.

"He was up in LA, and he tried so hard and failed and his soul was absolutely crushed, and you had no idea," I said. "You had no idea how crushed he was."

"We thought he was okay," said Mom.

"He was so sad," I said. "And all I did was kick him when he was down. I was bad to him. All because of a stupid thing I did."

I wasn't yelling at my parents. I was yelling at myself.

Mom held me. "I'm not going to say what you did wasn't stupid," she said. "But I will say you shouldn't ever feel like you have to do or be something you don't want to just to impress people who don't know the real you."

"What Mom said," said Dad.

I looked at them. "Are you guys serious?"

Mom and Dad looked at me: *Yes?*

"All you guys do is try to impress other people," I said. "Trey Fortune."

"That's work," said Dad. "That's different."

"Is it?" I said.

"Everyone has to put on a face for work," said Dad. "You will, too."

"Gray was the one who keyed your car," I said.

Dad's brow flashed with disbelief. "Why?"

"Dad, what was the name of Gray's last band?" I said.

Dad took a breath, but no response came out, because he did not know.

"*Endscene,*" I said. "It was *Endscene.*"

Dad shifted his weight, rapped twice on a chair as if to test its material strength, and grimaced, as if something had suddenly gone bitter in his mouth.

"I'm a good dad, aren't I?" said Dad.

My eyes instantly dilated with panic. Had I just done something horrible? "Of course you are."

"You're the best dad," said Mom.

"Am I?" said Dad, and released two heavy teardrops.

"You are," I said. "You are the best dad."

"Why is everyone crying?" said Gray.

We looked up. We rushed to the side of the bed.

"Ungh," said Gray. "Is my head open or something?"

"You okay?"

"I am not okay," said Gray.

"You have to be okay, stupid," I said, hugging him as best as I could through all the equipment. I wanted to hit him, too, but I cried instead.

"Are you in pain?" said Mom.

"Nn," said Gray.

"I'm gonna call the nurse right now, buddy," said Dad.

"It's fine," said Gray.

"Where's the stupid call button," said Dad.

"I said it's fine," said Gray.

Everyone froze. Gray squeezed his eyes shut and held a breath for a long moment.

"I'm sorry I keyed your car, Dad," he said finally.

"You heard that," I said.

Mom and Dad leaned in to hold Gray's hand, Gray's shoulder. It was awkward, but they didn't seem to notice.

"Are you angry with me?" said Dad.

Gray sighed a big sigh, like this was a stupid question. "Ten bands in three years," he said. "You guys could've come to one of my shows."

"Oh, Gray, honey—" said Mom.

"You were busy, and that's fine," said Gray. Something occurred to him that was painful enough to bring tears. "All I needed was for you to ask me—one time—how things were going. That's why I keyed your car. Your stupid, poser, look-at-me car."

Mom and Dad flinched, as if they realized they'd been touching the wrong person.

I watched as Dad cycled through emotions: anger, forced calm, remorse. He spoke quietly.

"Buddy, if you want to do music, then I promise I will support you one hundred percent," he said.

"I let that go, Dad," said Gray. "I made my peace with it. Just didn't think it would turn into all this."

"I'm sorry," said Dad. "We let you down."

"We're both sorry," said Mom.

Gray reached out, wincing slightly, and squeezed both their hands. "Just—we're all in the same house now, okay? Let's be in the same house together."

"We're glad you're home," said Dad, somewhat missing Gray's point, but hopefully not by much.

"I mean, you went to Sunny's freakin' show," said Gray. "Didn't it feel great to be there?"

Mom gazed at me with sparkling eyes. "You were such the rock star."

Finally I found myself laughing, and it felt good. "I am so not."

"Yeah you were," said Gray. "You just put your mind to it and bam, one month later you're playing Miss Mayhem. That's you, man. You just go ahead and do whatever the hell you want. Like you always have."

I blinked. *I have?*

The machines beeped and beeped.

"Sun," said Gray. "I'm really, really sorry I messed everything up."

"None of that matters," I said, and I meant it.

"I'm so stupid," said Gray.

"You're not stupid," I said.

"I am," said Gray.

"Maybe a little stupid."

Gray laughed, then grit his teeth to cough. Mom fetched him a cup of water the size of a thimble that would be later billed to us as PATIENT HYDRATION × 1 UNIT(S) for $300.

"You know the last time I played at Miss Mayhem was the last time I played anywhere?" said Gray. "It became all auditions for original studio work toward the end."

He chuckled at those last words: *toward the end.*

"It was?" I said with a frown. Gray had mentioned playing Miss Mayhem. All this time, I had imagined Gray playing all over the city and beyond. Pay-to-play probably had become unsustainable.

The three of us—me, Mom, Dad—sat and listened. We were finally hearing about Gray's time in Hollywood for real for the first time.

"Every producer was like, *You sound just like this band* or *that band, you need to work on defining your own sound,*" said Gray. He bobbled his head in mock imitation. "Like, *your own identity.* Like, *What makes you you?*"

"Is that why you let it go?" said Dad. "Because maybe all you need to do is work on coming up with—"

"Shh," I said. "Let him talk."

Dad nodded, with a look that seemed to say, *Let him talk, now why didn't I think of that?*

"The thing is," said Gray, "all those producers were right. Every gig, every audition, I sounded like a very, very good tribute band. But never an artist. I was very good at copying sounds and looks and trends the whole time I was in Hollywood. And all through high school. *God.*"

Gray nodded soberly at us—his head full of revelations jarred loose tonight—and we waited for him to continue.

"You know, when we moved to Rancho Ruby," said Gray, "on like day two, some kid asked me if I ate dog?"

"Me too!" I blurted.

Gray threw eyes at me with sudden concern—*Really? You got it, too?*

Mom reached out to touch my shoulder. "Why didn't you ever tell us?"

Dad fumed. "I'm calling the school first thing tomorrow."

"Please don't do that," I said.

Mom looked sick with worry. "It is pretty different here. Isn't it."

Gray and I just looked at each other and said nothing. Mom sagged. She knew that was a *yes*.

"I miss our old place," I said simply.

"Nn," added Gray.

Mom looked at Dad, who kept his eyes on the floor. She squeezed his hand. He squeezed back. It was the most physical contact I'd seen between them in years.

"Did kids at school say that stuff pretty often?" said Dad.

"Sure," said Gray with a shrug. "*Are you Chinese, do you know kung fu.* I even once got *Can you sing K-pop.*"

"I hate K-pop," I said with a groan.

"Actually K-pop does this amazing thing where it switches multiple, entirely different genres in the same track," said Gray. "It was kind of a huge inspiration for 'Beauty Is Truth.'"

The structure of "Beauty Is Truth" formed in my mind. Rock, trap, acoustic, all in a single song.

"I wrote 'Beauty Is Truth' just for myself," said Gray. "All that other music, pff—" Gray hid his face in his hands and spoke through them. "All that other music I made because I wanted friends."

"It worked," I said. "You were Mr. Popular."

"I was flavor of the week," said Gray. "For like a hundred weeks. It made me tired."

"You had so many friends," I said.

Gray disputed me with a look. "Not friends like Jamal. Or like Milo. Not even close. Do you have any idea how lucky you are?"

"I am?" I said.

Gray held his hands out, blatantly ripping off my hear-me-out pose. "You got to this new school, where you didn't know anyone, and everyone made fun of you, but bam, you went out and found yourself a couple of blood brothers for life. Because you're Sunny, and that's what Sunny does."

"It is?" I said.

"I always wished I had what you had," said Gray. "Because if you have that as sort of your foundation under your feet, you can do anything. You can become a rock star in a little over four weeks." He grinned and twinkled his hands, *voilà*.

He made me smile a lopsided smile.

"You three stuck together for years," said Gray. "No matter what people called you, like nerd, geek—"

“Okay,” I said.

“—dork, loser—”

“Okay,” I said.

“—virgin, weirdo—”

“We get it, honey,” said Mom.

“Thank you,” I said.

“You never cared what other people thought about you,” said Gray. “I always envied that. And you’re crushing it. ScreenJunkie, Miss Mayhem.” He paused. “Cirrus.”

Gray began crying in earnest now. “I really am super sorry.”

“Me too,” I said.

We cried together now, also something we hadn’t done since the day we left Arroyo Plato.

Coldplay

They discharged Gray a few hours later, once the IV drip ran out. It was almost five in the morning. The three of us tucked Gray into bed—a cozy little parade—and flumpity-dumped back up the stairs to let him sleep.

Yawning, I began a slow search for a glass to fill with water. Mom and Dad sat at the kitchen counter, both lost in thought.

"Mom?" I said.

"What, sweetie."

"Dad?" I said.

"Yap," said Dad. He stretched and yawned one of those great big dad-yawns.

"Are you guys happy?" I said.

"Hey, hey, hey," sang Mom in descending arpeggio. "What makes you say that?"

"I don't know," I said.

Dad sat straighter. "Do you want me to be more involved in

your fantasy gameplaying? Because I totally would love that, what ho, good sir."

"And you're fluent in Fakespearean," I said with a laugh.

"You're trying to tell us we work too much," said Dad. "Aren't you."

"I don't know," I said again.

Something dinged on Dad's laptop, momentarily pilfering his attention. Mom gently shut the lid.

I took a breath and said what I'd been wanting to say for years:

"You guys worked a lot less back at our old place."

I knit my fingers at my belly for a moment, then decided to stop. I put my hands on my hips instead. I wanted answers. I waited.

Dad looked at Mom. *You wanna tell the story?*

Mom looked back at Dad and touched his face. It was a simple gesture, one I didn't recall ever having seen. *You tell the story.*

Dad shoved his laptop away and heaved himself up onto the counter. "Once upon a time, a boy"—he pointed to himself—"met a girl"—he pointed to Mom—"and fell crazy in love."

Mom gripped his hand. I noticed that their rings aligned.

Rings, hands, Ring of Baphomet, Cirrus.

My gut twisted.

Dad continued. "The boy and girl got married, got jobs, me at Grandpa's office, Mom somewhere else, had kids"—he gestured at me—"and from that moment on worked day and night to make sure their beautiful new baby boys would never have to work day and night."

"And it was tough," said Mom. She shook Dad's hand as

if charging into battle. "Every weekend—every free minute—became a pressure cooker situation."

"I don't really understand what that means," I said.

"You will," Dad said, and then caught himself and *brrt* shook his head like a broken robot. "I mean, I hope you never do, is what I meant."

"Honey," said Mom.

"Sorry," said Dad.

"What I'm saying is they wanted to make sure their two beautiful boys always had enough," said Mom.

I looked around at our outrageous custom kitchen. "Uh, I think we have enough."

Dad's face tightened with sorrow. "But these two parents, they were so busy chasing the next dollar they forgot to pay attention to how many they already had."

Both Mom and Dad fell silent. I let my arms drop. I had been demanding answers from them, and now that I had them, I only felt a growing melancholy.

You forgot to pay attention to a lot of things, I wanted to say.

"We forgot to pay attention to a lot of things," said Mom.

"I spend all my time trying to keep a super-duper positive attitude," said Dad quietly. "More like super-stupid attitude."

Dad-joke, I thought, but didn't dare say anything. I was so grateful for these words that I just held my breath to hold on to the moment.

Dad slid off the counter. Mom stepped forward. I stepped into their arms.

"We're gonna work on working less," said Mom. "And not keeping up with the Joneses. Eyes on our own paper. Right, honey?"

"Right," said Dad.

She pounded hard on his kidney, causing minor renal stress. "RIGHT?"

"Right, *god*," groaned Dad, just like Gray would.

"Big baby," said Mom, and succumbed to a yawn so big it almost made her tip over.

We released, and I caught a glimpse of Mom wiping her eyes.

"Good night," said Mom.

"Don't worry about Cirrus," said Dad.

"Dad," I said, walking away.

"Lights will guide you home," said Dad. "That's 'Fix You' by Coldplay."

"Coldplay is U2 for beginners," I said, and threw them both a weary smile. I shouldered my GeoCities hip bag. "I'm gonna shower now."

"Coldplay rules," said Dad.

"Sunny drools," said Mom, and high-fived Dad.

I headed upstairs. The sight of Gray's room stopped me, pulled me in.

I yanked off my Ring of Baphomet and placed it exactly where I had found it so long ago. I cut a square of paper and covered the IM on the IMMORTALS flyer, restoring it to its original torn state.

I reset the steel chair, smoothed the bed. I set things into the milk crate—cables, adapters, blablabla—and dug out the old iPod from my bag to shove it deep under everything. I placed the crate back under the desk right as I had found it.

I went to my room, scooped up a bunch of Gray's old clothes, and went back to stuff them in Gray's closet where they belonged. I stripped down to my underwear and put those clothes in there, too.

Then I stood in the shower for a half hour. I usually never took showers this hot. Hot showers loosened your skin's essential oils, making you more prone to dryness and itching that only fed the global lotion and moisturizer industrial complex.

But this felt good. I stared at my feet, wishing it were as simple as letting everything be rinsed down the drain.

I got out, put on my flannels, and put my slippers into position for the morning. I bit down on my night guard.

I began texting *I'm sorry* to Cirrus, but deleted it after quickly realizing how insulting that sounded. I resolved to talk to her in person tomorrow.

I lay down, clapped off the lights. Outside, the sun was already rising.

I didn't come close to anything resembling sleep. I fantasized about donating all the contents of all my white plastic containers, then rinsing out the containers with a garden hose and donating those, too. I fantasized about donating all my clothes, then wearing nothing but white for the rest of my life to erase myself into a state of superblankness. I would spend years like this and grow into something not quite adult and not quite child. I would become something society didn't have a name for yet.

I didn't, of course, because I still had a responsibility to Jamal and Milo and DIY Fantasy FX. If they'd even still have me.

Don't you dare call us losers, Milo had said.

I flung off the covers, jammed my feet into the slippers. I sat there, just breathing. I put on my big wired headphones and cued up a classic I had considered during my rock research that literally had only three chords and elementary-level drum and bass parts. I slid the volume ever higher. Come at me, noise-induced hearing loss.

A-with the record selection, and the mirror's reflection, I'm a-dancin' with myself.

"Dancing with Myself," I decided, was the official anthem of heartbroken nerds everywhere.

Believe

When I awoke, it was late afternoon. I had slept the day away. If I could sleep the year away, I would. But that wouldn't solve anything, and things badly needed solving right now.

The room was full of stale sunlight that reflected off my white airtight plastic containers with an orange-yellow glow. They always looked kind of pretty this time of day. They were a testament to years of accumulating, organizing, and building. I hoped they still meant something.

I got up, changed into horrible cargo shorts and one of my favorites, a near-mint-condition vintage F*cked Company shirt from 2003. I sonic-brushed, water flossed, and went downstairs to make a solitary late lunch–slash–extremely early dinner of an egg white salad on high-fiber bran toast and a bowl of cubed cantaloupe.

I figured I should tell someone where I was going. I searched the house. Gray lay in his bed downstairs, peacefully snoozing with an open book by his side.

The kitchen was empty; Mom and Dad hadn't come down from their bedroom yet.

I let everyone sleep in.

I stood ready on my Velociraptor, feeling like a daredevil in my helmet and skid pads. I opened the garage. I felt like someone should know about this big thing I was heading off to do, and I couldn't think of anyone to text.

Hey, I wrote Jamal.

Hey, I wrote Milo.

I waited five whole minutes. I knew they'd seen my messages because, like fools with a death wish, they kept their phones in their pockets at all times.

Neither Jamal nor Milo wrote back. They were mad, or pretending to be busy, or both. Today, I would make it up to them. I would fix things. *I will try to fix you.*

Six hexes upon you, Dad, for forcing Coldplay so deep into my head.

I glided out of the garage with telemark grace. I went slow down the hill. What could I possibly say to Cirrus? I did not know. The important part was to get there before I chickened out and went back to hide in my beautiful warm bed for the rest of my life.

Her condo looked unchanged. I absurdly wanted it to have morphed drastically, to reflect how I was feeling. But why should it? Why should anything?

I kicked my kickstand, marched up to the front door, and rang the bell. The doorbell stared back at me with its little impassive video eye. A moment passed. Then ten. I rang again. Did she see me?

I backed away, looked up at her window. The curtain twitched.

"Cirrus," I called as quietly as I could, which was stupid because it was impossible to shout softly.

Nothing.

"I need to explain myself," I said.

The window slid smoothly open four inches. Her hand emerged, flung a rose petal, and retreated to slam the glass shut again.

I scrambled for the petal.

It was not a petal.

It was a guitar pick.

My heart sank into my stomach to be digested and later excreted out as so much waste down the toilet and into the sewer system to eventually become invisible food for so many tiny ocean dwellers. I put the guitar pick in my pocket. I understood.

I would go put the guitar pick back in Gray's room, where it belonged.

The ride back up the hill seemed to grow steeper and steeper with every lunge of my legs. When I reached Jamal's, I cruised up the herringbone driveway, through the carriage house, across a sunlit atrium, and into the guest villa garage, which was open.

Jamal and Milo were there. They watched in silence as I kicked my kickstand and removed my helmet and skid pads.

"We just finished setup," said Jamal. "Your services are not needed."

Ouch. Critical hit.

"Maybe I could sing the narration?" I said. "Ha ha?"

Milo shook his head slowly. "Too soon."

"I came to tell you I'm sorry," I said. "For everything."

"Is Gray sorry, too?" said Jamal.

"Actually, he is," I said. "More than you might realize."

Jamal and Milo looked at each other, then me.

Milo's jaw was set tight. "Nn."

"Well, the rest of high school should be very awkward from here on out," said Jamal. He raised his eyebrows. "Track's gonna be awkward. Lunch should be exceptionally awkward."

A hundred seconds passed. I couldn't think of a single thing I could say in that time.

"You said we were losers," said Jamal.

I struggled. "I didn't mean *loser.* I meant—"

"Sounded like *loser* to me," said Jamal. "Milo?"

"Me too," said Milo.

More silence. My mind was freezing to a halt.

"You know," said Jamal, "I used to think that hey, worst-case scenario, we would make fools out of ourselves before our big fake band breakup. We're used to being thought of as fools. I can do fools."

I looked back at him. "I really didn't think that things would—"

"I didn't think we would wind up being *hated,*" said Jamal. "Loathed and despised. Oh no. That was unexpected."

I shut up. I glanced at Milo. His eyes sat in a bar of LED light, unwavering.

"You realize the whole school knows what we did?" said Jamal.

"I'm sorry," I said. "I'm sorry I said—what I said."

"So you are officially admitting you did in fact call us *losers* last night," said Jamal.

"I am sorry I strongly implied you were losers by association, thereby effectively inflicting the same damage as if I had called you losers directly," I said.

"That apology is wholly unsatisfying," said Jamal. "I mean wholly."

"I've been ashamed for a long time," I said.

Jamal and Milo stopped what they were doing and stared.

Milo took a step. "Of what?"

"Of myself," I said.

"That's stupid," said Jamal.

"Jamal," said Milo.

"It is, because when you first came to Rancho Ruby, we all thought you were the coolest dude," said Jamal, irritated.

I gave a pained look, because that was the best thing to hear at the worst moment.

"You guys ever wonder why I never talk about my old house in Arroyo Plato?" I said.

Jamal and Milo eyed me, cautious, curious.

I took a breath, exhaled. "You're not gonna believe this, but me and Gray used to be best friends."

I saw Milo melt a little. Jamal stayed firm. *Go on,* he nodded.

"You're definitely not gonna believe this," I said. "But me and Gray used to LARP together."

Milo and Jamal quirked at the same time, in exactly the same way.

"No," said Jamal.

"He was Dungeon Master, in fact," I said.

"No," said Jamal.

"Shh," said Milo.

They were listening. I forged on. "We moved here, for reasons I'm still getting my parents to fully recognize, and right off the bat I got crap left and right from kids. Gray, too. You know what I mean."

"Pshh," said Jamal and Milo, nodding.

"Gunner came after me, we had to stop gaming, all that," I said. "Gray had to ditch me, because he had his own classmates to deal with. Suddenly I was on my own."

"Nn," said Milo.

"What I mean to say is, when I moved here, that was the first time I'd ever been called a loser in the most serious kind of way." I rubbed and rubbed the back of my hand. "I wanted to hide in a hole and die. But I couldn't, so I closed myself up. I watched my step. I got cynical."

"You weren't always cynical?" said Jamal.

"I built my weird fortress of storage cubes—"

"Fortress of solitude," said Milo sagely. "You were protecting yourself."

I jabbed a finger. "Exactly. But the thing is?"

They listened once more. On a computer screen, I could see a clock ticking away. I could not let them—us?—them?—miss the livestream with Lady Lashblade.

"The thing is," I said, "there was no protecting myself. Because I started to believe the bullies. I started to believe I was a loser. I never meant to call you guys losers. I was talking about me."

"You're not a loser," said Jamal. "I just told you that."

"And I know that now," I said. "Because what also happened

when I moved to Rancho Ruby was I met these two clowns, and they became my best friends, and it's because of them that I'm not a loser."

Jamal's eyes fell. He was still mad. But I knew he hated being mad.

Milo gazed at me with eyes of encouragement. *This is good. Keep going.*

"No cynicism or fortress of solitude or whatever could ever protect me from my own shame," I said. "You guys did."

"Sun," said Milo.

"You are my protectors," I said. "I'd be dead and buried in a baseball field if it weren't for you."

I realized I was trembling and breathing hard. My nose was running for some reason. I wiped it. Jamal and Milo glanced at each other, then back at me, then at the ground. They were thinking. Perhaps judging.

And why shouldn't they? Wouldn't I, if I were them?

I didn't know what I expected out of saying everything I'd just said. It would be naïve to think they'd take me back just like that, everything instantaneously forgiven.

I suddenly felt very exposed. I had the overwhelming urge to sprint home and hide in my room. So I got on my bike.

The computer screen twitched.

"It's fifteen minutes to live," I said. "Have a great show."

Back on the street, I refused to cry. There was no such thing as biking and crying.

It was slowly dawning on me that I no longer had any friends.

At least Gunner was my friend, right?

No crying while biking.

The ultimate irony was that, until recently, I'd finally no longer felt like a loser. Gunner had gone from bully to friend; I had Cirrus; I'd faked being a rock star, only to find I possessed the skills to actually *be* a rock star.

Now I was alone, with nothing else to do but help pick up the pieces of my broken brother, Gray.

As for Cirrus, I would see her in the halls and across the clover field at track, and our eyes would never meet again. In the larger scheme of things, I would become the school's village idiot—a loser of my own making.

Maybe there was a chance Milo and Jamal and I would still be friends, albeit in a completely different capacity. Like classmate friends—those kids you hung out with at school but nowhere else, capable of only the shallowest of conversation.

Or maybe we wouldn't at all.

Maybe we would just be acquaintances, and nod at one another in the hallways, and that would be it.

In one fell swoop, our flux capacitor now sat splintered apart into separate arms, flux things, whatever. I didn't even really like that movie all that much. Not even when Jamal and Milo and me watched it for the first time in Milo's backyard when we were kids, and his mom set up the sheet and the projector and his dad gave us all the homemade elote corncobs we could eat and—

"Sunny," shrieked Milo.

I looked back. On a conventional bike, such a lookback would surely cause an instant loss of control and inevitable crash followed by property damage, personal injury, or even death and dismemberment. But not on the ultra-stable Velociraptor® Elite.

Milo was piloting a miniature electric bike with his legs frogged out, clown-style. Behind him was Jamal. They were somehow riding the squirrelly thing together.

"Sunny," cried Jamal.

"Turn around," said Milo.

"Huh?" I said.

"It's three minutes till livestream, not fifteen," said Milo. "Lady Lashblade messaged in to say she's ready. Jamal, tell him."

"Sunny," said Jamal. "We forgive you."

"You don't have to," I said. "I wouldn't forgive me."

"Shut up with that self-pitying nonsense," said Jamal. "No one could know what they'd do if they were in your shoes—that's beside the point."

"Although I'm glad I wasn't in your shoes," said Milo.

"We need you," said Jamal.

"For the livestream?" I said.

"No, you idiot," said Jamal.

"I'm kidding," I said. "I need you guys, too."

"This is all wonderful," said Milo. "Now bang a yewie."

"Huh?" I said.

"Turn the heck around and come back with us!" said Jamal.

"Check one two syphilis," I said.

"Levels are good," said Jamal.

"Cuing in Lady Lashblade," said Milo.

We all held our breath as a rectangle appeared on-screen with her eminence herself. Lady Lashblade was one of the few prominent women of color in the world of role-playing games and was known for changing her hair into something architectural in its splendor every week. This time it was done in overlapping lacquered sheets bursting from a spiky halo in the back. A hippogriff pin held the whole thing together. Her eponymous eyelashes sparkled and matched the pin's crimson hue.

"Good afternoon, fine sirs," she said. "It's such a pleasure to be a part of your wonderful show."

"The honor's all ours pleasure is we're so glad to have you thank you this evening," we all said at once.

"Oh my," said Lady Lashblade. She got down to business. Livestream shows were nothing for her. "What's your preferred format?"

"Hi, I'm Sunny," I said. "Uh, so, um, it's twenty minutes of banter, and ten minutes of product intro and demo, then thirty minutes Q&A with the audience."

"That's typical," said Lady Lashblade, taking a sip of red wine through a straw in a crystal goblet.

"So I'm the funny one," said Jamal. "And Sunny's the Idea Guy."

"I'm the therapist philosopher," said Milo, crowding into Jamal's mic. "Sorta like an Oprah but not quite as good a listener, especially when I get nervous—"

"Fellas, fellas," said Lady Lashblade. "Just be yourselves. You're gonna do gr-r-reat."

Lady Lashblade was right. Of course she was right. She was Lady friggin' Lashblade.

We began the livestream.

We were ourselves.

And we did just gr-r-reat.

The viewership was ludicrous, in the tens of thousands. We gained hundreds of followers. Once those people started telling other people, Lady Lashblade gained hundreds of followers, too. Understand that these weren't ordinary followers—nothing like those drive-by scrollers who followed Skittles Official on a whim. These were hard-core fans. The type who made—never bought—their own cosplay. The kind who LARPed even in the rain. The kind who religiously made the pilgrimage to Fantastic Faire every year.

As we wrapped up the livestream, she said it.

"I look forward to seeing all of you at the Faire in—what—just a month now!" she said. "All my close friends will be at my booth, including these good sirs we've all just had the pleasure of learning from, DIY Fantasy FX. If their schedule allows, that is."

My face froze. So did Milo's and Jamal's. Jamal inched his face away so that he could freak out properly off-frame.

"I bluh-bluh-believe we're free?" I said.

"We'refreewurrfreewurrfree," said Milo.

"See you there!" said Lady Lashblade. She wiggled her sparkling fingers to deliver her catchphrase: "Make and believe."

"And cut," said Jamal. "We're out."

"Goddess of the game I worship thee Lady Lashblade!" I screamed.

"I'm still here," said Lady Lashblade.

"Thank you, Lady Lashblade!" we all screamed.

"You guys are so cute," she said, and vanished with a wink.

Jamal fetched us Ramunes, which we slammed open and raised for a toast.

“Guys,” I said, exhaling after a long pull, “I vow from this day forth to never betray you again. To never act without your consent if that consent involves all of us. I vow—”

“Whatever! Lady Lashblade!” said Jamal and Milo.

I couldn’t have agreed more.

Beautiful

Back home, evening.

I checked my phone out of the same helpless desperation of pathetic phone users all over the world.

Farewell, friend.

A cartoon version of Cirrus gave a sad smirk, blinked, smirked, blinked.

When had she sent this? What did this mean?

I watched the looping animation for a full minute. I gained no insight.

Dad came floating out from the dark. "Hey, bud," he whispered. "We watched your internet show. You guys were great."

"You did?" I said. "How did you even know we were on tonight?"

"You have a real broadcaster's voice," said Dad.

I didn't know what to say. My family was watching? And they liked it? But they weren't into the lifestyle. What would they even get out of it?

Just take the compliment, dummy.

"Thanks," I said.

He paused, then added, "Cirrus's parents told us about it."

All sound cut out for a moment, like it did sometimes. I pictured Cirrus, just beyond the upper window of her condo, watching on her phone along with thousands of others. Had she heard about DIY Fantasy FX from someone? Gunner? Artemis?

Did she hit the heart button?

"They told me something else," said Dad. "You're not gonna like it."

Farewell, friend.

"Their LA project is tied up in city hall," said Dad. "So they're gonna do a short gig in Yiwu."

"Is that inland?" I said.

"It's four hours south of Shanghai."

"China!" I shrieked.

Mom appeared in her pajamas. "Who's shouting?" she said, but fell quiet when she saw Dad and me.

"How short is a short gig?" I yelled.

"Just a few months," said Dad with a one-armed shrug.

"Honey, it's twelve," said Mom. "With the option to renew their contract if the government likes what they're getting."

"I was trying to soften the blow," said Dad.

Oops, mouthed Mom.

"A year?" I wailed.

"What's with the shouting?" said Gray from the landing below.

"Go back to sleep," said Mom.

"Oh, snap," said Gray. "You told him about tomorrow."

"Tomorrow?" I howled.

"Please, lower your volume," said Dad. "They leave first thing in the morning."

I sat right down in the foyer, among all the shoes. We Daes did not line up our shoes. Cirrus did, though. So I began lining up every last shoe, down to the millimeter.

"Sun?" said Mom.

I picked up my shoes, lined them up, and flung them both across the room. I took out my phone.

Hello? I wrote.

You're leaving?

Just like that?

Hello?

Cirrus did not blow a single bubble back.

"She's right down the street and I can't even reach her," I said.

My phone was a useless prehistoric piece of junk. I might as well have been staring at a loose bathroom tile in my hands. After tonight, Cirrus would be gone. And she would be gone forever, because Cirrus was highly skilled at being gone. She went gone every couple of years for her whole life. She was expert at it.

Cirrus had chosen to go, in fact. *I changed my mind,* she perhaps told her parents. *I'm ready for another adventure.*

And from the window she watched, no doubt, as Rancho Ruby and all of California became just another piece of vanishing landscape making way for the endless scrolling Pacific. She would chalk up this whole Sunny episode as one of her weirder duty stations, then safely detonate it from a distance like she'd had to do with all of her other memories in order to protect her heart.

And then I'd never see or hear from her again for years and years. Maybe in some inconceivable future we'd meet in some dumb shopping mall with our spouses and kids in tow, and have that awkward catching-up conversation adults seem to always be having even though all they'd rather do is sit on a couch and binge old shows until their toes became sharp roots that anchored them to the ground to draw up minerals that would soon calcify every vein in their body and render them into an anomalous state scientists would not quite be able to call death.

Mom knelt and simply put her arm around me.

"Listen," said Dad. "This might not be what you want to hear right now, but . . . you're young . . . and . . ."

"Dad," said Gray. He had emerged fully, and wore horrible baggy sweats and a horrible baggy hoodie. In one hand he held an acoustic guitar. In the other, a beautiful sunburst mandolin.

"Lemme handle this," said Gray.

"Okay?" said Dad, perplexed.

"Sunny, get up," said Gray. "Let's go."

"Go where?" I said. "For what?"

"Oh my god," said Mom, sweetly realizing some mysterious something. She gave Dad a squeeze. And then she gave him a little kiss. The kiss seemed to squirt a shot of understanding into Dad's brain, because he brightened like a little bulb.

"Might as well try," said Dad to Gray.

"Do or at least try, there is no do not," croaked Gray.

"Never attempt to quote *Star Wars* again," I said.

Gray opened the front door with a Picardian flourish. "Engage."

We walked outside in the chill of the deepening night. Gray tuned the guitar as he walked. It was the first guitar he ever got, way back in freshman year of high school: a little parlor-size classical with nylon strings. He made me wear it.

"You know that song 'You're Beautiful' by James Blunt?" he said.

"That song is so cheesy," I said. "Milo's mom piped stuff like that when he was a baby in her tum-tum."

"That's the song you're gonna sing," he said.

"Doesn't he say, *I will never be with you*?" I said.

"That line is precisely what makes it a great love song," said Gray.

I grappled with the paradoxical logic of declaring your love for a person by singing about how you'll never get to be in a relationship with them. Maybe the yearning alone made a persuasive case?

"Are we seriously doing this?" I said.

"*You* are seriously doing this," said Gray. "I sure couldn't. The vocals are way too high. But falsetto's in your wheelhouse. Plus you know all the words."

This was actually true. I used to sing along with the song every time it came on in the car in grade school. Funny that Gray remembered such a small detail.

"Chords are super simple," said Gray. "Capo the eighth fret, play G, D, E-minor, C, then for the chorus go C, D, E-minor, D, C, D, and back to G. Just follow my lead."

"You're serious," I said.

"What else are you doing tonight?" said Gray. "She friggin' leaves tomorrow."

I went through the chords with Gray, who guided me along by playing lead-in notes on his mandolin.

Down the hill was Cirrus's condo. I stopped walking, but Gray restarted me with a push of his hand.

It dawned on me—again—that after tomorrow morning Cirrus would be gone. What would a late-night serenade even accomplish? Would she reverse course yet again and ask her parents to drop the project and stay put, all for the chance to be with someone she could never quite trust?

If it were me, I would start learning my basic Mandarin.

But it wasn't me, and I couldn't deny that I harbored a tiny crumb of hope that a miracle would happen. This crumb came from the same crappy, tasteless loaf of bread shared with lottery ticket owners, children still believing in Santa Claus (bless them), and every game show contestant ever, including and especially the defunct *X-Factor.*

We reached her condo. An automatic floodlight flooded us with light.

"That's your cue," said Gray. He stood some feet apart to give me more of the spotlight, then counted us in.

Suddenly I was freezing. My hands were freezing. But I clipped on the capo and played the first G, remembering to add the little hammer-on detail.

"Here we go," said Gray. He led me in with the familiar solo melody. It was a simple phrase played twice over four bars at a leisurely pace, giving me a full eight bars to clear my throat and my fears and just dive in to the song's oddball fake-out fragment of a first line—

My life is brilliant

—sung before the actual real beginning of the song, which we soon reached in three short bars.

My love is pure
I saw an angel
Of that I'm sure

VERSE 1 ⟶ CHORUS
VERSE 2 ⟶ CHORUS
BRIDGE ⟶ CHORUS

Simple as can be. My voice slotted in so comfortably at this high register that I didn't have to worry about hitting the notes. I didn't have to worry about remembering the lyrics, either. My performer's brain was freed up to go for style points, and I tried my best: adding in grace notes and voice cracks here, mumbles and slurs there. Gray had been right: falsetto was in my wheelhouse. The perks of being a castrato.

Cirrus's condo remained dark.

I glanced at big brother Gray now and then. He nodded like a grinning idiot. He strummed quietly along at mezzo piano in support of my mezzo forte. Because he wanted to make sure everyone knew who the star was.

It was a short song, not much longer than three minutes. But still, it managed to convey an entire journey of stupefied longing by a hopeless (and hopelessly stoned) romantic on a train in love with a girl across the car. I kind of wished Gray hadn't made me play this song, whose last line, as a friendly reminder, was:

I will never be with you.

But the song also had a charming ironic quality to it, something English, and the English ironic-ness suited Cirrus, so whatever, it didn't matter at this point. Because now we had reached the end.

The timer ran out on the motion sensor floodlight, and it turned off.

"That was wonderful," said a voice. An older woman's voice. Cirrus's mom?

I looked up. Still the house was dark. The voice wasn't coming from there.

It was the condo next door.

"Uh, thank you," I said. I waved an arm to turn the light back on.

"I loved singing telegrams when I was a child," said my favorite somnambulist.

Gray spoke at a slow, constant pace. "It's not a telegram. It's a serenade."

"Uh-oh," said the woman.

Gray whispered to me, "You wanna try another song?"

The woman heard him. "I would love another song, but the Sohs left an hour ago. They won't be back for months."

"I thought it was tomorrow morning," said Gray.

"They got a great deal on first-class seats," said the woman.

"Sorry to disturb your sleep," I said.

"You are very talented," said the woman. "You are a natural."

"I mostly fake it," I said, and walked away.

V

Patiently watch and you'll see them come back:
summertime meteors dazzling on black.

Doomed

What else was there to say?

Nothing.

I had just serenaded a painted box.

Like one of the millions of wretched unwanted outcasts silently screaming at the murderous uncaring world for even the tiniest shred of attention no matter how sneering and disdainful, I launched the monopolistic social media photo sharing app known as Snapstory. The Chinese city of Yiwu, according to my teary-eyed research, was home to the world's largest wholesale market of dollar-store knickknacks that was ten times larger than the biggest mall in America. I wanted to see it through her eyes. I needed to.

But she was not on Snapstory.

I deleted the app. What was the point of using an app that had no one on it?

I drove Gray to LA—he had left his wallet with his driver's license at Miss Mayhem—and being back on Sunset had felt like self-inflicted punishment. It had stung to see the club's marquee blank and stripped of letters. Also stinging—and surreal—was the sight of three neighborhood homeless people each wearing Immortals shirts. They must've been abandoned, then donated by the venue. Cirrus would've been heartbroken. Or then again not, because now at least someone who really needed a shirt now had a shirt.

None of this should have happened.

If I had just been normal, Cirrus would've told her parents she wanted to stay and finish out Ruby High, and she would still be here.

Anyway.

School was school.

What was there to say about school?

Lockers. Class bells. The pantheon of student archetypes.

There were old friends, like Jamal and Milo.

There were new ones, like Gunner and August. They joined the SuJaMi guild, forming what I supposed was the SuJaMiAuGu crew now. It was actually kind of nice. Also inevitable, really, since we all shared a ludicrous history that stuck us together like wet gummy bears.

Gunner still bullied me, but now with body slams and bone-crushing high fives. I went to his games now and then, when they didn't stir up too many memories. He came to my parties (bearing dice), and I went to his (bearing beer).

Was he the Bully anymore?

Was I the Nerd?

Maybe forget that pantheon.

I walked the halls, dressed neither in extinct dot-com swag

nor Mortals-era black. I wore a plain tee shirt and plain jeans. My style had no name, because I was still figuring it out.

Wherever I walked, I caught the Look.

It was a different Look now, of course, always accompanied by whispers. I was sure everyone had some version of what they imagined had happened the night of the talent show. It didn't matter. Interest would fade, like interest tends to do at school. The rumors would dry up. The Looks would cease. And I would slide back into obscurity from whence I had come.

I would just be a guy named Sunny.

There was Hot Girl Artemis, still at the locker next to mine.

"Hey," I said.

"Hey," said Artemis.

She'd been typing something on her phone. I stared at it, wondering if I could ask about her friend and fellow incompetent trackmate. Wondering if I even had the right to ask.

"You, ah, ever hear from . . . ?"

"Cirrus is fine," said Artemis, bound by loyalty to never betray any report beyond the most trivial minutiae. "She says China is really pretty."

I pictured Cirrus's mouth forming the words of that anodyne statement:

China is really pretty.

"This is on that AlloAllo thing?" I said.

Artemis answered only with a nod. She knew she couldn't give me Cirrus's handle, and I knew I was in no position to ask for it.

Gunner shattered the awkward moment by giving me a backslap strong enough to loosen phlegm from my lungs.

"Hey, Gun," I said.

"Hey, Sun," said Gun.

He turned to Artemis for a slower, more sincere "Hey." He ran a hand through his hair, clearly to see if she would notice, and was thrilled when she actually did.

"Your fantasy football post was funny," said Artemis.

Gunner whipped forth twin finger pistols. "It's just D&D for jocks, loll."

And Artemis laughed!

Before I left, I reminded Gunner: "Livestream tonight."

Gunner knew I meant DIY Fantasy FX, and nodded. As I walked away, I saw him murmur to Artemis, "We broke a thousand followers this week—it's pretty cool."

It *was* pretty cool. It might not be the kind of cool that other people would readily understand, and I was fine with that. It felt cool to me.

The vice principal called out, "Brain train's leaving Grand Mental Station, all aboard."

Mr. Tweed very gently encouraged me to take sanctuary in the music room to develop what he perceived to be true musical talents hidden amidst all the fakery, but I wasn't ready to reenter that room yet.

I needed a reason to make music, and my reason had flown away first class.

At track, I stared wistfully at the girls' team, willing Cirrus to appear alongside Artemis, then stared down at the clover. I flipped off the poor little plants with one finger, two, one, two.

"Let's go," said Coach Oldtimer.

“Yes sir,” I said, rising.

“We’re hopping bleachers today,” said Coach Oldtimer.

“Yes sir,” said Jamal.

The three of us rose like old men on a cloudy day.

Out of sheer boredom I found myself actually trying.

I ran my long jumps and averaged five meters, a new personal best.

Milo threw the shot put an incredible twenty-two meters, which nobody noticed because still nobody cared about shot put.

Jamal got the high bar stuck between his legs while midair and abraded the groin muscle next to his right testicle.

One evening, I suited up for a ride. Gray poked his head up from his basement staircase and asked if he could come, too, and of course I said yes.

So Gray and I hit the streets together.

“So, I start tomorrow,” said Gray.

“The new job?” I said.

Gray ratcheted his pedals backward a full revolution. “That’s next Monday. Tomorrow’s recording.”

“Recording,” I said.

“I’ve been talking with this married musician couple on Stalker Classifieds,” said Gray. “Legit veterans looking to experiment and create a new sound. They liked my reel.”

“You have a reel?” I said.

“It’s just one song,” said Gray.

I wanted to jump a curb with joy. There was as yet no such thing as an elliptical stunt league, which was a baffling mystery to me. Maybe I would create one—everyone would find elliptical tricks extremely cool, perhaps at something like the X Games.

We zipped past Cirrus's condo, now her old condo. The vestibule had a little log-pile of forsaken newspapers.

We reached Jamal's house and made our way to the back garage, where Jamal, Milo, Gunner, and August already were.

We parked our bikes, said hi, and toasted with Ramune sodas. Gray was immediately entranced by Jamal's music workstation. The two of them began geeking out over crafting beats and patterns, then stringing those patterns together to make the epic, ever-evolving soundtrack of our evening in real time.

Milo showed Gunner all the props we'd made. After asking dozens of technical questions, he enveloped an unsuspecting August in the bright green bolts of Raiden's Spark. August retaliated with a shot from the Crucifix Slayer—an electroplated PVC crossbow able to launch marshmallows up to ten meters. And before we knew it, the four of us were having a battle in the herringbone courtyard.

Jamal had a collection of fancy hats, so we wore fancy hats. As Dungeon Master, I dictated the parameters of the current sticky situation, and then we would work together—or not—to solve it.

We were LARPing again.

We were finally here.

Fantastic Faire, where the Delgado Beach and Glass Harbor freeways meet, take Exit 28b toward Hardware Gloryhole Parkway.

We crossed under a wrought-iron gate into a dusty canyon of hay bales on a sawdust floor. There was quite a queue to get in—people young and old, dressed as elves, orcs, Stormtroopers,

Doras, SpongeBobs, anything and everything. We walked right by them all.

"There's a woman in a chain-mail bikini," murmured Gray in awe.

"Yap," I said, striding.

"That green guy is totally naked," said Gunner with wonderment.

"Nekkid!" said Oggy, his eyes so big the balls nearly ejected.

Gray, Gunner, and Oggy had all agreed to come—and even dress up—to support me as duty-bound friends. They had no idea how marvelous this nerd prom actually was, or how much celebrity they would receive.

I beamed with hometown pride, bless-this-mess. "Welcome to Fantastic Faire," I said.

We turned right, flashed our EXHIBITOR badges at a cigarette-smoking knight standing before a velvet rope, and—boom—passed right on through.

Then we emerged into the Faire proper: a vast village of buildings from every style and era—as long as those styles and eras never actually existed in reality—all under a canopy of crisscrossed lines of colorful antiqued bunting.

I was a paladin in chrome craft foam, wielding a steam sword hissing mist*.

Jamal was a wizard in a sand nomad's robe covered in runes glowing green and able to shoot lightning from his fingertips**.

---

* Same mechanism as Esmeralda's Veil, but in a melee weapon with the switch hidden below the sword hilt and a white noise generator.

** Electroluminescent sheets sewn into windows cut out of the fabric, powered by a Li-ion waist pack. Two Raiden's Spark mechanisms concealed in each arm sleeve.

Gunner was a crusty, leathery orc with an explosive mace in his green hand*.

Gray was in an ornate suit of fabric armor, which he thought looked cool but actually meant he was a ranger, one of the most useless character types in modern gameplay**.

Milo was a Spartan halberd soldier in nothing but a steel codpiece, fire-red cloak, and rock-hard exposed abs***.

Oggy was medieval Oggy****.

"Step back," cried Jamal to the smiling crowd. He shot lightning at them, then retracted the wires to shoot again. "Make way!"

Gunner played his part with surprising élan, snapping and cracking his mace at happily shrieking kids and Faire-goers shooting video.

"Make way, I say!" cried Milo with a flourish of his cloak, causing women and men alike to suddenly thirst for cool water on such a sultry hot day.

"Lady Lashblade demands our presence!" I cried, and sliced a white arc before a dad holding up a camera.

The crowd loved us, and we loved them back.

I was home.

When we reached the stage, Lady Lashblade hugged us all (especially Milo, and twice). She was smaller than I thought, but

---

* Concealed cap-gun mechanism with additional white LED flash effect.

** Don't make fun; Gray had been out of the game for years. He thought a ranger was a type of vehicle.

*** Just abs.

**** No change.

no less powerful. Within minutes every wooden bench in the sunken outdoor auditorium was occupied with the most wonderful, most motley cast of characters all wearing their secret fantasies and desires quite literally on their sleeves.

She introduced us one by one in a voice so big it needed no amplification.

"Bless this space with your rapturous applause for the dark sorcerers of DIY Fantasy FX!" she roared.

The crowd clapped and clapped. And then they grew quiet. Dragon pilots sat still. Death set his scythe down so people in the back could see. Daimyo parents shushed their little samurai children.

They were waiting for the *magic*.

So I threw the cover off a nearby barrel full of props. We'd spent every night perfecting all of them.

One by one we thrilled the audience not just with fancy effects, but with instructions and expert tips on how to make their very own props that were Cheap, Readily available, Easy to assemble, Awesome in effect, Portable, and Safe.

Magic for everyone with a little bit of money and time to spare.

None of the props were for sale. We were here to give away knowledge, not things.

After our presentation, we lined up for a group bow as Lady Lashblade handed out flyers with our name on it. Our name!

"Make and believe!" chanted everybody.

"You're gonna get a bazillion subscribers after this, so be ready," she crooned into my ear. "Bank some content and keep on banking it."

"Thank you," I said.

"When the first advertisers start coming, call me," she said. "I'll help you out. You guys have merch potential up the hoo-ha."

I wanted to cry. "Thank you so, so much, Lady Lashblade."

"Please," she said. "Call me Destiny."

We signed flyers.

We shook hands.

We posed for selfie after selfie with fans old and new.

Gunner sat at a little stump off to the side, talking excitedly about something as Oggy rested at his feet. Gunner was talking with a maiden in modern dress. The maiden was Artemis, and she looked happy. Gunner looked happy. I was happy for them both.

Gray had doffed his regalia, declaring loudly that it was *too friggin' hot*, adding *god*.

After a solid hour, the crowd finally began moving on to explore the rest of the Faire. I had broken character long ago. I was a babbling little boy in a costume jumping up and down. We all were.

"That was awesome!" I cried. "That was awesome!"

Jamal stopped jumping abruptly and pointed. "Dude."

"That was awesome!" said Milo and Gray.

"Dude," said Jamal.

I looked.

In the trees beyond stood a sylph. There were lots of sylphs at the Faire, but this one was like no other.

For she glowed.

She glowed the purest blue.

Light burst through from beneath her white bodice and white skirt. Behind her sprouted an impenetrable steel fan of radiating wing blades, each polished to intensify the luminescence. The wing blades were each tipped with crimson triangles of blood—this sylph had seen battle, yet not a stain marred her garment.

The astonished crowd around her throbbed as she took a step beneath the branches of the tree and changed her hue to bright yellow, then orange. In the shade she was even more brilliant.

I wanted to know how blinding she would be in the darkness of night. I had never wanted anything worse.

She drew me toward her with a simple curl of outstretched fingers. I let my sword fall. I ignored the amazed cries of my compatriots.

I went.

"You look incandescent," I said.

"They're actually LEDs," said Cirrus. "In Yiwu you can get fifty thousand three-meter strands for a hundred bucks. I learned how to install and configure a controller on Nerdsweat."

"I know Nerdsweat," I said.

"These metal blades took forever to cut and form," said Cirrus. "I almost chopped my fingers off. Then I almost burned them soldering on all the individual servo motors."

"Servo motors?" I said. "For what?"

Cirrus gave me a look: *You'll see.*

"Let's just say I watched a ton of NeoForge videos," said Cirrus.

"I know NeoForge," I said.

"You better," said Cirrus. "Those guys follow you. Everyone follows you. Because they know no one else comes close to DIY Fantasy FX, led by one Sunny Dae."

I nodded with sheepish pride, because it was true. We had

the most, *best* followers of anyone in the entire Do-It-Yourself Fantasy and Science Fiction Cosplay Special Effects Maker category. And on every video since the talent show, I was the host. The front man, you could say.

"I've been exploring your strange little world," said Cirrus. "It's quite nerdy."

"I know," I said.

"Obsessively nerdy," said Cirrus. "The arguments people get into—Dumbledore versus Gandalf?"

"Yap," I said, like *What can you do?*

"I wish you'd just shown me the real you when we first met," said Cirrus.

I paused. "Do you miss Rock Star Sunny?"

Cirrus sucked her teeth and thought. "I mourned him. I did. One day I met him, and then one day he just went away."

"I'm so sorry about everything," I said. "I am an idiot."

"But not all of him went away," said Cirrus, catching my eyes with hers. "I saw him in your videos. Not Rock Star Sunny or Nerd Sunny, but a kind of pure Sunny-ness."

"A Sunny-ness," I said, with a chuckle.

"Anyway, I'm an idiot, too," she said. "Because I'm here."

"I missed you."

"I missed you more," said Cirrus.

"Not as much as I missed you, though," I said.

"Shut up," she said. "Listen. The Yiwu thing ended sooner than expected. Yay. I made my parents move us back here instead of some other new city."

I blinked with surprise. "Did they freak?"

"Not as much as I hoped," she said. "But I'm trying to get over that. They are who they are."

"You're really back," I said.

"There's that famous Californian endless summer I keep hearing about," said Cirrus.

"I can show it to you," I said.

She took a step closer. "I liked your video. I liked it a lot."

I took a step, too. "Thanks."

"I'm not talking about Esmeralda's Veil," she said. "I'm talking about the other one."

What?

"From my doorbell," she said.

Cirrus's doorbell, with its little impassive video eye.

She smiled, took a breath, and quietly sang.

"You're beautiful. You're beautiful."

And I sang with her.

"You're beautiful, it's true."

We kissed, and the beautiful nerds around us laughed and cheered.

It was much too much attention for Cirrus, I guessed, because she activated individual servo motors to draw her wing blades down around us and shut out the crowd, creating a gleaming dark hood where she glowed and glowed, her light pinging back and forth from metal to metal.

She closed those deadly sharp blades tight and offered no possibility of escape.

I was doomed.

Acknowledgments

Greetings, adventurer! You have reached the Realm of the Acknowledgments. I hope you had a fun journey. I know I had a ton of fun creating it. For this is my *fun* book: my happy, goof-off, slap-silly story very intentionally designed to bring desperately needed joy and light to what was a very difficult and mind-bending year.

Anyway, you know those people I thanked for *Frankly in Love*? They're still here, and still wonderful. Our adventuring party includes:

Jen Loja, our fearless, lawful-good level 27 warrior leader, along with her compatriot Jocelyn Schmidt.

Jen Klonsky, a chaotic-good rogue with at least 19 charisma. I can't believe I'm lucky enough to work with a publisher like you.

The wise clerics Elyse Marshall and Lizzie Goodell of the publicity clan.

All those within House Marketing: Her Benevolence Kara Brammer, the neutral-good ranger Alex Garber, the lawful-evil drow druid Felicity Vallence, and the loyal warlock apprentice James Akinaka. And we cannot forget Shannon Spann, a sorceress of unspecified level who can teleport between the worlds of TikTok and Rec-A-Reads at will.

Felicia Frazier, lawful-good level 25 sorceress, and all her anointed wizards in sales.

Caitlin Tutterow, Theresa Evangelista, and Eileen Savage, lawful-good monks blessed with 20 points of constitution each, as well as shadow rogues Laurel Robinson, Elizabeth Lunn, and Cindy Howle.

Those mystic seers perched high atop Alloy Mountain: Les Morgenstein, Josh Bank, Sara Shandler, Joelle Hobeika, and Elysa Dutton.

I must include the traveling bard Timba Smits for his beautifully precise and evocative cover art, as well as the greatsword barbarian Judy Bass.

Ensconced within the central tower of Yoon Castle, there is always Lady Nicola, my eternal love. Together we are ruled over by the kind but very confusing Queen Empress Penny. Sound the butt alarm!

I have to end by thanking my big brother, Danny, artist, tinkerer, and archnerd, who I have always looked up to, and still do. As kids we conquered the Tomb of Horrors atop the pool table plains at the house of the O'Bitz brothers, and Danny was the best Dungeon Master ever.